PRAISE FOR

'Robert Bryndza's characters are so vividly drawn—even the slightest character—and fully human and uniquely imperfect. His plots are clever and original and cool, and his sense of timing is excruciatingly flawless.'

AUGUSTEN BURROUGHS, *NEW YORK TIMES* BESTSELLING AUTHOR OF *RUNNING WITH SCISSORS*

'A rising star in British crime fiction.'

IRISH INDEPENDENT

'A riveting page-turner. An astonishingly good plot with perfectly drawn characters and sharp, detailed writing.'

ROBERT DUGONI, #1 *WALL STREET JOURNAL* BESTSELLING AUTHOR

'It is impossible not to root for the feisty, flawed Kate.'

DAILY MAIL

'You can't help turning the pages hungrily to see what happens next!'

THE TIMES

ALSO BY ROBERT BRYNDZA

KATE MARSHALL CRIME THRILLER SERIES

Nine Elms

Shadow Sands

Darkness Falls

Devil's Way

DETECTIVE ERIKA FOSTER CRIME THRILLER SERIES

The Girl in the Ice

The Night Stalker

Dark Water

Last Breath

Cold Blood

Deadly Secrets

Fatal Witness

ROMANTIC COMEDY SERIES

The Not So Secret Emails Of Coco Pinchard

Coco Pinchard's Big Fat Tipsy Wedding

Coco Pinchard, The Consequences of Love and Sex

A Very Coco Christmas

Coco Pinchard's Must-Have Toy Story

Miss Wrong and Mr Right

Raven Street Publishing

www.ravenstreetpublishing.com

Copyright © Raven Street Ltd 2023

Robert Bryndza has asserted his right to be identified as the author of this work.

Cover design by Henry Steadman

Ebook ISBN: 9781914547096

Paperback ISBN: 9781914547102

Hardback ISBN: 9781914547119

ROBERT BRYNDZA

A **KATE MARSHALL** THRILLER

DEVIL'S WAY

For Janeken Skywalker, my first reader

You must be proud, bold, pleasant, resolute,
And now and then stab, when occasion serves.
— **Christopher Marlowe, Edward II**

PROLOGUE

Thursday June 21st 2007

Jean Julings knelt down inside the small tent and tucked her three-year-old grandson, Charlie, into his sleeping bag. He had a tousled mop of white-blond hair, and his face was flushed with tiredness from fresh air and fun. He held onto a small brown teddy bear who had one eye missing.

'Did you have a fun day with your gran?' asked Jean. Charlie nodded sleepily and grinned, showing his perfect white baby teeth. 'Good boy. And what about Button-Eye? Did he brush his teeth?'

'Top and bottom,' said Charlie, holding up the teddy bear. Jean laughed, and her heart swelled with love for the little boy.

'Good. It's just as important for a teddy bear to brush his teeth. They eat all that honey.' Her knees clicked as she sat back on her haunches and reached for the small battery-powered lamp, which was casting a soft yellow glow.

'No, light on,' Charlie whined. His little brow creased, and he kicked his feet inside the sleeping bag. Jean flicked it off, and a soft glow remained inside. The moon was full, and it shone through the canvas.

'Look at that. We don't need a light. We have God's night-light in the sky,' said Jean, stroking his soft blond hair. 'It's not scary when the moon is so bright at night, is it?'

Charlie shook his head and tucked Button-Eye under his arm.

'I'm just going to go outside for some fresh air,' she said, patting the pockets of her shorts and feeling the pack of cigarettes and the lighter in the left-hand pocket.

'No...'

'I'll only be a few minutes. And then I'll come back in, and I'll tell you a story if you're still awake. Okay? I'll be outside, and you can say "Gran", and I'll hear you and come back inside. Yes?'

Charlie nodded.

'Good boy.' Jean kissed him on the cheek, and as she crawled out of the tent, she saw that Charlie's eyes were already fluttering closed. They'd been on the go all day, playing and paddling in the river. He'd be asleep in a flash.

Jean crept out of the tent doorway onto the long, matted grass outside and pulled down the zip behind her. The tent was pitched under the broad canopy of a vast, ancient oak tree, and its thick, bare branches reached far out like ragged arms casting malformed shadows across the grass. Jean stood up, hearing her knees click again. She took out a cigarette and lit up, exhaling into the night sky. Stars twinkled above, and she listened to the nearby river running into the gorge. It seemed louder at night. The moor stretched away like a blanket of blue satin, dotted with rocks, and a faint mist clung to the troughs and lowland areas.

Directly to her right, across a short expanse of grass, Devil's

2

Tor towered above everything. Despite its imposing height, the stack of rocks looked very zen and calming, as if a giant had stacked a pile of large smooth stones on top of a grassy platform. At its base, and in shadow from the bright moonlight, was another tent belonging to Jean's daughter, Becky, and her partner Joel. The canvas was dark, and it looked like they were already asleep.

God, this place is beautiful, she thought. When she finished her cigarette, she stubbed it out carefully with the bottom of her shoe and slipped the blackened butt into the packet. She was about to back into the tent when she heard a faint voice calling her name.

'Jean!'

She saw a dishevelled figure appear behind the Tor and stagger into a patch of moonlight on the grassy platform.

'Jeeean!'

It was Declan, her sometime partner of many years. Jean cursed under her breath and, checked that the tent was zipped up. Seized with urgency, she hurried off across the long grass, terrified that Declan would wake the family up and cause a scene.

She ran up the grassy bank to the platform to try and stop him from coming down, and she was out of breath when she reached him. Declan was dressed in the same ripped jeans and striped T-shirt he'd been wearing when he'd turned up by the river that afternoon.

'What the hell are you doing? I told you this afternoon you're not welcome here!' she hissed.

He smiled, and a flash of his yellow teeth appeared through his thick beard. She had a cold feeling of dread when she saw he was carrying a bottle of whisky, with only a few inches of amber fluid left inside. He swayed on his feet, holding the bottle up to her mouth to try and make her drink.

'Don't!' she said, slapping it away. 'Charlie's asleep, and so are Becky and Joel.'

'I know,' he said, reaching out to grab her breasts. He staggered forward, pushing her back into the shadows against the high stones of the Tor. She could smell his sour, nasty breath as he pressed against her. She managed to push him off and wrestle herself free, coming to stand back out in the moonlight. He looked surprised. 'You really aren't any fun anymore, now you're sober...' He lifted the bottle to her mouth, but she swiped his hand away. She didn't feel fear. She wasn't scared of him anymore. Jean felt a fierce need to protect Charlie from him. She grabbed the bottle and twisted it out of his hand, ignoring his protests.

'Where's your car?' she asked. His eyes rolled back in his head, and he pointed vaguely to the other side of the grass platform, pursing his lips. Jean grabbed him by the collar and marched him around the Tor.

'Easy, *easy!*' he shouted. A small scrubland car park on the other side of the Tor led away to a gravel road. Jean saw his clapped-out blue Renault parked in the middle. The engine was still running, and the driver's door was open.

'Can I come and see you tomorrow?' asked Declan as she dragged him down the shallower grass slope to his car.

'No. I've told you. That's it. We're finished.'

A few feet from his car he stumbled on the uneven rocky surface and fell flat on his face. He let out a groan. Jean stood back and watched impassively as he got up. He teetered on his feet, fixed her with a mean, glassy stare and came close to her again.

'I heard your bitch daughter, in her tent, *screwing,*' he said,

4

his face twisting into a snarl. 'She sounded like she was enjoying it, more than you do, I'm sure.'

Jean slapped him around the face, and he struck back with a backhanded smack. She tottered and tripped over, landing on hard rock. She watched as Declan staggered, unperturbed. The side of her face stung, and she put her hand to her lip. There was no blood, but her ears were ringing. It wasn't the worst thing he had done to her.

Jean felt rage. Pure rage. She got up, grabbed what was left of the hair on the back of his head, and pushed him through the open door into his car.

'Where are your keys?'

'What?' he whined. She roughly searched his pockets and pulled out the car keys.

'I'm not leaving,' he said, folding his arms.

'You are. You're leaving now. It's the middle of the night.'

'Have you got any drink?'

'No.'

'You're an ugly bitch,' he said.

'And you are a flaccid waste of space.' She meant this to hurt him, but he smiled and started laughing, his yellowing teeth showing through his beard again.

'What time is it?'

'The pub up the road has a lock-in, one of the locals told me. You could be in time if you hurry,' she said, feeling a flash of inspiration. She couldn't believe he bought this, but Declan was a raging alcoholic. He closed the door, and she watched as his zeal for booze took over. He switched on the lights, and as the car lurched into a turn, the long grass was briefly illuminated. She thought she saw something move in the shadows, and then it was gone.

'Please, God, let him die in a ditch. Don't let him hurt

5

anyone but himself,' she said. Jean watched as the headlights moved down the road and then vanished. Relief flooded over her, and her shoulders sagged. She put her hand up to the side of her aching head. The roar of the river seemed louder in the dark.

Charlie, she thought. Jean hurried back around the Tor and down the other side of the slope. How long had he been left alone? It was only a few minutes. All was silent in the field. An owl hooted, the branches of the enormous tree creaked in the soft breeze, and the two tents were still.

As she drew close to their tent, the nightlight flicked on inside. Relief washed over her as she rounded it and her daughter Becky poked her head out. She was wearing her pyjamas, and her face was clean of make-up. Her brow was creased with concern.

'Mum. Is Charlie with you?' she said.

'He's not in the tent?' said Jean, feeling panic return.

'No.'

Jean pushed past her and looked inside. Both sleeping bags were empty, and she felt her stomach drop.

'He must be with Joel,' she said, coming back and seeing Becky's worried face.

'No, Mum, he's not. I thought I heard him outside our tent. That's why I came out to look for him. Why aren't you with him?'

'I went for a cigarette. Just for a minute,' said Jean. The lie dropping out of her mouth without any preparation needed.

'What if he went down to the river? I don't know if it's rained, can you hear how loud the water is?' said Becky. Her voice had a tinge of hysteria.

'Let's look. Charlie can't have wandered far,' said Jean, trying to keep calm. The fact that Becky was more scared than angry frightened her.

Becky woke Joel, and they all found torches and started to search, taking in the river, the rocks on the Tor, and the surrounding fields. The arcs of the light from their torches swept across the dark landscape, searching. The river was higher than it had been the day before, and as Jean shone her torch over the dark raging torrent, and called out Charlie's name, her voice seemed to get swallowed up by the darkness. She felt sick as the minutes passed, turning to an hour, then two. Charlie was nowhere to be found. Around 4am, the sky started to turn light, and this was when they called the police.

As the sun rose over the moors, a police car arrived, then two more.

The search began in earnest, but they never found Charlie.

1

ELEVEN YEARS LATER
Thursday 7th June 2018

The morning started out as regular as any other. Private detective Kate Marshall woke at six, just before her alarm, and automatically reached for her swimming costume, which was hanging on the chair beside her bed.

Kate swam in the sea every day of the year, come rain or shine, but it was these sleepy summer mornings, when the breeze was light, and the silvery fingers of dawn were just breaking above the horizon, that she loved the most. Her house was perched on top of a cliff in Thurlow Bay, on the south coast of England. It was a quiet spot, five miles outside the University town of Ashdean. After a quick slug of water from the tap in the kitchen, Kate opened the back door, which led out to a small terrace and a sandy path and blearily picked her way down to the beach.

The sand was soft, and she felt the prickle of the marram grass underfoot as it levelled out at the bottom of the cliff, and she walked through the dunes. The grass was tall, covering the high mounds and sheltering her from the breeze coming off the water.

As she emerged onto the beach, the first rays of the sun peeked over the horizon, hitting a large pool of seawater on the beach with a sparkle. To her left, she could see all along the craggy Jurassic coastline to Ashdean, which sat in a small horse-shoe-shaped bay. To her right were the cliffs, dotted with an occasional house, and a black outcrop of rock jutting out into the sea formed a barrier to the west. Kate thought a couple of the surfers staying at the caravan park opposite her house might already be in the water, but no, she had the beach to herself.

The wet sand was solid and cool under her feet. She dropped the towel a few metres from where the swells broke and stepped into the surf. The waves rolling in were knee-height, and she felt the zing of the water on her skin.

The sand dropped away as she walked through the breakers, and taking a deep breath, she dove in. Kate first noticed something was wrong when she came up for air, and she felt a current pulling at her waist, like invisible yet solid fingers.

And then it all happened so fast; she glanced back at the shore at the vast shimmering pool of seawater, saw the deep channel of white water rushing back from the large pool into the sea, and there was a violent pull on her legs. Kate was dragged under, her legs spinning around her head, her nose and mouth filling with water, and she realised too late that she'd swum into a deadly riptide.

All her years of sea swimming fell away, and she was caught in a blind panic of survival. The speed and power of the riptide were sudden and terrifying. Kate was dragged away from the shore, tumbling over and over. She saw flashes of the sky, the empty beach and a glimpse of her house on the cliffs, now far away, and then she was yanked violently back down under the water. She coughed and gagged, and her throat filled with seawater.

On the other side of town, Tristan Harper, Kate's partner in the detective agency, shifted in the driver's seat of his Mini Cooper. His back hurt, and his butt was going numb. He checked his watch and saw it was coming up to 6.10 am.

'Come on, please. Go to work,' said Tristan, keeping his eyes on the yellow front door of a terraced house further up on Walker Avenue. It was a neat road of terraced houses in the 'posh' part of Ashdean. The house belonged to an architect called Terrance Trent. He was in his early fifties, and his wife had hired Kate and Tristan to prove he was having an affair.

He heard a door slam to his left and turned to see an older lady emerging from the gate of the house he was parked outside. She wore a faded pink tracksuit, and her short jet-black hair was set in a very tight perm.

She came to his window, knocked on the glass, and then stood back with her arms folded.

Tristan looked back at the yellow front door. Terrance Trent was due to leave for work at any minute. He wound down his window.

'Can you *please* tell me *why* you have been sitting outside *my house* since three o'clock this morning?' the woman demanded. '*Well?*' She spoke grandly and seemed to emphasise random words. Up close her face was covered in thick, pale foundation, and she'd overdrawn her lips in scarlet. The crown of tight jet-black curls on her head reminded Tristan of a glistening plate of winkles. He wondered if it was a wig or a terrible dye job. He glanced back at the yellow front door, which remained closed. Tristan had been parked on Walker Avenue since 11pm. He'd moved the car twice, coming to settle outside this lady's house an hour before she'd noticed him, at 2 am. A car drove past, and an elderly man came out of a front door further down on the opposite side of the road, followed by an equally elderly brown dog.

'I'm waiting for someone,' said Tristan, adding, 'This is a public street.'

The woman's eyebrows shot up.

'For your information, *this* is a *private residential street*. Why are you parked outside *my* house?'

'Because there was a parking space free,' said Tristan, trying not to lose his rag with this rather insane-looking busybody.

She pursed her lips and came closer, dipping down to peer into his car. The seat next to Tristan was littered with empty sandwich packets and a long lens camera. There was a bottle of peach iced tea in the cupholder, but it no longer held iced tea after Tristan had been forced to pee in it at half past four in the morning.

'You look *fishy*. Like you're up to no good. Are you a *journalist*?'

Just then, Tristan saw the yellow front door open, and Terrance Trent emerged, walking at a pace with the young woman on his arm. He was dressed in a sharp blue pinstripe suit. The woman wore the same white mini dress, high heels, and fur coat she'd been wearing at eleven o'clock last night. 'I know *everything* that goes on around here,' the woman boomed. 'I am *chairlady* of the local neighbourhood *watch*.'

Tristan's heart plummeted in his chest. He wanted to pick up the camera and get the photo, but it was too risky. If this old bagged twigged he was a private detective, she could tip off Terrance and tell him he was under surveillance, which would mean losing a hefty fee for the agency. Terrance and the young woman got into his car and then drove off in the opposite direction.

Tristan sighed and sank back into his seat.

'*Well*? *What* do you have to say for yourself?' said the woman.

'I work for the council. I'm checking no one is leaving wheelie bins out after collection,' he said.

'*Ah*,' said the woman, smiling and nodding approvingly. She tapped the side of her nose and seemed to accept this explanation. She leaned closer. 'There are a group of *students* opposite, number four, who a *very guilty* of that and deserve a fixed penalty notice,' she said.

'Number four,' said Tristan.

'And of course, *my* wheelie bin goes out less than an hour before collection, and I whisk it back inside *the moment* it's emptied.'

'That's good to hear.'

Terrance Trent worked all day, so he was unlikely to be home before the evening. Tristan looked up and down the street, smiled, and thanked the zealous informer. When he started the engine and pulled out onto the street. He could see the woman in the rear-view mirror, watching as he drove away.

2

When Kate opened her eyes, she was in a small hospital room. The bed she lay in seemed surrounded by white, and it was swaying. Her throat felt sore and her skin clammy. She moved her head, and pain exploded like the worst hangover. *Did I drink? Please, no,* she thought. She took some deep breaths, but it felt like an effort, and there was a wet rattling in her chest.

And then it came back to her. She hadn't fallen off the wagon after thirteen years of sobriety. Her last memory had been the sheer panic that she would drown. Kate shifted in the bed and saw a drip in her arm and wires attached to her chest. A forest of coloured lines was moving silently across the screen of a heart monitor on the right-hand side of the bed. The relief that she hadn't drunk was replaced by the memory of being dragged down into the water.

A row of glass windows looked out onto a corridor outside, and a doctor appeared in the open doorway and knocked on the frame. He looked young, in his late twenties, with thick dark hair and glasses. He smiled.

'Hello, Kate,' he said, coming into the room and standing at the end of her bed. The way he said her name made Kate think they knew each other.

'Hello,' she tried to say, but her voice came out in a croak. She swallowed, but her throat felt dry and filled with needles.

'You've been unconscious for some time. We had you in intensive care,' said the doctor. He took her chart off the end, flipping over the pages. Kate rubbed at her throat and swallowed, wincing. The bed seemed to rock and shift underneath her. 'You had seawater in your lungs. We had to intubate,' he added. She coughed, which seemed to activate a dull thudding pain to add to the symphony in her head.

'How long is *some time*?'

'Almost twenty-four hours,' he said. The closed curtain on Kate's right billowed out, and she heard murmured voices from the other side. It opened a crack, and a nurse put her head through.

'Sorry, Doctor Harris, do you have a minute? Mrs Julings is, out of sorts,' she said. He put down the clipboard on the bed, nodded and followed her through the gap. The nurse gave her a nod and closed the curtain behind them. Kate leant forward to reach for the clipboard, but the exertion made her dizzy. She lay back, sweating and breathless. The doctor and nurse spoke softly from the other side of the curtain, and an older woman's shrill voice cut through.

'Doctor, please, give me something stronger. They bloody hurt. You can look at them for as long as you want, but it's not stopping the pain!'

Kate's nose seemed to reboot, and she caught a nasty smell of pus, and then the other hospital aromas seemed to flood her senses; disinfectant, floor polish and another clinical funk that she couldn't quite put her finger on. She jumped when the woman screamed.

'Christ! Warn me next time!'

'Please, Jean. Calm down. The doctor will be all done in a moment,' said the nurse in a sing-song voice.

'Don't you tell me to calm down!'

'Okay. Jean, we're all done,' said Dr Harris.

'Please. Cover me up. Even the air on them hurts,' moaned the woman in a desperate voice. There was some more shuffling, and then Dr Harris slid back through the curtain, followed by the nurse carrying a cardboard bowl filled with soiled dressings. Kate caught a glimpse through the gap of a tiny woman with a fuzz of treacle-coloured hair barely clinging to her head, sitting back in the bed with a sheen of sweat over her face.

'Where were we?' he said, coming back around the bed. The nurse left the room, and the smell of pus and infection wafted over them with an eye-watering intensity. Kate swallowed with difficulty as he pulled a tiny pen torch out of his pocket and shone the light in her eyes. It seemed to blaze against the back of her head. Dr Harris seemed satisfied and pocketed the torch.

'You have the beginnings of a lung infection, pneumonia, which would be expected after the water in your lungs. We have you on a very strong course of intravenous antibiotics, and we need to keep monitoring you for a few days,' he said, indicating the screen Kate was hooked up to. She could still see a blaze of gold from the torch.

'How did I get here?' she asked, suddenly putting together the memory of the riptide, being pulled out to sea. 'And where is here?'

'Ah, I think you were pulled out by a couple of surfers?' he said, consulting the chart again. 'I believe they called the emergency services.'

'Which emergency services?'

'The lifeboat.'

Kate felt mortified, hearing this. 'Who were the surfers?'

'I'm sorry. I don't know. But you were very fortunate.'

Kate saw her mobile phone sitting on the top of the cabinet next to a box of tissues and some water bottles. Dr Harris followed her gaze.

'Your son has been here whilst you were unconscious.'

'Jake is here? He's flown home?'

Dr Harris hesitated.

'I don't know. There was a chap called Tristan here, is he not your son?'

'That's my business partner,' said Kate. 'Does my son know I'm okay?'

'I'm sure the nursing staff will have been in contact with your next of kin.' Dr Harris looked at her chart again. 'I see that your occupation is private detective. That's a first. I've never treated a private detective before,' he said, looking down at her with a smile. 'I'll check on you again in a few hours. You're doing well, but you can't mess about with pneumonia. It can quickly turn nasty.'

Kate felt emotion overwhelm her. Hot tears coursed down her face, and then, without warning, a massive slick of snot ran down her chin. Dr Harris offered the box of tissues from the tall cabinet, and Kate took one, pressing it to her face. He nodded awkwardly and left the room. Kate reached for another tissue, but she was hit by dizziness and nausea. She lay back, panting and sweating, and stared up at the ceiling. Sea swimming was something she did every day. What happened? How could she have been so stupid as to get caught by a riptide?

3

It was a busy Friday night, and Ashdean seafront was crawling with noisy teenagers on their way out. Tristan sat in his car on the promenade outside his flat, feeling exhausted. He'd been awake for more than two days and couldn't summon the energy to get out and cross the pavement to his front door. For a moment, he watched the Ferris wheel on the pier. It had a large video screen in the centre, with psychedelic patterns whirling as it spun, criss-crossing like a crazy cartoon eye. It went in and out of focus as his eyes drooped.

He'd arrived at Kate's house just as she was being carried off the beach on a stretcher, and he watched for a long, terrifying two minutes as the paramedics fought to restart her heart.

Tristan and Kate had grown close over seven years working together, first when she had taken him on as her research assistant at the university when she lectured in criminology, and then as her partner in their burgeoning detective agency. He'd spent the day at the hospital, and relayed the good news to Kate's mother, Glenda, that Kate was out of intensive care and stable, and now the adrenalin that had kept him going all day after no sleep had drained away.

There was a bang on the car window, and Tristan jumped, opening his eyes. A group of teenagers were walking past, dressed up for a night trawling the bars in Ashdean, and one of the young guys grinned and then gave him the middle finger. His mates all laughed, carrying on along the promenade towards the pier. Tristan picked up his phone and dragged himself out of the car.

When he opened the front door to his flat, he was met by his sister, Sarah, putting her finger to her lips.

'I just put Leo down,' she said in an exaggerated stage whisper. Tristan followed her into the living room, where baby clothes and nappies were piled everywhere. Sarah's husband, Gary, was redecorating their new house, so Sarah and nine-month-old Leo had come to stay for a few days. He saw that Sarah had a cup of herbal tea and her Kindle on the coffee table. 'I'm keeping the telly off because the walls here are paper-thin. I'd forgotten how you can hear every noise. Doesn't it drive you mad?'

'I don't really notice it,' said Tristan in a low voice. He went to the dark kitchen, opened the fridge and took out a beer. When he turned around, Sarah was standing in the doorway. The light illuminated the room, and he saw that everything had been cleaned and reorganised, just like when Sarah had lived with him before she met Gary.

'Have you eaten, Tris?' she said, continuing with the stage whisper. He glanced back into the fridge. The top shelf was now filled with jars of baby food.

'Not yet.'

'I thought you might have grabbed something. That's why I closed up the kitchen,' said Sarah, pulling an awkward face. The clock was ticking loudly. Tristan was about to say something when they heard the next-door neighbour slamming their door. It wasn't loud, but a moment later, there was a wail from upstairs as Leo woke up.

'For fuck's sake!' hissed Sarah. 'I just got him down!' Fuming, she went stomping off up the stairs. Tristan sighed, opened the freezer, and dug out a pack of potato waffles. He put four into the toaster and went into the living room with his beer.

A couple of minutes later, Sarah came downstairs carrying Leo, whose face was bright red as he cried. Putting down the beer, he held out his arms, and Sarah handed him over.

Tristan sat down on the sofa and jiggled the little boy on his lap.

'What's wrong with our little Leo?' he said, peering at him and pulling a funny face. Leo abruptly stopped crying and regarded him thoughtfully, and then his little red face broke into a gummy grin. He gave a final blast of crying, hiccupped and began playing with his T-shirt material. Leo traced his tiny fingers across the tattoos on Tristan's forearms, and the black band tattoo on his left tricep.

'He's always so calm around you, Tris,' said Sarah. The toaster popped up in the kitchen.

'They pick up on your emotions – in general, I mean,' Tristan added quickly.

'I'm just scared of doing it wrong,' said Sarah. She held out her finger, and Leo grabbed it. Tristan looked at her tired face. She'd been pregnant twice before Leo, losing the babies at three months and then four. Her third pregnancy with Leo had been stressful and complicated and, now, nine months on, she was still a nervous wreck, thinking she might do something wrong.

'You've already done the hard work, making him. And what

a perfect little boy. They broke the mould with you, Leo, didn't they?' said Tristan.

'He won't stop crying. He cries all the time. The doctor says he's fine, but...'

'Sarah. Babies cry, dogs poop, water is wet, and the world keeps turning.'

She was silent and then nodded.

'Yes. I know.'

'You know what else people do?'

'What?'

'Eat. My potato waffles just popped up.' He grinned, tilting his head towards the kitchen door. Sarah smiled and rolled her eyes.

'Do you want brown sauce?'

'That would be divine.'

Tristan ate with Leo sleeping on his shoulder, and he told her about his day and what had happened to Kate. Sarah listened gravely.

'She's lucky there was someone there in the water. I'm glad she's okay,' she said.

'Are you?' he said, raising an eyebrow. Sarah had never liked Kate and took every opportunity to comment on her. She pulled an indignant face.

'I might not be her greatest fan, but I draw the line at wanting her to drown.'

'That's nice of you,' said Tristan.

'Although, haven't I always said it's dangerous to swim around there? Does she take a proper float with her? Like the one Pamela Anderson had in *Baywatch*.'

'I was never really into Pamela Anderson,' said Tristan, keeping hold of the sleeping Leo as he leant forward to put his empty plate on the coffee table.

'I'm sure if Kate had had one of those red floats, then she wouldn't have got into trouble,' said Sarah.

'Kate's a strong swimmer.'

'Yes, but how old is she? Fifty?'

'She's forty-seven.'

'Is she? She looks a lot older... I suppose you'll have to pick up the slack at the agency now that she's out of action? And what about the caravan site? This is your busiest time, with the summer holidays coming up. Is Jake coming back from university to help out?'

Thankfully, Kate also owned the caravan park opposite her house, and the income from it was used to prop up the agency in lean times.

'No. We've got the manager now for the caravan site. As far as I know Jake's staying in California for the summer.'

Sarah raised an eyebrow.

'What do you mean, as far as you know? Did you tell him about Kate?'

'I don't have his number. I spoke to Kate's mum, and she said she'd keep him updated.'

Sarah looked back at Leo.

'That's another of my fears, that Leo will grow up to hate me,' she said.

'I don't think Jake hates Kate.'

'But they have an awkward relationship. His father is a convicted serial killer. Kate lost custody of him when he was small, because of her drink problems.'

'Kate's mum looked after him.'

'Yes, but she still lost custody.'

'No, Kate and Jake are okay, now,' said Tristan.

'Are they? Why did he choose to go to university in America?'

'I don't know, Sarah. Lots of people study abroad.'

Sarah nodded. Tristan could tell she was in the mood to pick at Kate.

'How many cases have you got on the go?' she asked.

'We're busy,' lied Tristan. The number of cases they had on the go was always a worry. There never seemed to be enough. He thought about returning tonight to try again to get a photo of Terrance Trent, but he knew he had to sleep.

Leo shifted, and the warmth of the little body on his shoulder and the soft baby smell reminded Tristan of how exhausted he was.

'Have you managed to sort things out with your friend, Ade?' asked Sarah.

'No.'

'That's a shame. I like him. I suppose it's awkward when your friend gets drunk and then makes a pass at you.'

Tristan nodded. 'He's got issues with the booze and post-traumatic stress from his work in the police. I just feel sad about it all, really.'

'He's a lot older than you. And you are so out of his league.'

'Sarah, that's not nice.'

'You're a catch. You should see how many heads you turn when we go out. I just want you to find someone, like I found Gary.'

'I'm not really looking, right now.'

'Oh. Can I ask you something?'

'What do you mean? You've been firing questions at me since I got home. I feel like a contestant on a gameshow. You don't want to set me up on a date again, do you?' said Tristan, his heart sinking at the thought.

'No. Do you think Leo is going to get Gary's nose?'

Tristan laughed.

'There's a good chance he will.'

Sarah pulled a face.

'I love everything about Gary, apart from that.'

'What about your nose?' asked Tristan.

'Mine's fine, but you've got a lovely Roman nose. I'm hoping the genes from our side of the family will win through.'

Tristan looked at Leo with his cute little button nose, fast asleep on his shoulder.

'I think it's a lottery, but he'll be a looker, either way.'

Sarah nodded and smiled. Tristan gently handed Leo back to her.

'Now, if this interview is over, I need to sleep. I've been awake for almost two days.'

'Just don't worry about Kate. She's in good hands in the hospital,' said Sarah. Tristan nodded.

'Thank you.'

'And Tris?'

'Yes?'

'Can you make sure you put the toilet seat down? It drives me crazy when you leave it up.'

Tristan gave a salute and went upstairs. Just as he sank down on the bed, he heard Leo start to scream again, but exhaustion pulled him into a deep, dreamless sleep.

4

Kate woke, confused and coughing in the dim light. She couldn't catch her breath. She hacked and retched and then managed to gulp in some air. She sat back, panting, her eyes and nose streaming, and reached for a tissue. She tried to breathe evenly. When she closed her eyes, she could feel herself turning over and over as she spun through the water, catching glimpses of the rocks at the bottom of the sea. She opened her eyes. The screen beside her bed glowed with different coloured lines, showing her vital signs. Kate concentrated on it until they stopped spiking so rapidly. She cleared her throat and had to spit into a tissue.

'You all right, love?' asked a voice in the darkness. Kate turned and could make out the shape of the older lady hunched down under the covers. Her small head seemed to float above the blankets.

'Yes.'

'You don't sound okay.'

'I'm sorry if I woke you up.'

'You didn't wake me up, love. I can't sleep. What are you in for?'

Kate gripped the sides of the bed, still feeling the rocking motion of the sea.

'I...' It felt difficult to admit what had happened. 'I almost drowned, which is embarrassing.'

'Why?'

'I swim every day.'

'Were you in a swimming pool?'

'No. The sea. I swim in the sea every day.'

The old lady shifted under the covers and cursed.

'You'll be okay, though. I heard the doctor.'

Kate could hear a tinge of bitterness in her voice. She was about to ask her neighbour what she was in for, but the older lady changed the subject.

'You see that light out there?' The large glass window looked out onto the corridor and the nurses' station opposite. On top of the high counter was a lamp in a green shade. 'It keeps me awake. I've asked the nurse to move it, but she won't. She's a right bitch.' Kate's heart sank when she heard the woman talking like this, and she wished the curtain was drawn between them. The older lady didn't wait for her to answer. 'Always pulls when she's changing my dressing. She's got a whiff of the sadist in her, but it's subtle, very subtle.'

Her voice was gravelly, and Kate was glad she couldn't see her face. She sank back in the bed and squinted at the walls. There was no clock, and Kate didn't know where her phone or watch was.

'Do you know what time it is?'

'Just before two.'

'Only?' said Kate. She was now wide awake. The thought of the hours left until the sun came up filled her with dread.

'I can never sleep.'

'How long have you been here?' asked Kate.

'This time? Two weeks. I've got ulcers on my legs, and the infection gave me blood poisoning.'

'Sorry to hear that.'

'I'm Jean, by the way.'

'I'm Kate. Hi.'

Kate heard a rustle and then cursing, and Jean rang the bell by her bed. A moment later, a nurse, who looked only in her twenties, came to the door.

'Everything all right, Jean?' she asked crisply.

'Please. Can you move that light off the desk?' asked Jean.

The nurse sighed and checked the watch pinned to her lapel.

'Jean. I've told you before that we have to have a light on at the nurses' station. We need to be able to see. The light has a shade; it's the lowest wattage. Would you like me to draw your curtains?'

'No! I can't sleep in such a confined space. I don't know why you can't put blinds in those windows.'

'We have to be able to see you, so we can take care of you,' said the nurse. She was keeping her voice light, but Kate could tell this was a conversation she'd had before. 'Do you need anything, Kate?' she added, her voice softer.

'No. Thank you.'

'Okay. I'll just be out here.'

The nurse left the room and went back to sit at the desk. The counter was very high, and as she worked at her computer Kate could only see the very top of her head.

'I'm not being fussy,' said Jean now they were alone again.

'Of course not,' said Kate, thinking the opposite.

'Are you married?'

'No.'

'Kids?'

'I've got a son, Jake. He's in his third year at university in California.'

'I've never been to America. Never been nowhere much. I went to France for a pound a few years back. You remember that deal they had in the back of the newspapers? I went to Calais. It was quite nice, apart from all the French people.'

'Yes, Calais is quite nice.'

There was a moment of silence and Kate closed her eyes.

'I heard the doctor say that you're a private detective?'

Kate hesitated. She just wanted to sleep.

'Yes. I am.'

'I've never met one before. I thought private detectives were all men.'

The way Jean said the word 'men' indicated to Kate that her history with the opposite sex hadn't been happy.

'A lot of them are,' said Kate.

'Have you solved lots of cases?'

'A few.'

'Have you ever had a case where you've had to find someone who went missing?'

'Yes. Most recently a young woman.'

Jean was quiet for a moment, then she asked in a small voice, 'Did you find her?'

'Yes.'

'Yes?' Jean replied, her voice hopeful. Kate sighed. 'Oh. She was dead, wasn't she?'

'Yes, she was.'

'How did you find her, and where? You can tell me.'

'We found her skeleton, buried in a wood.'

There was another long silence and then Jean blurted out, 'My grandson went missing. It was on a camping trip, and we had a green tent. That's why I hate that lamp at the nurses' station.' Kate looked at it again. The light glowed through the green fabric shade, slightly mottled like canvas. It did look like a tent, a small one pitched on the wooden surface. 'I only left him for a few minutes... When I came back, he was gone.'

'When did this happen?' asked Kate, her interest piqued.

'Eleven years ago,' said Jean, and the sadness in her voice broke Kate's heart. 'For a long time, I thought that he might be out there, somewhere, still alive, but he was only three when he went missing. How would a three-year-old survive out there all alone? And, of course, there are lots of people who will take a three-year-old child for a reason.' Her last words hung in the darkness for a long beat.

'What does your daughter think happened?' asked Kate.

'She's dead. Killed herself, four years ago. Couldn't cope with the loss. Blamed me. Becky... That was her name. She was Becky.'

There was a long silence, and Kate could feel herself drawn to the story.

'The doctors can't understand why I have these ulcers and why they're not healing. They think it's my immune system, but I think it's the poison inside me coming out. Like acid, it seems to keep coming.'

Kate sat up in bed and sloughed off the covers. She slid her feet out, ignoring the dizziness, and scooted over to the edge of her bed to reach out to Jean. She found her hand and squeezed it.

'Oh, you made me jump.'

Kate could feel a little resistance, so she let go and shifted back into bed.

'Thanks, love,' said Jean. Kate thought she'd gone too far with this display of affection, but Jean cleared her throat and said, 'Can I tell you the story of what happened?'

'If you feel up to it,' said Kate.

'No, but I want to tell you,' replied Jean.

5

'Devil's Way is in the eastern part of the Dartmoor National Park, a few miles from the town of Bovey Tracey. It's named after the river next to the Devil's Tor. My daughter, Becky, and her partner, Joel, had the idea for us all to go camping.'

'Joel is Charlie's father?'

'Yeah. Joel comes from quite a well-to-do family. They weren't thrilled that he got together with my Becky. And then, when she fell pregnant with Charlie, they pretty much disowned him. Money was tight. They were only young when all this happened, in their early twenties. I was only in my forties. I know. I look older than I am,' said Jean, seeing Kate's reaction. 'I'm only fifty-five, but you try living the last eleven years of my life. And things weren't straightforward before it all happened, either.'

Kate nodded, shocked to learn that Jean was only eight years older than her. She looked to be in her late sixties.

'That's how we ended up camping. We had no money, but we were blessed with the beautiful countryside on the moors... Joel picked the place. I thought we'd be staying at a nice campsite with communal toilets, a little shop, and other kids for Charlie to play with. I was shocked when we arrived on the open moor. No loos. The nearest pub and shop were six miles away. We pitched our tents next to Devil's Tor. It was beautiful, and Charlie was excited. It was the first time he'd been anywhere, really.'

'Where did they live?' asked Kate.

'With me, in my one-bedroom flat in Exmouth. I'd taken them in when Becky fell pregnant, and Joel's family didn't want anything to do with him. They were on the list for a council flat.'

'Were you all sharing the same tent?' asked Kate.

'No. I put me foot down at that. Becky and Joel were in one tent, and me and Charlie had the other. The first night we slept like logs, but the next morning, I was up early with Charlie who was still excited. So excited. He wanted to paddle in the stream and go looking for frogs. He was obsessed with frogs. We let Becky and Joel sleep in. Then around eleven-thirty, I noticed that the car was gone. I called Becky, and they were miles away on the other side of Dartmoor at some music festival, and she was already drunk. They'd left Charlie and me with only a bit of bread and margarine. I couldn't drive anywhere. She said that Joel had been offered a gig at the last minute, playing with a band and that they would be back later. When I told her we didn't have much food left, she told me to go and pick blackberries!'

'Blackberries aren't ripe until July or August,' said Kate.

'I know. Can you believe it? Stupid girl. I shouldn't speak ill of the dead...' Jean was quiet for a moment and shifted uncomfortably in the bed. 'Anyway, it didn't matter in the end. Charlie was so excited about everything and anything, and we played and paddled. Two o'clock comes by, and then three, four, five, six! Becky and Joel finally rock up just before eight with food for a barbeque.'

Jean sighed, and there was a creak as she shifted again in her bed.

'What happened when they got back?' asked Kate. When the pause was long enough, she felt comfortable interjecting.

'I was mad, but I kept my mouth shut until after we'd eaten. I pulled Becky off to the stream and was about to let her have it, but she told me Joel had earned a hundred quid playing the guitar for this band. Their guitarist had come down with something. She gave me half the money for house-keeping, and then we were okay. We came back from the stream, Joel lit a fire, and we toasted marshmallows and ate loads of chocolate. They'd bought some of my favourite drink, Babycham...' Jean sighed. 'I can still see that night so vividly, us all being together by the fire. Happy. You know those summer nights that seem to go on for hours after the sun sets?'

Kate nodded. 'Yes.'

'When the sky stays burnt orange and the sun glowing low on the horizon. It felt like it was just God and us sitting there that night. And I'm not even religious... It was the longest day of the year, the twenty-first of June. Anyway, around nine-thirty, when it was getting dark, Charlie was finally tired, and we all turned in for the night. After he was down, I went to have a cigarette. Charlie didn't want me to go, but I was only going to be outside the tent.' At this point, Jean's voice faltered, and she sat up in bed.

'Are you okay?'

'Yeah. Just trying to get comfy. I left Charlie, and I went up onto the Devil's Tor. It was only a hundred metres away from the tent, if that. And...'

Jean put her hand to her mouth as if this part of the story made her feel sick.

'It's okay,' said Kate.

'No. It's not okay. I was only gone for a few minutes, and when I came back to the tent, Becky was just coming out. She said Charlie's sleeping bag was empty. The weather had turned quickly. There was a strange mist hanging over everything, sort of knee height and very thick. I first thought Charlie had come looking for me and got lost in that mist. We looked around the tent, then Becky and Joel's. I went back up to the Tor and searched the base. It was like a series of stones stacked on top of each other, very smooth, there was no way that he could have climbed up. I clambered to the top, scratching my arms on the way, and when I got there, I looked out over everything to see if I could see him. Becky and Joel searched the stream. Nothing.'

Kate could hear that Jean was out of breath.

'It's okay.'

'Even after all this time, I can feel it. I can smell that night. You know when you've got tanned skin? I can still smell that summery scent, mixed with the cold fog in the air. I can almost feel the moisture on my tongue.'

'When did you call the police?' asked Kate.

'We should have done it right away, but none of us wanted to admit it was serious. A couple of police came out, and they started to search the area... Then it got light. The sun came up, and it was so hot. There were more police, and then the Dartmoor National Park got a search party together. Nothing. It was like he'd vanished into thin air.'

'And you said this was eleven years ago?' asked Kate.

'Yes,' said Jean. 'And I haven't had a good night's sleep since then. Charlie would be almost fourteen now if he were alive. They think he might have fallen in the river and been washed away, but we don't know. He just vanished. It's what pushed Becky over the edge. The lack of answers. No closure. She eventually broke up with Joel, and got into drugs.'

There was a long silence in the dark, and then Jean said, 'Do you think you can help me find him?'

6

Kate woke up, disorientated, after another night of strange, vivid dreams. She was drenched in sweat and felt an incredible thirst. The room was bright, and a group of young men and women filed past the window. Kate pushed back the hair stuck to her damp forehead, and it all came back to her. She was in hospital, but she couldn't remember falling asleep.

The bed next to hers was now empty, and the bedding had been stripped off the mattress.

There was a creak and a low rumbling, and a nurse who looked familiar from the previous day came bustling into the room with a medicine trolley. She wore a red tabard over her blue uniform with DRUG ROUND IN PROGRESS, DO NOT DISTURB written in white letters.

'Hello, Kate. How are we today?' she asked chirpily, stopping the trolley beside the bed and unhooking Kate's chart from where it hung on the end.

'Where's Jean, the lady from the next bed?' asked Kate, hearing her voice was croaky and thick with sleep. 'She's not dead, is she?'

The nurse peered over and hesitated, with a rictus grin on her face.

'I can't talk about other patients due to data protection.'

'If she's dead, then there's no more data to protect,' said Kate. The nurse from the previous evening's shift came to the door.

'Dawn. Jean Julings. I've just had to send her records over to The Lawns. A place came available for her early this morning.'

The nurse left, and there was a rattle as Dawn put some pills in a little paper cup which she handed to Kate.

'What are The Lawns?' asked Kate. She remembered Jean's story from the night before and wasn't sure if it was a dream.

'It's a residential care home,' said Dawn.

'Do you know why they moved her?'

'Probably because she was blocking a bed that could be used for someone sicker.'

'What's this?' asked Kate, peering at the tablets nestled at the bottom of the cup. Dawn consulted the chart.

'Levofloxacin is an antibiotic for your chest infection. You have an antihistamine for the motion sickness you've been experiencing, and a mild sedative to help you rest. Rest is essential, and you must drink plenty of fluids.' Dawn took the empty plastic jug from beside the bed, went to the sink in the corner, filled it, and poured Kate a glass of water. 'Here, drink.'

Kate took a long pull, wincing at the tepid water, which seemed to have a tinge of chlorine.

'When can I leave?'

'That's up to the doctor and the results of your next chest x-ray. You had seawater on your lungs. Seawater has all kinds of bacteria, which is fine normally, but when it gets into your lungs, it can cause many problems. We need to keep you under observation.' Dawn flicked through Kate's chart, and her brow furrowed. 'Hm. You have significant scarring on the liver.' She looked down at Kate. 'How many units of alcohol do you drink a week?'

'None. I'm sober thirteen years.'

'Ah,' said Dawn, nodding. 'Okay, I see...' Her eyebrows shot up into her hairline, and she murmured, 'He's prescribed Diazepam.'

'I never had a problem with drugs. I'm in recovery for alcohol addiction,' said Kate. She noticed Dawn's eyes swivel around to the large bottle of hand sanitiser by the sink.

'The doctor should be round later. You ring the bell if you need anything.' She put the chart back on the end of the bed, and the rictus grin was back on her face. Dawn swivelled her trolley and left, removing the bottle of hand sanitiser on her way out.

Kate sat for a moment, feeling despair. *The nurse thinks I'm going to drink the hand sanitiser.* She downed two more glasses of water and then got up to use the bathroom in the corner of the room. On her way back, she realised she was no longer hooked up to the IV line and the heart monitor. She sat on the edge of the bed, feeling a little dizzy from the exertion and ran over what she could remember about her conversation with Jean the night before. It had happened. Hadn't it?

Kate reached to her locker by the bed and opened the door to the compartment at the bottom. Her mobile phone was inside and she saw a small wash bag that Tristan had brought her. Kate switched on her phone and was about to look up 'Charlie Julings missing' on Google when it rang. It was Tristan.

'Hello,' he said, sounding happy to hear her answer. 'Are you okay?'

'I think so. I'm off the machines and IV.'

'Do you feel better?' he asked. Kate hesitated. She no longer felt unwell in her body, but her mind was a mess. She could feel a dark cloud of depression forming, and the sense of embarrassment and failure loomed large.

'Yes,' she lied.

'Any clue to when you're going to be discharged?'

'I don't know. I hope in a couple of days. How are things in the office?'

Tristan hesitated on the end of the phone.

'I finally got the photo of Terrance Trent. I took a punt and got up early this morning. By pure luck, I pulled into a parking spot outside his house and bam, out he came with this young girl, holding hands. I emailed it over to his wife.'

'Good work,' said Kate.

'Are you all right to talk more?'

'Of course.'

'We've just had an email query from a solicitor, Steve Dexter, based in Exeter. He represents a woman called Jean Julings. He said you know her?'

Kate sat back in the bed and felt a surge of relief and excitement. It had happened. She had had the conversation. Kate quickly outlined what Jean had told her the night before.

'A missing person's case. Do you want me to set up a meeting with him?'

'Set it up for Tuesday. Hopefully I'll be discharged by then.'

7

Kate spent Sunday sleeping, and she was pleased the bed beside her remained empty. At 8am on Monday morning, a different doctor examined her. She scrutinised Kate's latest x-ray and deemed her fit to go home.

It all happened so fast, and by nine, Kate was up and dressed, clutching a bag of medication, and waiting outside in the warm sunshine for a taxi to take her home. Kate was thankful that Tristan had brought her an old tracksuit and trainers. Still, she didn't have any underwear – he'd probably been too embarrassed to root through her knicker drawer.

The taxi driver was of the miserable variety, which Kate was glad for. She couldn't face making conversation on the short journey home. When the driver pulled off the motorway and onto the clifftop road leading towards Kate's house and office, a warm breeze floated through the window, and the sea sparkled below.

Kate usually felt at peace when she saw the vast expanse of water stretching away to the horizon, but today it made her feel uneasy. They passed the two wooden clifftop houses, which were let as holiday rentals, both with cars outside, and then further down, the caravan site. It was at full capacity, and a few campers were sitting in the sunshine. The surfers who had pulled her out of the water were renting a caravan, and she was embarrassed to bump into them. Kate leant down and busied herself with her paper bag of medication on the floor, and as they passed the campsite shop with the agency office above, she kept her head down.

Kate paid the driver and then hurried inside her house. The hallway led into a vast living room. A picture window ran all along the back wall looking out to sea. The other walls were covered in bookshelves stacked untidily with novels. The furniture was old and heavy: a battered sofa, coffee table, and an upright piano, which Kate didn't play, against one wall. The house had initially come with Kate's job as a lecturer in criminology at Ashdean University. Her friend Myra had owned the campsite next door, and when she died two years ago, she'd left it all to Kate on the condition that she follow her dream and start up her own detective agency.

Myra had been Kate's sponsor in Alcoholics Anonymous as well as her friend, and right now, in her vulnerable state, she missed Myra more than ever. She moved to the kitchen and stood silently, listening to the clock ticking.

You know, you could have a shot of whisky? said the voice in her head. The one that seemed to be getting louder over the past few days. *Think how good you'd feel if you fixed yourself a nice hot toddy. You've proved to yourself that you can do without. It's virtually medicine – and you've been ill. Take it.* Kate looked out of the side window. The campsite shop sold alcohol and lemons... And there was a jar of honey in the back of the cupboard.

Her phone rang, and she was glad for the distraction. It was Jake on Facetime.

'Hi Mum,' said Jake, his face filling the screen. It looked like he was in his dorm room.

'Hello, love. What happened to your hair?' she asked. When they'd spoken a week ago, his brown hair had been shoulder length, and he'd had a beard. His hair was now cropped very short, and he was clean-shaven.

'I fancied a change,' he said, running his hand over his head. 'More importantly, are you okay? Grandma has been keeping me updated. I tried to call you a couple of times.' His brow furrowed, and Kate felt the balance shifting for the first time in their relationship. He was fixing her with the same concern she'd often had for him as a small boy.

'I'm home.'

'Have you told Grandma?'

'Not yet. It all happened so quickly.'

Jake nodded. He looked good, but the scruffy tousled boy was gone. He looked like a man. It threw Kate for a moment.

'What happened, Mum? You're such a strong swimmer,' he said.

'I am a strong swimmer. It was a riptide, and I wasn't paying attention.'

'Are you still going to meetings?'

'Of course. This doesn't have anything to do with that,' said Kate, hearing the defensive tone in her voice. Jake put up his hands.

'I'm just asking.'

'And I'm just telling you, it was an accident. I am *allowed* to have an accident. It doesn't have to be connected to... anything else.'

Jake nodded.

'I know. But I'm far away, and I worry. I tried to call you a couple of times. Grandma said you had your phone in the hospital, but I haven't heard from you.'

'Jake, you can stop telling me off? Did Grandma also say that I was in intensive care? And that I stopped breathing?'

'No.'

'Well, there you go. I didn't know what day it was. However, I'm home now and on the mend.'

Jake nodded, and they were silent. She heard some noises in the background, people laughing.

'Do you need me to come home?' he said.

'No, but I thought you were coming back for the summer?'

His brow creased.

'I've been offered a summer internship here in LA... It's at a film company. A very prestigious one. And it's paid, too. I know I'm majoring in English Lit, but being in Los Angeles amongst all these film people and creatives, I think I've caught the bug. Or at least this internship will help me make up my mind if I want to pursue a career in film and TV.'

Kate could feel her heart sinking, but she kept her face neutral.

'That's brilliant. Of course, you must take it.'

'Really? I worry about you, and after what happened...'

'You shouldn't. Things are going well here. I'm busy and happy. I would have loved to see you, but you'll be home for Christmas?'

'Of course,' he said. 'And we'll talk lots, as usual. And I might be able to come back for a week or so at the end of the summer.'

'Jake. It's your future.'

'Can you promise me one thing?'

'What?'

'That you'll take care swimming. I know you don't want to hear this, but you're getting older.'

'You're right. I don't want to hear that. I'm forty-seven, not seventy-four!'

'Sorry, Mum. I'm only saying this because I love you.'

When Kate came off the phone, she made herself a cup of tea, went upstairs and crawled under the covers. She lay staring at the ceiling and tried to process her conversation with Jake. *I should be happy*, she thought. *Isn't this what I always wanted for Jake? For him to be successful and happy?* He'd had a rough start in life, and he had to carry the legacy of his father. Despite all that, he was studying abroad and making a life for himself.

However, there was a selfish part of Kate that wished he'd come home. She shook the thought away and tried to get some sleep.

8

The next day, Kate and Tristan met with Dexter Solicitors in Exeter. The solicitor's office comprised two small rooms above a bakery on a quiet street a few hundred yards from the city centre. It was a hot day, and it felt stuffy in the office.

'Jean was due to join us on speakerphone, but the mobile phone signal is bad at the nursing home where she's convalescing,' said the solicitor, Steve Dexter. He was a tall, skinny man who looked to be in his mid-thirties. His black hair was styled in a greased quiff and he had on thick-framed glasses. His black suit had seen better days, with shiny elbows and frayed cuffs. His office was a tribute to disorder. Every wall was filled with bookshelves packed with sagging lever arch files, and his large desk was stacked high on either side with paperwork. His desktop screensaver was an image of Roy Orbison. He had a cardboard folder on the desk in front of him.

'Could we open a window?' asked Kate.

'Sorry, they don't open,' he said. 'Jean has asked me to apologise for her absence today. It's all happened rather fast.'

'We're pleased to be here and working for Jean,' said Kate,

still feeling out of sorts and sickly. Only the day before, she'd been lying in a hospital bed, and now she was zipped up in her best trouser suit to discuss a new case. She unbuttoned the black jacket and cleared her throat, hoping she wasn't about to have another coughing fit.

'Jean is more than just a client to me,' said Steve. 'I was close friends with her late daughter, Becky. And I dealt with Becky's funeral and the paperwork when she passed...' He took a deep breath and looked at them keenly. 'If I'm honest, I'm sceptical about Jean spending what savings she has left on this investigation. The family has suffered so much with the loss of Charlie, and then Becky's death.'

'I'm just as surprised as you,' said Kate. 'I've only spoken to Jean once, and that was when we were in hospital beds.'

'And I've never met Jean,' added Tristan. 'I hope you've taken the time to look at our agency website and google the cases we've worked on.'

Steve looked between Kate and Tristan.

'You understand that the likelihood of finding Charlie alive is almost zero.'

'Yes, we know,' said Kate. 'But if we can find out what happened to Charlie, it would give Jean closure and peace. This is delicate, but can I please ask how Becky passed away?'

The door opened and hit the wall with a thump. An older woman came bustling into the room carrying a round tray of mismatched coffee mugs, all filled to the brim and steaming. She wore a boxy grey trouser suit, a white blouse and a pair of flip-flops. A pair of spectacles hung over an ample bosom, and she had a second pair balanced on her nose with thick greasy lenses. She looked like she was suffering in the heat more than Kate. She was breathing heavily as she walked over, trying not to spill the contents of the overfilled mugs.

'It was Jean who found Becky. She'd hung herself from the light fitting in the living room,' said the woman, steering herself and the tray towards the table. 'The fitting collapsed. The crown mouldings gave in with the weight of her. Not that she was fat. Becky was a slip of a girl, weren't she, Steve?'

Steve didn't look pleased with the interruption. The woman put the tray down and carried on talking.

'Just before she died, Becky was deep into drugs.' She tutted and shook her head at the memory. 'Jean tried to help her so many times. And Steve, he was a real rock for her... And I did what I could. I hosted the intervention.'

Something about how she said 'hosted' made it sound like a catered event.

'I'm Sadie, by the way, office manager and Steve's mum. It's nice to meet you.' She held out her hand. Kate and Tristan shook hands with her, and Kate liked her instantly. She was a real contrast to her snooty son. 'I'm so pleased that you're going to investigate what happened. Charlie, he was such a dear little boy. The apple of Jean's eye. After everything she's had to cope with in her life, it's just cruel what happened to Charlie. You read about those cases where children go missing, and you never expect it to happen to someone you know so well. I've told Jean for years that she should hire a private detective. The police have been next to useless... You'd think that children go missing every day.'

'Well, sadly, they do,' said Kate. 'Did you know over 112,000 children are reported missing in the UK every year?'

'You're kidding?' said Sadie, appalled.

'Lots of them are found, but it's still a horrifying statistic.'

'What are the chances of you finding Charlie?'

'I'm not going to lie. Slim. But we have a strong record with finding missing people,' said Kate. There was silence. 'Do you know Jean outside of work?'

'Yes. Me and Jean go way back. We were both in the dreaded children's home together. That bonded us, and here I am. I was fifty last year, and we're close. Steve and Becky used to play together.'

Steve pursed his lips and gingerly lifted one of the dripping mugs off the tray.

'Thank you, Sadie,' he said. Kate and Tristan exchanged a glance. Was he one of those odd people who call their parents by their first name?

'Sorry about the mess. The capsule machine is broken. I hope you don't mind instant?' Sadie added, picking up the mugs and blotting them underneath with a wad of tissue.

'Instant is fine, thank you,' said Tristan.

'I read that *National Geographic* article about you both online. It's so impressive how you found out who killed that journalist. And I like that you're a local boy,' she said to Tristan. 'Jean's made the right choice with you two. I just hope she'll be better soon and able to go home. She has terrible trouble with ulcers. You should see them. Have you ever seen venous ulcers?'

Kate and Tristan shook their heads. Sadie put up her hand.

'Awful they are, so painful, and sometimes they never heal! Jean has terrible varicose veins. She won't mind me saying, I'm sure. All the jobs she's ever done have had her on her feet all day; cleaner, barmaid and what-have-you. And she got these ulcers from the veins on the backs of her thighs breaking. Can you imagine? She can barely sit or move when they erupt.'

Steve gave Sadie a look.

'Anyway. It's nice to meet you both. I'll see if I can get Jean on the blower. She wanted us to put her on speakerphone so she could join this meeting, but there's terrible mobile reception at

The Lawns, and the nursing staff are funny about her using the landline.'

Steve cleared his throat, and his look of annoyance almost made Kate laugh.

'Well, I'll be outside if you need me.' She backed out of the room with a smile. Steve waited until the door was closed before continuing.

'Sorry about that,' he said, sliding the two chipped Smarties-branded coffee mugs to Tristan and Kate and keeping the Cadbury's Crunchie-branded one for himself. 'Sadie... my mother is a good secretary. It's just keeping the boundaries sometimes is, er...' He picked up the folder.

'What's Joel, Charlie's father, doing now?' asked Kate.

'He runs a pub on the other side of Dartmoor near Belstone.'

'Is he married?'

'Yes. He has two young girls with his second wife. He's on holiday in Spain with his family.'

'Does he know that Jean is hiring us?' asked Tristan.

'I don't know. This has all come together so fast.' He took a piece of paper from a pile next to him. 'Now. I received a copy of your business contract. Everything looks acceptable, but you'll be dealing with me regarding finances.' He took a silver pen from his inside pocket and signed the contract with a flourish. 'Jean kept some newspaper clippings and the photos she took during that fateful camping trip. It's not much to go on, but I thought you should have them.'

'What about contacts? Are there any details of the police officers who worked on the case?' asked Tristan.

Steve shook his head.

'Jean hates the police. If I'm honest, she never had a good relationship with any of the police officers who worked on the case. She even told the lead detective to eff off.' He slid the folder across the table to them. When Kate picked it up, she could feel it was very slim.

'If I can take a moment to speak as Jean's friend and not her solicitor, please be mindful of her vulnerability. The statistics you quoted are horrific. And even if you do find Charlie, I don't know if it will give her the closure she wants. Please, don't get her hopes up, and know when to let her down gently.'

'Of course,' said Kate.

He nodded and smiled. 'Thank you. I wish you both the best of luck, and I'll help whichever way I can.'

9

'Are you okay?' asked Tristan. He was driving them back from the meeting with Steve Dexter, and he could see Kate looking very pale beside him.

'I just need a moment to catch up after everything,' she said.

Privately, Tristan thought it was a little too soon for Kate to be back at work, but he kept this to himself. She wouldn't react well to being told to stay in bed. She cleared her throat, and it descended into a rattling coughing fit.

'Do you need some water? There should be a sports drink rolling around in the back.' Kate pulled out a tissue, undid her seat belt and, still coughing, found the bottle, opened it, and took a sip.

'That's better,' she said, her eyes still watering. 'I think it's the air conditioning in the car making me cough.'

Tristan switched it off and opened the windows. Kate's phone rang in her suit jacket, hanging over the back of her seat. She turned, rummaged in the pockets, and pulled it out.

'Oh, it's Jean,' she said.

'Put her on speakerphone,' said Tristan. Kate answered.

'Alright, love? Can you hear me?' said Jean, her voice sounding tinny and far away.

'Yes. I'm here in the car with my partner in the agency, Tristan,' said Kate.

'Hello, Jean,' said Tristan, taking care not to say 'hi'. He remembered a dinner lady they had at school called Jean and how the students had constantly goaded her, shouting '*hygiene!*' at every opportunity.

'Hello, Tristan,' said Jean. 'Are you local or from up country?'

'Local,' said Tristan. 'Ashdean born and bred.' He didn't have much of an accent. Sarah had made an effort to eradicate her West Country accent, and it had rubbed off on him. Jean's was subtle, but he could hear the trace of a West Country twang in her voice.

'I'm sorry I missed the meeting. I'm sitting in the staff toilets,' she added. 'Would you believe it's the only place with a decent mobile phone signal? Was everything all right with Steve?'

'He was very accommodating,' said Kate. 'And I just want to say how pleased we are to work on this for you.'

'Yes, well. Just keep telling me everything straight. I don't need things sugar-coated. Did Steve give you the folder with the photos?'

'Yes,' said Kate, holding it in her lap. They'd looked through it, and it contained a few dog-eared newspaper clippings and photos of the tents pitched next to the Devil's Tor. 'We did some internet research before the meeting and found a couple more articles.'

'You won't find much online. Sadie's been having a look for me. Did you meet Sadie?'

'Yes,' said Kate.

'She's a good pal, is my Sadie. We go way back. When Charlie

51

went missing, the story was in the local news, but then, it seemed to all go quiet.'

'There were a lot more local newspapers eleven years ago that could have covered the story. We want to check out the microfilm archives in Exeter,' said Kate. She hadn't mentioned this to Tristan and when he glanced over, Kate raised an eyebrow in question and he nodded.

'Good luck with that,' Jean said, her voice full of gloom.

'It would also help if we could come and talk to you, properly, in a few days to find out from you exactly what happened. In detail.'

'I'll tell you whatever you need. I'm paying, aren't I? I'm always here on the phone when I can get a bloody signal. I don't have email or what-have-you.'

'The phone is fine,' said Kate. 'But can we come and visit you?'

'Of course! I'm not in prison,' she snapped. There was a long pause. Tristan wondered why Jean sounded so hostile. Maybe it was nerves.

'How is your relationship with Joel?' asked Kate.

'I know who Joel is! He got re-married. He runs a pub near Belstone with his wife. They've got two young girls. We're not in contact, much. I do know that he's on holiday in Spain.'

'Could you tell him you've hired us to investigate Charlie's disappearance? It will help if we don't have to cold call him. Or you could get Steve to call him?'

'Yeah. I'll get Steve to ring him. Let him know,' said Jean. They heard her sigh. 'Is that all you need from me for now?' she added.

'Yes. Can you suggest a time when we can come and talk to you?' said Kate. There was a click as the call got cut off.

'Do you think she hung up, or the signal was bad?' said Kate, looking at Tristan. He shrugged. 'She was so open with me when she spoke in hospital.'

'Maybe she felt self-conscious being on speakerphone. I haven't met her yet,' replied Tristan. 'And she's hired us to "find" Charlie, but what we're going to do is give her a conclusion, do you know what I mean? And most likely Charlie is... dead.'

When Tristan pulled off the main road down towards Kate's house, he noticed her duck down and busy herself with the contents of her bags, spending a long time searching for her keys. She didn't sit up until Tristan pulled into the carport outside her house. Kate let out a long sigh and closed her eyes. Tristan rolled up the windows and switched off the engine.

'I don't want to keep asking this, but are you okay?' he said.

Kate hesitated and then nodded. Tristan could see she was too tired to go to the office, so he suggested they work in the house.

'I can make the tea,' he said when they were inside.

'A coffee, please. Strong,' said Kate, sinking into one of the easy chairs next to the picture window. She clutched the folder and opened it on her lap as Tristan went into the kitchen and filled the kettle.

There was a packet of photos with the PRONTAPRINT logo. When she opened it, she saw the negatives sticking out of the pocket in the front. It had been a long time since she'd seen a packet of photos.

The photo on top was a small square. The edge had been torn off and then stuck back on with sticky tape. It was a picture of a little boy standing in front of a white door with a silver handle above his head. He had white-blond hair and was wearing a pirate outfit with a black patch over one eye. He was an angelic little boy, grimacing with a row of very white, straight teeth and rosy cheeks.

Kate turned the photo over, and written on the back was "Charlie's first fancy dress party".

She flicked through the other photos which were of the campsite at Devil's Tor. Two tents were pitched, one under the tree and the other next to the Tor. The tree branches seemed to reach several metres in each direction and had no leaves, even though the photos had been taken in June. The grass was long between the tents. A red Renault was parked beside the Tor.

There were other photos of a young, stocky man with long dark hair tied back in a ponytail and wearing a Led Zeppelin T-shirt. He was leaning into the car's boot next to a thin, red-haired woman who had her back to the camera. She was wearing tiny cut-off denim shorts and a sleeveless T-shirt. Charlie stood a few feet away, watching them, holding a long stick. In another photo, Jean was standing under the tree, with Charlie sitting on her shoulders. She looked so young and had thick red hair down to her shoulders and a silver nose ring. Kate could not contemplate how this was the same wizened woman she'd seen in the next hospital bed.

Tristan came into the living room with two mugs of coffee and looked at the photos over her shoulder.

'Anything?' he asked.

'They're photos taken before Charlie went missing,' said Kate lingering on the smiling photo of the young Jean with Charlie. She flicked through to the next image. 'Oh, there's one of the police.'

It was a picture of a group of three police officers searching the moorland around the tents and Devil's Tor. Their squad car was parked next to the Renault. Tristan peered closer at the photo. One of the police officers was close to the camera, and he'd taken off his cap, presumably to wipe his forehead in the heat.

He was a tall, solid-looking man, and his short dark hair was plastered to his head. His face looked like a beef tomato. *It must have been a hot day*, thought Kate.

'Blimey. That's Ade,' said Tristan, taking the photo from her.

'Ade, your friend, Ade? The retired ex-police officer?' asked Kate. She realised she didn't know his surname.

'It looks like him.'

Kate took the photo back and peered at the man.

'Well spotted. He looks so different. Thinner, and less flamboyant. Do you think you can ask him about the case?'

'He might just have been the responding officer,' said Tristan.

'Yes. But he's worth asking.' She glanced at Tristan's face. 'What?'

'I'm not really talking to him right now.'

'Why not?'

'I used to go for a drink with him at the pub every week. A few weeks ago, he got drunk, or drunker than normal, and he tried it on with me.'

'Oh,' said Kate, thinking back to the things she'd done under the influence, and quickly putting them out of her mind.

'I tried to give him the brush-off nicely, but he didn't take it well.'

Kate hesitated and peered at the photo again.

'He was ranked a DCI, I didn't know that,' she said, holding it up to show the pips on Ade's uniform. 'He could have worked this case. We don't have much to go on right now, and Steve said that Jean didn't have a good relationship with any of the police officers who worked on the case. This could save us a lot of time.'

'All right,' said Tristan. 'I'll go and talk to him.'

10

The next morning, Tristan got up early and went to the gym. He'd arranged to visit the Devil's Way campsite later that afternoon with Kate, so after his workout, he came home to get changed and then steeled himself to visit Ade.

Ade lived at the opposite end of Ashdean's long seafront promenade, in the basement flat of an old Victorian townhouse. It was the second to last building on the seafront, close to the university building. When Tristan reached the gate, he saw the curtains were closed in the front window. He went down the steps to the small mews courtyard, which had a cast-iron bench against the wall, and on the front doorstep were six packages of various shapes and sizes.

Tristan stood for a moment, suddenly feeling nervous. He put his hand to the brass door knocker when the door opened. Ade's face registered surprise, and he clasped a hand to his chest.

'Jesus, Miss Marple. Do you want to give me a bloody heart attack? What are you doing, hovering on my doorstep?'

Ade was a different man now from the picture of the police

officer in the newspaper article. He was slimmer, and his hair was a magnificent mane of dyed chestnut brown, which flowed down his back. Ade had a neatly trimmed beard, and wore an emerald green velvet dressing gown. Miss Marple was Ade's nickname for Tristan, which he'd coined when he heard Tristan was working as a private detective.

Ade didn't seem annoyed or even acknowledge that there was anything wrong. Tristan opened his mouth but was unsure where to start.

'I was going to knock,' he said.

'Were you now? What stopped you?' asked Ade, peering up at the sky and blinking in the bright sunshine. He looked back at Tristan and raised an eyebrow, challenging him.

'I was worried about all the parcels on your doorstep. I thought you might be dead.'

'Dead, dear? Me, dear? No, dear. My time is far from up. This is par for the course of a Wednesday morning,' he said, indicating the parcels on his doorstep. 'It's my latest eBay haul. Now, make yourself useful, and grab a couple on your way in.'

Ade's flat was decorated with dark wooden furniture upholstered with multi-coloured cushions. The walls had a midnight blue, flock wallpaper covered in stars and moons. The tiny basement flat didn't feel dingy because seven Tiffany lamps were lit up on every surface. Two huge bookshelves were packed with books and DVDs, overflowing onto the floor and the large coffee table. A small galley kitchen led off to the living room, and Tristan followed Ade through. The kitchen was beautifully clean and ordered compared to the rest of the house. Herbs were growing in little clay pots on the windowsill, and Ade had somehow managed to fit an Aga into the small space. Despite the summer weather, Tristan could feel it was kicking out some heat.

'You can put the packages down there,' said Ade, indicating a small round wooden table by the door, with a bowl piled high with passion fruits and avocados. Above it on the wall was a poster of the Jonas Brothers. 'Would you like some tea or coffee?'

'Tea would be lovely.'

'Tea it is then,' he said, fixing Tristan with a stare for a moment before moving to fill the kettle.

'Listen, Ade,' said Tristan.

'Yes. We need to talk about what happened.' Ade swivelled around on his heels and put the kettle on the Aga. He put his hands up. 'I was in the wrong. I'm sorry.'

'It's okay.'

'No. It's not. And I mean it. I'm sorry. You must know how gorgeous you are, Tris?' Tristan didn't know what to say. 'Well, you are. But it's no excuse. I know that we are just friends. And even though I would give anything for a roll in the hay with you, what's clear is that you just want to be friends. And your friendship is more important.'

There was an awkward pause, and Ade turned back to the sink.

'I'm sorry if I gave you the wrong idea,' said Tristan. Ade put up his hand.

'You didn't. It was me and the demon drink. I should never touch Campari. I lose all inhibitions.'

'Yes,' said Tristan, thinking back to what happened, walking home from the pub when Ade tried to kiss him. He turned back to Tristan, and there were tears in his eyes. It looked like the memory was painful for Ade, too.

'I'm sorry, Tris. I shouldn't have. Can we go back to being

friends? I'm so grateful you came here and made the first move to fix things.'

'Of course,' said Tristan.

'Good,' said Ade with a smile, dabbing his eyes. 'Do you like ginger nuts?' he added.

'If you're talking about biscuits, then yes.'

Ade laughed, and Tristan felt they were back on an even footing. Although, there was the delicate issue that he hadn't come to see Ade just to make things up. When they had their tea, they came to sit on the bench outside the front door.

'How's work?' asked Ade, slipping on a massive pair of Jackie-O sunglasses. Tristan told him what had happened to Kate.

'Jesus, but she's okay now?'

'She's shaken up. But one good thing came out of it. She met a woman in the hospital who's hired us to look for her missing grandson.'

'As you do.'

'I'm not joking.'

Tristan briefly outlined the case and pulled the newspaper article out of his pocket to show to Ade.

'Hang on a mo,' said Ade. He took off the sunglasses and searched in the folds of his dressing gown, taking out a packet of cigarettes, a lighter, and then a pair of thick, brown framed glasses. He put them on, took Jean's photograph from the Tor, and peered at it.

'Oh, dear. Yes. That's me. What a porker. And who cut my hair? It looks like whoever did it put a bowl on my head and cut around it.'

'I wanted to know about the case. Do you remember it?' said Tristan. 'It was eleven years ago that Charlie Julings went missing.'

The sound of laughter on the promenade and waves breaking on the beach floated down into the courtyard.

'Yes. I do remember it,' said Ade, handing the photo back and taking off his glasses. He tapped a cigarette out of the packet and lit up.

'Did you work on the investigation?' asked Tristan, watching him as he exhaled smoke.

'Is that why you came here today?' he said, fixing Tristan with a keen stare.

'Yes. And I wanted to sort things out.'

Ade flicked ash on the ground, pursed his lips, then abruptly got up, went back inside, and slammed the front door.

Bloody hell, thought Tristan. *Has he gone off in a huff again?*

11

Tristan got up, went to the door, and tried the handle. It was open.

'I'm just through here, Tris,' shouted Ade. Tristan moved through to a small room at the back of the flat that he hadn't seen before. It was a tiny office filled with metal shelving and all kinds of folders and paperwork. Tristan watched as Ade searched through a pile of files on the top shelf. 'These are copies of my old pocket notebooks.'

'Notebooks from what?'

'It's the notebook you get issued with as a police officer. It's an official document,' Ade said, putting a folder back and teasing a yellow one from the shelf below. Tristan moved to help him, lifting the stack above the folder so he could pull it out.

'It isn't strictly legal for a police officer to make copies of his notebooks, but I worked with a slippery bastard superintendent who altered his... I won't go into it now,' he said. He opened the folder.

'Here we go! June 2007,' he said triumphantly. He pulled out a bunch of photocopied sheets. Tristan followed him back into the living room. They sat in opposite chairs, and Ade started looking through the pages filled with his neat handwriting.

'June 22nd, a mobile phone call came into control at 4am,' he read. 'We got the call from the little boy's father, Joel. He'd sounded very distressed, saying his son had been missing for a couple of hours.'

'They noticed Charlie was missing at 2am?' asked Tristan. Ade nodded.

'We were called out from Okehampton, where I was working, and it took us about forty minutes to get there. My colleague was a very nervous driver. There were no streetlights on the moor; it was only just getting light. We arrived at Devil's Way around four-forty,' he said, finding the correct page.

Tristan had started to make notes on his phone.

'What was your colleague called?'

'I can't remember, he was a uniform officer, quite cute,' said Ade.

'Are you still in touch?'

'I can't remember his name, so no.' Ade carried on reading in silence for a moment. 'Ah, yes! The grandmother. Jesus, she was a piece of work.'

'Jean Julings?'

'Yes. When we got there, it was a surreal sight. The sun was just coming up, and Jean and her daughter, Becky, were fighting. Physically fighting, rolling around like two WWE fighters in the long grass next to one of the tents. They were both bloodied and bruised. Joel was trying to pull them apart.'

'Why were they fighting?' asked Tristan.

'Becky blamed Jean for the boy getting lost. We thought he had wandered off on the moors. However, Becky was convinced that Jean's boyfriend was responsible for Charlie going missing.'

'Boyfriend?'

'Yes,' Ade said, consulting his notes. 'A guy called Declan Connoly. He was there with Jean just before the boy went missing. Declan Connoly was already known to the police. A few weeks before, an officer caught him in a pub with an underage girl. Someone had rung the police saying he was buying this girl drinks. She was only twelve. The police got there before anything nasty happened, and the girl seemed to be with him voluntarily. There was some confusion at the time if she was an underage prostitute,' said Ade, reading from neatly written notes in black ink. 'Declan also had a prison record. He'd spent time inside for burglary and GBH. He'd been in an on-off relationship with Jean Julings for years, ever since they were young. Later that morning, one of the backup squad cars who came to help with the search found him in his car in a ditch a mile from Devil's Way.'

Ade looked up from his notes.

'Did you say you've been hired by Jean Julings, the grandmother?'

'Yes,' said Tristan. 'What did the police do when they found Declan?'

'They took him to Exeter A&E where they checked him over. We were in the middle of organising a search. Dartmoor National Park got involved. They recruited a big group for the search, which we conducted for the next twenty-four hours, but we never found the boy. We called in the scent dogs, and they followed it to the river, if I remember, and then the trail went dead. It led us to believe he fell into the water and was swept away. The river was churning and raging when we came down to do the search.'

'Anything else?' asked Tristan. Ade checked his paperwork.

'That was as far as I went with it, but I do remember that the police took in Declan for questioning a week later. And they found some of Charlie's blood in his car.'

'Where?'

'In the back seat, I think. The police brought in Jean for questioning, and she stuck up for Declan. He'd taken Charlie and Jean out for the day a few weeks before the disappearance. Charlie had been playing in a park and cut his hand on a piece of glass. He said that's where the blood in the car came from.'

'Did the police charge Declan?'

'No. We didn't have enough evidence. The daughter, Becky, confirmed that Charlie had cut himself.'

'What happened next?'

'I don't know, Tris. I didn't move forward with the case. I was reassigned to something else. I think that's when things went cold. The evidence pointed towards the boy falling into the river. It was a raging muddy torrent,' said Ade. 'We couldn't cross it with the sniffer dogs, and the search party made up of locals had to be very careful, too.'

'Had it rained?' asked Tristan.

'I can't remember,' said Ade. 'Like the Tor, the river's called the Devil's Way, and it runs into the Devil's Gorge. At the base of the gorge, the water disappears into a strange sinkhole, like a bubbling cauldron.'

'If Charlie fell into the river, could he have been washed down the gorge and into this sinkhole?'

Ade sat back and thought for a moment.

'The sinkhole was covered by a grate, so the boy couldn't have gone down it. That grate would have stopped him. That's what kept the case open and unsolved, as far as I can remember,' he said.

'Do you have the names of the other police officers who worked on the case?'

'I'd have to go back over my notes. You should take a look at Devil's Way. I'd be interested to see what you think.'

As Tristan leafed through the photocopied notes, he could tell that Ade's interest had been spiked about the old case.

'Thank you for helping me,' said Tristan.

'I've got nothing better to do,' said Ade airily. 'And, if I'm honest, I've missed your ugly mug.'

Tristan smiled.

'I've missed yours, too.'

'Cheeky.'

'Can I have copies of those notes?'

Ade looked down at the paperwork for a moment.

'You are the mistress of manipulation, Miss Marple. *If* I let you have copies, you have to know that these don't officially exist, understand?'

'Understood.'

'Good. Now have you got time for another cuppa before you go?'

12

It had been a hot day, and the sun was still shining bright when Tristan picked Kate up just after 5pm. She had been sleeping most of the day, and felt only a little better.

The journey from Ashdean to Bovey Tracey on the edge of Dartmoor took about forty minutes. They rode in silence, watching the beauty of the coastline roll out. When they reached Bovey Tracey, the dual carriageway became a single-lane road for a few miles along the edge of Dartmoor. They had to go slowly for the next ten minutes as the road surface alternated between tarmac and a gravel track across the moorland. Then trees rose out of the landscape, and the road entered a tunnel of ancient oaks, blocking the sunlight. They continued driving in the gloom for a few minutes until the tunnel of trees thinned and the road banked down on a steep hill. At the bottom was a deep ford where the water was rushing across the road. Tristan slowed the car and came to a stop at the edge.

'I hate fords,' he said.

'Me too,' agreed Kate. She already knew they would have to

drive back in the dark, and she suddenly felt uneasy. They should have left it until the next day.

'We do want to see Devil's Way in the dark. To get an idea of what it was like when they were camping,' said Tristan, seeming to read her mind.

Kate peered at the water in the gloom, surging silently past.

'Just go very slowly,' she said. Tristan pressed his foot down gently on the gas and steered the car into the water.

'Are fords normally this deep?' said Tristan, looking out the car window as the water spattered up the glass.

'This is a mini, and it rained last night,' Kate replied. She gripped the side of the door and felt the wheels shift under them as they reached the middle of the ford. The car lurched and seemed to leave the road and float for a moment, and then there was a roar as the wheels gripped the tarmac. Tristan regained control as they drove up and out of the water on the other side.

The road wound down through another steep tunnel of trees, where it grew so dark with the surrounding thick foliage that Tristan flicked on the car's headlights. And then they burst out of the trees into the hazy sunlight and open moor. It was now a quarter past seven, and they passed a couple of tors casting long shadows. The road was now just an earth track, which threaded its way down across a broad platform of moorland stretching far away to the hazy horizon.

'Okay. This up ahead should be Devil's Way,' said Tristan, peering at the GPS on his phone.

'Is this the only route to Devil's Way?' asked Kate. Tristan took his phone out of its holder and handed it to her. She zoomed out of the GPS map, where the expanse of green on both sides was moving past. 'The is the only road. The other sides of the Tor are open to the moorland and the Devil's Way river.'

The road straightened up as it led them down to a deep groove in the fields, and then it banked sharply up. When they reached the crest of the hill, they saw the Devil's Tor in the distance. It stood out and looked like a giant had stacked a pile of pebbles on a raised platform of rock and grass.

As they drew close, it grew bigger and towered above them when the dirt road ended. There was a small patch of flattened ground on the roadside of the Tor, but Tristan drove around the large grass base, and on the other side, they saw the ancient tree from the news reports about Charlie's disappearance.

Kate hadn't thought much about why the place was called Devil's Way – living in Devon and Cornwall for so long, you became blasé about these names. When they got out of the car, they looked over the short expanse of grass to the tree. It had no leaves, but the branches were ancient and thick. They reached out to make a vast canopy in all directions, so the tree cast shade even without leaves. A flock of black crows perched high on the branches at the top of the tree, and when Tristan closed his door, the sound echoed like a gunshot. The birds took flight with a collective caw across the blue sky.

There was a thick silence in the air and no breeze. As Kate and Tristan stood in the quiet, the sound of running water started to echo around them.

Tristan locked the car, and they walked up the grassy slope and around the stacked stones of the Tor. The landscape was so vast that their perception of distance was slightly skewed. Kate couldn't work out how far they could see. The moor was twenty miles wide from east to west, and at three hundred and sixty-eight square miles, there were lots of places for a small child to get lost.

'Let's take a look at the river,' said Kate. They walked down the grass slope on the opposite side. They passed between a cluster of granite boulders at the base and emerged next to a fast-running river winding through a rock seam. It was idyllic and surrounded by mossy boulders and grass on the banks. When they reached the water's edge, Kate could see it was about ten metres wide and very clear. It wasn't deep, perhaps a metre or more. Tristan slipped off his flip-flops and sat down on a rock, dipping his toes into the water.

'Wow, that's cold. Lovely and cold,' he said. Kate followed and sat down beside him. She pulled off her shoes and sighed with pleasure as her bare feet hit the cool running water. Tristan slid off the rock and waded out.

'I'm trying to remember how tall a three-year-old is?' asked Kate, looking at Tristan. The water came up to the top of his thighs at the deepest point in the middle. She thought back to when Jake was three of four, but during this period, she'd been in the worst grip of her alcoholism. Her memory of that time was hazy.

Tristan turned to her and exhaled, arching his shoulders and blowing out his cheeks at the feel of the cold water.

'A bit below my waist? My nephew is nine months old, and he's about this big,' he said, holding his hands a couple of feet apart. Kate laughed.

'You're what? Six feet tall?'

'Six two.'

'If Charlie had fallen in here, he could have easily drowned.'

'It's quite a gentle stream,' said Tristan, wading back to her. 'Ade said the water was churning and raging when they came down to do the search.' He turned slowly in the water and trailed his fingers across the surface as it moved around him with lazy ripples.

Kate stepped down into the water and joined him. The river bed was covered in large smooth stones and a little gravel. She waded out to a rock poking out of the middle of the stream and climbed up on it. From this vantage point, she could see that the river came from across the moors, passing the tree at a distance. It carried on for twenty metres in the other direction and then turned dramatically to the left, vanishing behind a massive outcrop of pearl-grey granite on the nearside bank.

'That's the Devil's Gorge,' said Kate, pointing to it. 'Let's have a look.' They waded back to the bank, and Tristan helped Kate out of the water. They set off along the river bank, carrying their shoes and walking barefoot on the soft moss and grass. The ground stayed level, but as they walked, Kate saw how the water level banked down. When they reached the rocky outcrop, the banks narrowed, and the river moved fast, the water white and churning between large boulders. The terrain was growing rougher on the feet, and Kate dropped her shoes and slipped them on. Tristan did the same.

They climbed up over the rocky outcrop, which at the top was a smooth shelf of granite. Kate grabbed Tristan's arm when they found themselves on the edge of a steep drop. The river lurched sharply to the left where the water was forced into a narrow channel and fell into the gorge with a roar. A footpath began next to the waterfall and sloped gently down into the gorge. Tristan went first, and they picked their way down the narrow path. There was no guard rail to stop them from falling thirty feet down, and in places, Kate held onto the wall.

As they descended, Kate felt a chill in the air in the shadow of the gorge. The waterfall roared and echoed around the rocky walls above.

The path came level with the water at the end of the gorge and a high rock face covered in dripping moss and ferns. The trail ended a few feet from a waist-high metal barrier with a grille. Next to the path, the rushing water was funnelled into a space about a metre wide, and pushed through the grille, which was blocked in places with pieces of wood, rubbish, and strands of soggy tissue paper. On the other side of the grille, the water was swirling around in a vast pool several metres wide, and vanishing with a roar into a black void like a plughole in the centre. The sounds of the water here were so loud that Kate had to raise her voice and shout.

'Where does it go? Does that lead to an underground stream?'

Tristan pointed to a battered metal sign tacked to the rock above.

THIS IS THE DEVIL'S WAY was written in tall black letters.

13

Kate and Tristan stood beside the roaring water for a long time. The metal grille was made of thick iron and coated with layers of paint. It was a metre high, and if either one had stepped into the rushing water, the grille would protect them from being pulled into the pool and the sinkhole on the other side.

'Do you think Charlie could have climbed over this grille?' said Tristan, having to shout over the sound of the water. He moved closer to the top of the grille. There was a waist-high metal bar halfway up, running horizontally with a rusting padlock in the centre. The bar was a way of stepping up, like over a farm gate. Tristan used it to pull himself up, straddling the grille effortlessly.

Kate moved closer. She could smell the dampness in the air, and here the gorge's walls were covered with dripping green moss, adding to the gloom and infusing the air with a chill, despite the summer weather.

Still straddling the grille, Tristan pulled a till receipt from his pocket, folded it in half, and made a small paper aeroplane. He threw it over, and the paper plane swooped down and landed on the idling water at the pool's edge; it floated for a moment before it was grabbed by the swirling current. They watched as it spun anti-clockwise, moving faster as it was pulled towards the centre. It became a blur as it turned, and then it vanished into the black hole.

Kate thought of Charlie. If he'd wandered off alone and ended up here, could he have climbed over the grille and fallen into the pool? Had he gone down into the sinkhole, never to be seen again? She shivered in the cold and dark of the gorge.

'Please, come down, and let's go,' she said. Tristan stepped down, and they started to climb back up the trail. The walk back to the river seemed more protracted, and where the fronds of moss and ferns had appeared so summery before, they were now cast in shadow, and a couple of times, Kate thought she saw movement, a fleeting glance of someone or something. When they were back at the top of the smooth rock, Kate saw the sun was now low on the horizon. It was eight-fifty, and the sun would soon set.

'It must be creepy here the second it gets dark,' said Tristan, echoing her thoughts. Kate looked across past where the river took a turn into the gorge. A narrow footpath on the other side of the river led further away to a thick wall of gorse and foliage. Beyond this were dense trees.

They walked back along the riverbank to the car, and by the time they were back at Devil's Tor, the sun had set, and Dartmoor stretched out in front of them in the darkness. The moon was a pale silvery disc, and several stars appeared in the blue-black sky. The river sounded quieter now, shifting past them here like black ink. Kate shivered. She loved the water, the sea, lakes, and streams during the day, but open water in the darkness terrified her.

The Tor seemed taller in the failing light, like a vast

skyscraper with no windows, reaching high above the stars. It made Kate think of a sci-fi movie, and for a moment, she wondered if the legends were true and if strange creatures, like goblins and elves, lived inside. This was the problem with the deepest moors – legends played on your mind. And at night, rationality left you.

They moved around the grass platform to Tristan's car. Like the Tor, the ancient oak tree now seemed immense in the twilight.

'How can anyone want to camp here?' said Tristan. 'It's bloody creepy.'

'Jean and her family had no money, and it was free,' said Kate.

'Do we really think a three-year-old would wander off alone here at night? I'd be too scared to leave the tent for a pee.' Kate nodded. It was a good point.

'Jean and Charlie slept in their tent under the tree. It's not a great distance between the two. Joel and Becky pitched theirs next to the car at the base of the Tor.'

She took out her phone and found Jean's photos. Tristan came around to look at the screen. One photo had been taken from a similar angle to where they were standing. A small red domed tent was pitched under the tree, and closer to the camera, next to the Tor was an identical tent in blue with Joel's car parked next to it.

Kate estimated the expanse of grass between the tree and Tor was twenty metres wide. It was almost dark, and the stars were bright in the sky. The moon cast the stretch of ground between the Tor and tree in a pale glow.

'Charlie could have easily walked over to his parents' tent,' said Kate.

They walked to the tree. It took around twenty seconds. The

vast branches of the old oak, gnarled and bare, seemed to move and surround them.

'I'm finding this a bit eerie,' said Kate, looking up. 'And we're together. I don't think a three-year-old would want to cross this short expanse of ground in the middle of the night, let alone walk all the way down to the river.' The branches creaked and keened in the silence, and a far-off owl hooted.

'True,' said Tristan. 'But that's not to say he wasn't a tough little kid.'

'Okay. Jean said it was just dark when she put Charlie to bed. She came out of the tent to have a cigarette after he fell asleep. That's when she heard Declan's voice calling her from up there on the Tor. It was dark, but she said the moon was full. It was midsummer night, June 21st, so it wouldn't have got dark until after nine thirty.'

'Ade said Joel called the police at 4am, and Joel said on the phone that they'd discovered Charlie was missing at 2am,' said Tristan.

'Which is five hours difference. Is Jean lying about the length of time she was up on the Tor with Declan?' asked Kate.

'Jean heard Declan's voice up on the Tor when she was here under the tree. That means that Charlie could have woken up a bit later, come out of the tent, and heard Jean talking to Declan. That could have made him want to walk towards her voice.'

Kate nodded.

'That's when he could have got lost. He could have taken a wrong turn through those boulders and ended up by the river.'

The moor around them was now dark. They could just see a faint orange glow over the hills of the towns and villages on the other side of Dartmoor. Kate saw the windows of a house glowing in the distance, very faint. It wasn't part of a town or village; it was a house alone on the moor. Kate shivered and crossed her arms over her chest.

'We need to talk to everyone,' Tristan said. 'Jean, Joel... Declan, if we can find him. Oh, and Sadie in the solicitor's office. She's Jean's friend, and she clearly loves to talk.'

'I've got us booked in at Exeter records office tomorrow morning,' said Kate. 'I want to look through everything written in the press about the case before we talk to people. Shall we go?'

'Yeah,' said Tristan, shivering. 'Let's get out of here.'

14

Early the following day, Kate and Tristan arrived at Exeter records office. It was housed inside a wing of Exeter Cathedral, and was calm and peaceful this June morning. Kate loved the smell of books; that dusty dryness mixed with grease and a slight undertone of mould.

'We'd like to access your microfilm records of local newspapers,' said Kate as she and Tristan signed in.

'Do you have a period and a particular paper in mind?' asked the young woman at the front desk. Devon and Cornwall had a plethora of local newspapers.

'Could we start with June to August 2007, and then May and June 2014, for all of these, please.' Kate dug around in her bag and handed over a list of fifteen local newspapers. The young woman raised an eyebrow.

'Okay, this might take a bit of time to gather,' she said.

Kate loved working on the microfilm machines. There was something sturdy and definite about them. Information on the internet could be changed and wiped. There was something about the microfilm which comforted her. You could burn it, yes, but it remained constant and uneditable.

Kate and Tristan sat side by side on two microfiche machines, tucked at the back of the records office, up against the wall, behind a long row of shelves containing law reference books.

'This is everything we have for those periods,' said the young woman, returning with a plastic container stacked with tiny boxes holding the microfilm rolls. 'With the May to June 2014 records you've requested, things are a little patchy. Quite a few of the titles on the list you gave me have now shifted to an online presence through the Devon Live website.'

'Okay, thank you,' said Kate. They'd requested the 2014 records to see if anything had been written about Becky Julings's suicide.

They divided up the stack of microfilm boxes and started to whizz through. The local papers only produced a weekly edition, so they began with the date of the first issue after Charlie went missing on June 21st 2007. They already had a couple of press cuttings from Jean, but Kate wanted to see how the local news covered the aftermath of Charlie's disappearance. There was often a more nuanced approach to local news and more detail, often omitted in the national newspapers where space was at a premium. They were looking for names of police officers, first responders and anyone else who might crop up.

'I have the name of the lead police officer who took over the case. DCI David Falstaff,' said Kate.

'Here's an article from the end of June,' said Tristan. 'There's another name, a Detective Inspector Lewis Tate.' There was silence for a moment as he read. He had a pen between his teeth, turning the handle on the side of the microfilm viewer as the black and white newsprint whizzed past on the screen. 'DI

Lewis Tate was tasked with organising the search with the Dart-moor National Park office. That's all it says.'

Kate dug around in her bag and found her phone. She googled "Detective Inspector Lewis Tate, Devon and Cornwall police." One of the first results made her sigh.

'What?' asked Tristan.

'Lewis Tate was in prison for dealing drugs and stealing drugs from the police evidence store. He went down in 2011 for six years. He must be out now.' Kate made a note of this on her pad.

'What about DCI David Falstaff?' asked Tristan.

Kate typed on her phone.

'It looks like he's still in the force. He's now superintendent. There's an email for his office.'

There were many articles written during the week Charlie went missing, but they all said similar things. The police revealed the details of Charlie's blood found in the back of Declan's car two weeks after the disappearance, and that they brought him in for questioning before releasing him without charge.

'It seems like the story went away pretty fast when they couldn't charge Declan,' said Tristan as the morning wore on. 'And it never made the national newspapers.'

'Charlie went missing at the end of June 2007, and a week later, Gordon Brown took over from Tony Blair as Prime Minis-ter. It was all the newspapers could talk about.'

As the time passed, their spot behind the rows of dusty books began to feel airless. They were staring at a high wall of breeze blocks, and the hot summer sun seemed to press at the corners of the long blinds pulled down over the glass.

'Did Jean talk about a court ruling to get a declaration of presumed death for Charlie?' asked Tristan. 'Look at this.' It was an article dated July 11th 2014, a written statement printed in the *Okehampton Times*.

In the High Court of Justice Chancery Family Division
Case number. 32498569328

In the matter of an application for a declaration of the presumed death of **CHARLES ROBERT JULINGS**. *A claim has been issued in the High Court of Justice, for a declaration that* **CHARLES ROBERT JULINGS**, *whose last known address was* **FLAT 4, LINK LANE, EXMOUTH, DEVON EX11 1BD** *is presumed to be dead. Any person having an interest may apply to the court to intervene in the matter.*

If you wish to apply to the court, you should do so at **DEXTER & ASSOCIATES SOLICITORS LTD** *as soon as possible, and if possible, within 21 days of the date of this notice. Delay may harm your prospects of being able to intervene.*

CLAIMANT: **JEAN ELIZABETH JULINGS**

CLAIMANT'S LEGAL REPRESENTATIVE: **STEVEN DEXTER, DEXTER & ASSOCIATES, BARFIELD HOUSE, EXETER, EX1 2RE (01483) 567932**

'No. I didn't know they'd applied for a ruling,' said Kate.

'That's not normal?' asked Tristan.

'It's quite an unusual thing to do, especially for a child. An application for a declaration of the presumed death is usually filed to settle legal matters, like an inheritance.'

'Charlie would have been ten years old when this ruling was filed in 2014,' said Tristan.

Kate was looking at the same time period, and a few minutes later, she found an article about the funeral of Charlie Julings.

'This is dated September 1st 2014,' she said. There was a black and white picture taken in a graveyard. A group of mourners stood looking at a small black headstone embossed with Charlie's name. It was piled high with flowers and some cuddly toys. Jean was standing next to Becky and Joel, clutching a white handkerchief in a black-gloved hand.

Underneath was written:

The funeral of Charlie Julings took place today at All Saints Church in Exmouth. Charlie went missing in June 2007 at Devil's Way gorge on Dartmoor. A search for many years failed to find any trace of the young boy. The family took the unusual step of applying for a high court ruling for a declaration of presumed death, which was granted in August. The official conclusion handed down by the high court is that Charlie fell into the Devil's Way gorge sinkhole and drowned.

'Why didn't Jean or Steve Dexter mention this?' asked Kate. 'If you decide to get a declaration of presumed death from the high court, it means that you've accepted the person is dead. It's a final legal decision. You have to print a statement of your intentions so the decision can be disputed if necessary.'

'Oh, Jesus. Becky killed herself four weeks after the funeral,' said Tristan. 'There's a death notice printed in the same newspaper on October 1st 2014.'

Kate sat back in her chair.

'This is strange. Why would Jean hire us now? The declaration of presumed death was applied for in her name. Has she got new evidence that makes her think Charlie is alive? And if she has, why hasn't she or her solicitor mentioned any of this?'

'Ade said that the police thought Charlie had fallen in the river from the first few days of the investigation. And the police dogs backed this up. They traced his scent to the river where it stopped.'

'But they'd been paddling and swimming that day in the river, which could account for that,' said Kate. 'I know, I'm being Devil's advocate,' she added, seeing his face. She looked at the pile of microfilm they still needed to check from the *North Devon Journal*, *Crediton Gazette*, and *Culm Valley Gazette*.

'The *North Devon Journal* ran the same stories almost word for word about Charlie's disappearance,' said Tristan as he whizzed through the June 2007 editions.

Kate was working through the microfilm articles in the *Crediton Gazette* when she saw the same name mentioned twice in quick succession. A social worker called Anna Treadwell. Anna had spoken to a news reporter about Jean and Becky Julings, saying there had been, quote, "problems in the family". Anna was quoted again in a *Crediton Gazette* article a week later. It stuck out to Kate because until now, the news reports had focused on Charlie going missing, and the only comments were of the family being "desperate" and "distressed" and Charlie being a "missing angel" etc. This Anna Treadwell seemed to be the only person criticising the family. Kate showed the articles to Tristan.

'Two weeks on from the disappearance of Charlie Julings,' said Tristan, reading aloud from the screen, 'the police have no suspects and no leads. One theory is that Charlie wandered off from the family tent and fell into the Devil's Way gorge. However, a local social worker, Anna Treadwell, is quoted saying there were "problems within the family" and "known issues around Charlie's care". What do you think they could be?'

'It could have been Jean's relationship with Declan. Ade said Declan had a police record, and there was that incident with the underage girl in the pub,' said Kate.

'But why doesn't this social worker mention that? This second article was published two weeks after Charlie went missing and just after the police released Declan without charge,' said Tristan.

'And we don't know enough about what was going on with Becky. Could she have been suicidal or have had mental problems before which had been flagged by social services?' said Kate.

She picked up her phone from the desk and typed in a Google search for "Anna Treadwell, Devon and Cornwall council social worker". She froze when the first results came up on the screen.

'What?' asked Tristan, seeing her face.

'She's dead. Eleven years ago, 8th July 2007, Anna Treadwell's body was found. She'd been the victim of a vicious hammer attack in her home,' said Kate. 'Two weeks after Charlie went missing.'

15

After their morning at the Exeter records office, Tristan and Kate stopped in a café for lunch, but Kate didn't have much appetite. She felt weak and washed out when they pulled up outside The Lawns nursing home.

It was a former cottage hospital on the outskirts of Exmouth with extensive grounds. They'd decided that Kate would go by herself and talk to Jean. There were delicate questions to ask her, and Kate thought Jean might be more open to talking one-to-one.

When she opened the car door, the heat from outside was fierce, but she felt cold and clammy.

'Are you okay?' asked Tristan. She could see the concern in his eyes.

'Yes,' she said firmly. Work had always been the focus that saved her. Work and purpose took her out of her head and out of her problems. She was determined to keep going.

'Do you want to call me when you're done? I can hang around.'

'No. I can get the 157 bus. It's only a fifteen-minute ride back to Ashdean. Tris, I'm fine. It's going to take a few days for me to get back to myself.'

'If you don't fancy taking the bus, I'm happy to come back.'

Jean had asked to meet Kate in the grounds of the nursing home. The reception area was brightly decorated, but there was a smell of sickness and floor cleaner, so Kate was pleased they would meet in the open air. She was shown out to the garden, where Jean was sitting waiting in the shade of a huge walnut tree. The vast lawn was dotted with patients on zimmer frames and being pushed in wheelchairs, and a gardener was digging over the soil in the rose patch. Jean looked better; her face had more colour, and she wore a bright, patterned summer dress. She pulled herself out of her chair and hugged Kate for a long moment.

'Thank you for coming. Sit down,' she said, indicating a chair. Jean eased herself back into her own with a grimace, and when she adjusted the hem of her dress, Kate saw a flash of the bandages wrapped tightly around her thighs.

'How are you? I brought you some sweets. I figured fruit was boring,' said Kate, taking a packet of Fox's Glacier Fruits from her bag.

'Thanks, love. The bloody ulcers on my legs are finally healing. I can cope with everything else now that those are better. You look a bit peaky.'

'I'm fine,' Kate said, wishing people would stop telling her she looked like crap. There was another silence.

'Where is your assistant? I wanted to meet him.'

'He's my business partner, but I thought it might be better if I came alone for our first proper chat,' said Kate.

'That sounds ominous.'

'I didn't know that you went to the high court and had Charlie ruled as presumed dead?'

A look of profound sadness moved across Jean's face.

'Yes. That was four years ago. I think that was a mistake.'

'Why?'

'Lately, I can feel Charlie, still alive somewhere,' said Jean, leaning closer and clutching her hand against her chest. 'I know it sounds barmy, but it's true.'

Kate looked at Jean for a moment. She hadn't mentioned she'd had this feeling when they were in the hospital.

'But you didn't feel it when you petitioned the court for Charlie's death certificate?'

Jean shook her head.

'No. I felt it for the first time shortly after Becky killed herself. It was that court ruling that tipped her over the edge. After we had the funeral, all hope in her died. And then she hung herself.'

'I'm so sorry.'

Jean straightened up in her chair, and seemed to close off a little.

'Anyway. You've signed the contract. You've got my money. What's happening with finding Charlie?' she asked, fixing Kate with a keen stare.

'We've been talking to a couple of police officers who worked on the case. They were both on call the morning that Charlie went missing.'

'What are their names?'

'Adrian Merton and Lewis Tate.'

'Nope, doesn't ring a bell.'

'We've also been doing some research, and we've flagged a few things I wanted to talk about,' said Kate. She was unsure how to approach what she said next. 'First of all, the timings of everything differ from what you told me in the hospital.'

'Differ? What do you mean?'

'You told me that on the night Charlie went missing, you put him to bed, went outside the tent for a cigarette, and that's when you heard Declan's voice up on Devil's Tor. What time was this?'

Jean sighed.

'I put Charlie down when it got dark. I remember it was well past his bedtime.'

'It was midsummer night, so it wouldn't have got dark until nine-thirty, at the earliest.'

'Then that's when it was – it was dark.'

'How long were you up on the Tor with Declan?'

'About ten minutes.'

'And after Declan left, you returned to the tent and found Charlie was missing?'

'No, that's not what I said,' replied Jean. 'When I came back, Becky was coming out of the tent. She said Charlie was missing.'

'So, this was just before 10pm?'

Jean hesitated.

'I think so. It was a long time ago.'

'Joel didn't call the police until 4am. That's six hours later. What were you all doing for six hours?'

'What do you think we were doing? Having a laugh? We were looking!'

Kate sat back and kept eye contact with Jean. 'Adrian Merton was the policeman who arrived first at Devil's Way. He said that you and Becky were fighting on the ground.'

Jean nodded.

'Becky blamed me. It had got heated, when we couldn't find Charlie.'

'Did you fight often?'

'No.'

'Why didn't you call the police earlier? Six hours seems like a long time to wait when you knew Charlie was missing.'

'I don't like the police. None of us does,' said Jean, fixing her with a cold stare. 'You and me, we come from different worlds. In my world, the police are evil bastards. They're the last people you call.'

'Even if a child is missing?'

'We thought he'd wandered off! He'd done it before, at the Magnolia shopping centre in Exmouth... And in a park one day when we had a picnic. We were looking, everywhere!' she insisted. 'You don't know what it was like, searching for hours, hoping he would just be around the corner. When Joel finally decided to call the police, it was like we had to admit he was gone. And the police judged us. They judged me when they heard about mine and Declan's history.' There was an awkward silence. Jean shook her head and looked away across the grounds. Kate knew that what she said next wouldn't go down well either.

'Declan Connoly was caught with an underage girl in a pub a few weeks before Charlie went missing.'

'Is that a question? Cos I sent Declan away that night when he showed up. I didn't want anything to do with him. That's what I told the police, too.'

'But you were both together, in a relationship for a long time?'

'Do you think Declan did it? Took Charlie?' asked Jean.

'He was there at the time Charlie went missing.'

Jean shook her head impatiently.

'The police questioned him. They found his car in a ditch the next morning. He was so drunk that he wasn't capable. And he wouldn't have taken Charlie. Declan is many things, but he's not—'

'A child killer?' finished Kate. She knew she was pushing it by saying it in such a blunt way.

Jean looked at the ground for a long moment.

'Declan is many things, but he's not a child killer. He's a useless druggie. My life with Declan meant I wasn't the best mother to Becky,' said Jean, her voice trembling along with her bottom lip. 'I did a lot of things I'm not proud of. I had drug problems in the past, and alcohol, too. Declan was a part of my life for a long time, but by the time Charlie was born, he was out of it, and I'd been clean for four years. I swear on Charlie's life, that's true. I left Charlie in the tent because I wanted Declan to go and leave us alone. I was protecting him.'

Kate nodded.

'Do you know where Declan lives now?'

'Yeah. I can give you his address. We're not in contact, really.' Jean looked up at Kate. 'People like you have no idea what it's like to try and turn a corner and get sober after making so many mistakes.'

'I do. I'm in recovery from alcohol addiction. I lost custody of my son, Jake, when he was six,' she said. Jean hesitated. Kate could see that this revelation had thrown her off for a moment.

'How did you get him back?' asked Jean.

'I didn't. My mother had custody until he was sixteen, and then Jake was free to choose.'

'Did he choose you?'

'Yes. And I used to see Jake during school holidays, and my mother always let him visit after I got myself sorted out.'

'Ah. So you had a nice middle-class arrangement? No social workers.'

'There were social workers involved. I know that a social worker expressed concern about Charlie in the weeks before he went missing. What was that about?'

Jean sat back in shock.

'You are a good private detective.'

'I need to know all the information, Jean. I'm not here to accuse you or to make you feel guilty, but if this is going to work, then I need to know everything.'

Jean searched her pockets and found a clean tissue.

'I had a neighbour upstairs who had it in for me. One night, a few months before Charlie went missing, Declan came to my flat in the early hours one morning, and we had a blazing row. This neighbour heard the commotion and called social services. Charlie wasn't even in the flat at the time. Becky and Joel had gone to Center Parcs with him. But still, social services sent this woman around.'

'Anna Treadwell?'

'Yeah. That was her. The bitch. You have been doing your research.'

'Why was she a bitch?'

'Cos she kept showing up, hounding us to try and catch us out. At times it felt like she wanted to take him away and keep him for her own. She wouldn't accept that Charlie was a happy little boy, which he was. I might have messed up in my life, but as far as Charlie was concerned, he was always immaculate. He always had food. And warmth. And love.'

Jean now had tears in her eyes, and she wiped at them with the tissue.

'Did you know Anna Treadwell was murdered?' asked Kate.

'No. I didn't know that. When?'

'Shortly after Charlie went missing.'

Jean put her hand to her mouth, and something moved across her face. Was it a realisation? Or shock? Kate wondered. It was a mere flicker, and then it was gone.

'Well. I wouldn't wish that on anyone.'

'Did Anna ever show up at your flat when Declan was there?'

'No.'

'Did you tell Declan about Anna taking an interest in Charlie?'

'I don't know. I might have.'

'What do you mean? What happened if you crossed him? Do you think he had something to do with Anna Treadwell's death?' asked Kate. Jean shook her head as if she had thought about it and then dismissed it.

'No. I doubt it. Declan had other interests than killing a social worker.'

'What interests?'

'Drugs. Booze. Women. I don't want to talk about him. I want to talk about finding Charlie.'

'We need to talk about him, Jean. Whether you like it or not, he could still be a suspect in this.'

'Declan is not the kind of man you'd want to cross.'

16

'Why isn't Declan the kind of man you'd like to cross?' repeated Kate. The sun was no lower in the sky, and the shade covering their chairs in the hospital garden had lengthened.

Jean's hands were shaking.

'I just want you to find Charlie. I don't want to have to dig things up!' Jean was now clutching the tissue, and her hands were shaking. Kate got up and crouched beside her chair.

'Jean. Jean, listen to me,' she said as Jean clamped her eyes shut and shook her head indignantly like a child. 'Anything you say to me will remain in the strictest confidence. Do you think Declan had anything to do with Charlie's disappearance?'

'No!'

A strong breeze blew through the garden, cutting through the afternoon's heat. It rustled the leaves on the walnut tree, and Kate felt a sudden strange melancholy dread. She often felt this when she took on significant cases; it was a feeling that time was moving fast, and she would be left behind. The case would go unsolved. She shook the thought away.

'Jean. What don't you want to dig up about Declan?' She sat back in her chair and gave Jean a moment to compose herself.

'Just talking about him makes me feel bad. He's ten years older than me, Declan. You probably couldn't tell now. We're both seen as old, but I was fifteen when I first met him, and he was twenty-five. That was a huge age gap.'

'Where did you meet him?'

'I was in a children's home from when I was four. My mum died, and I didn't have anyone else. I never experienced anything bad, if you know what I mean. I was two months away from my sixteenth birthday and I knew I'd be turfed out the day after I turned sixteen. They help you find a bedsit and whatnot, but it was a terrifying prospect to have to leave and go out into the world on your own. I met Declan around this time. He was part of a building crew who came to fix the roof on the building at the home,' she said.

'What was the home called?'

'Finbury House. Sounds posh, doesn't it? It wasn't. It's a few miles outside Exeter. It was one of those old manor houses that got commandeered during the war. All plasterboard partitions and Formica, and so draughty. The home closed a few years after I left. It's now a posh spa.'

'So you met Declan when he was working on the roof?'

'Yeah. It was summer 1980. A couple of us girls were asked to take out drinks for the workers, orange squash.' She smiled ruefully. 'That's when I met him, and then I started to spend time with him during his lunch breaks. One thing led to another. Like I said, I was only a couple of months off leaving, and I was a beauty back then,' she added to Kate as if she somehow doubted her.

'You were fifteen?'

'Yeah. I would skive off at night to meet him in the pub. This happened for a couple of months, and then, when I was sixteen, Declan asked me to move in with him. He had a bedsit in Taunton, and for a time, it was nice...' Her voice trailed off. 'And then he started to pester me about his friends who liked me. One of them came over for the night, and we all ended up, you know, in bed together.'

'Was it consensual?'

'I went along with it,' said Jean after a pause. 'He wore me down like he did with lots of things. First, it was one friend who became a regular thing with us, and then we went to a party that turned into wife-swapping. That was when I discovered he was whoring me out. For money.'

Kate didn't know what to say. She was shocked, but at the same time, she wasn't, so she just listened.

'I didn't think much of myself back then, and I still don't, but Declan had a way of convincing me that it was normal. He made me feel like I wasn't pulling my weight. I didn't have a job, I was on the dole, so there were times when he would charge men for a night with me. Some of them were respectable, smart and well-dressed. He said I was going to sleep with them anyway.'

'I know this might sound an odd question, but you said Declan was a builder?'

'Yeah, a jack-of-all-trades builder.'

'Were these men builders too?'

'No, they were respectable.'

'How did Declan know these men?'

'He had a way of ingratiating himself with people. He wasn't afraid or intimidated by posh people. Declan could go into a room and be the same with everyone.'

'What did these men do for work?' asked Kate.

'I never got that far. I remember some of the men having

nice suits and keeping their cash in one of those silver money clips. Lots of cash... I'm making it sound like I was a prostitute, but it never felt that way. The men he chose for me were always kind. Always decent to me.' She gave a huge sigh. 'I'm kidding myself, aren't I?'

'How long did this go on for?'

'Until I lost my bloom when I was nineteen, and I fell pregnant with Becky.'

'Who was the father?'

Jean bit her bottom lip, and Kate noticed for the first time that she had false teeth. They were very white and straight.

'It wasn't Declan. I'd left him. I got a job in a pub and started seeing the landlord. He was a good man, but he was in the middle of a messy divorce, and then just when I fell pregnant, him and his wife wanted to make a go of it. They got back together.'

'What did you do?' asked Kate.

'I went back to Declan. He took me in, and I had nowhere else to go. I'd lost my job at the pub. That's when stuff turned a lot darker for me. I had another man's baby growing in my belly, and Declan hated that. He started drinking a lot and drugging, too. He hit me.'

'While you were pregnant?'

'Yeah. Until I ran away one night when I was eight months pregnant. I was lucky to find a women's shelter. They took me in, and I stayed there until I had Becky and for the first few months after she was born. I eventually went back to Declan.' She smiled ruefully and shook her head. 'I thought he'd changed. And he did for a while, but the next few years were a pattern of him getting drunk and abusive. I finally broke free of him when Becky was three and got a council flat. But then

Declan wormed his way back in again.' Jean put her hands over her face.

'It's okay,' said Kate.

'No. It's not. I got into drugs. Becky was eight or nine, getting older. I don't know how it happened. I just, I tried it.'

'What did you try?'

'Weed at first, and then cocaine and finally heroin. I managed to keep things steady for a few years, but when Becky was fifteen, I lost it and ended up overdosing for the third time...' Silent tears ran down her face. 'I'd grown up with no one, and then I have a kid, and I put her in the same position. I got given a rehab place. It was rough, not like those American ones where you all bask in sunny gardens and sleep in private rooms.'

Kate nodded, remembering her own experience of an NHS rehab facility.

'What did Becky do?'

'She had some nice friends at school. One, in particular, Kelly-Jane, came from a nice family, and they were close. Kelly-Jane's mother offered Becky to come and live with them whilst I was in rehab, and she stayed there for nearly a year until she'd got her GCSEs; she got five A grades.'

'Did Becky come back to live with you?' asked Kate.

'She stayed living with Kelly-Jane's family whilst she did her A-Levels. She got a place at university. Then she fell pregnant with Charlie.'

At this point, Jean looked sadly out at the empty garden. Most of the other patients had gone inside, and Kate saw that visiting time would soon be over.

'And this was Joel who got Becky pregnant?' asked Kate.

'Yes. Joel was Kelly-Jane's older brother,' said Jean.

'Ah.'

'Yeah. The family weren't too happy, being quite middle class and all that. Joel didn't want to get married. His family turned their back on them, so suddenly the tables were turned, and they both came to live with me. Becky had been a nice little pet project for them when she toed the line. Their little Eliza Doolittle did ever so well at school. But then Eliza started carrying on with their darling son and got knocked up. Becky was suddenly just another working-class slag.'

'Where were you living?'

'I had my council flat, but Declan was still coming in and out of my life, so it was hard to keep clean. I vowed that I would be clean from when Becky had her baby, and I was. A few months before, I sorted myself out so I could help her with Charlie. And I swear on his life that I never did drugs again. I never drank. When Declan turned up that day when we were camping, he was drunk and out of it, and I was scared for Charlie.'

'And you tried to appease him,' said Kate. Jean nodded.

'I had to get rid of him without things getting nasty. He'd screwed me up, and it affected Becky. I didn't want him near my grandson.'

'How did you get rid of him?'

'He hit me, and then I dragged him by the ear and scolded him. He had quite an overbearing mother, and it sometimes worked when he was really drunk. He'd revert back to being a kid.'

Kate found Jean another tissue. She gave her a moment. And then knew she had to ask the question.

'The police said they found Charlie's blood in Declan's car—'

'That was from weeks before,' said Jean, slightly defensively. 'We'd gone to the cinema in Declan's car.'

'I thought you didn't want him near your grandson? And I thought you and him were no longer together?'

'That was just one time when I needed him to take us to the cinema. I'd promised Charlie the cinema. We stopped at a park on the way home, and Charlie cut himself on a small piece of glass by the swings. The blood came from there.'

'Are you sure you don't have any doubts?'

'I can't... I can't contemplate that Declan did that. He may be many things, but he's not a child killer.'

Kate looked at the insistence in Jean's face, and her heart sank. She was still in love with Declan. And love was blind.

17

Kate left The Lawns nursing home just before four. It was an awkward parting; she felt she knew much about Jean and her past, but the case was far more complicated than she'd first thought.

Kate came out onto the main road. She felt hungry, but the thought of eating a meal made her stomach turn. It was still hot, and a nice breeze was in the air. A newsagent's was on the other side of the road, and Kate thought she could stomach some chocolate. She waited for a gap in the traffic and then dashed across.

Inside the newsagent's, a small boy and girl stood at a glass-topped counter with a white-haired lady. An older man with a white fuzz of hair waited patiently on the other side of the counter as they chose a selection of penny sweets from different compartments under the glass.

'How much have we got left, Gran?' asked the boy, looking up at the older lady.

'You've got ten pence left each,' said the man, standing patiently with his hand in a clear plastic glove.

The two children turned their attention back to the glass. They were deep in concentration as they decided to choose the white sugar mice or cola bottle chews. The woman turned back and saw Kate waiting behind.

'Sorry, love. We won't be a moment. You'd think they were voting at the UN,' she said with a smile.

'No problem,' said Kate.

'I'd give anything to have their decisions,' said the man with a chuckle.

Kate looked around at the inside of the newsagent's. It was almost identical to the one she remembered as a child. The tabloid newspapers fanned out in a row on a long low shelf, and above, rows of magazines reached up to the infamous 'top shelf' near the ceiling. Kate noticed that the copies of *Razzle* and *Escort* now had white plastic covering the front.

Next to the till were rows of chocolate bars, and a couple of tall glass-fronted fridges hummed. Behind the glass, along with the Coke, Sprite and Fanta, were fizzy drinks she'd long forgotten about: Panda Pops, Cream Soda, Shandy Bass, Irn-Bru and Cherry Coke. The rest of the shop was filled with frames of greetings cards and a section for cheap toys.

As Kate watched the two small children, she thought of what she'd missed out on with Jake; the little things like trips to the newsagent's to buy sweets. Kate thought of Jean losing her grandson at such a young age. She'd always thought she lost custody of Jake, but Kate realised now that she never did. Her mother had taken over when she couldn't look after him. How hard had it been for Jean to let go of Charlie and acknowledge he would never return?

Kate thought back to the missing person cases she'd worked on. The outcome was almost always a corpse or the remains of the missing loved one. Jean had gone as far as applying for a death certificate for Charlie, but now she thought he was still alive and wanted to find him.

What had prompted this? Could it really just have been a feeling she had?

The bell jangled on the door, and the woman left with the two children. The old man smiled and asked if he could help her. Kate was suddenly seized with a silly thought. She was no longer a child with only fifty pence to spend. She could buy as many sweets as she wanted.

Ten minutes later, Kate emerged out onto the road with a plastic bag filled with cans of fizzy drinks, chocolate bars and penny sweets. Luckily, a bus was just pulling up opposite, going to Ashdean. She hurried across the road and bought a ticket.

The bus was empty, and as it lurched off, Kate wobbled her way down the aisle and sat on the back seat. She opened the plastic bag, took out a Curly Wurly, and started to eat, feeling better when the sugar hit her tongue. The bus journey was pleasant, and once they left Exmoor, it was a slightly bumpy ride along the coastal road. A well-thumbed edition of the *Okehampton Times* was on the seat behind, and Kate picked it up and began to flick through. There were the usual stories about local council budgets being cut and a visit from the mayor of Craon, the French town twinned with Okehampton. And then Kate noticed an article about house prices in the Devon and Cornwall area.

It began in the usual way, with the legitimate complaints about non-locals buying up property as holiday lets. Then there was a byline article titled: *10 of the cheapest houses for sale in Devon that are perfect first-time buys!* Kate read through the list, and a home second from the bottom caught her eye: 4 Kirby Cane Walk, Okehampton. It rang a bell in her mind. She rummaged around in her bag for her notebook. Flicking through the pages, she found the notes she'd made that morning in Exeter Records Office. Yes. Anna Treadwell had been found murdered at 4 Kirby Cane Walk, Okehampton.

'Jesus!' said Kate, loud enough for the bus driver to peer up at her in the reflection of his rear-view mirror. She checked the copy of the *Okehampton Times*. It was dated two weeks ago. The picture was of a run-down townhouse with what looked like metal grilles on the window. The garden was overgrown, and the description underneath read:

If you're prepared to roll up your sleeves and get stuck in, this two-bedroom house could be a tremendous first-home fixer-upper! On sale with Coveney Estate Agents for just £100,000, this modern townhouse offers a great investment opportunity and is described as 'requiring modernisation and TLC from a motivated buyer'. It provides an entrance hall, lounge, kitchen and dining room, utility, two bedrooms and a bathroom. The South Devon home also has gas central heating, double glazing, and a garden.

What an odd coincidence that this newspaper had been waiting for her on this bus. She peered at the photo of the townhouse.

Kate knew from her time in the police that houses were only boarded up with metal grilles when they were situated in a rough area, which this wasn't, or if the house had been empty for a long time and was persistently visited by squatters and arsonists.

Why had Anna's house sat empty for so long? thought Kate. *How gruesome had her murder been?*

18

It was late afternoon, and Tristan had just finished working out at the gym on Ashdean pier. He had been expecting to hear from Kate about her meeting with Jean, but when his phone rang, he saw it was Ade.

'You sound out of breath,' said Ade when Tristan answered. 'Are you having fun?'

'No. I'm at the gym.' Tristan grabbed his towel and water bottle from the floor next to the bench press and moved aside to let a guy use the machine. He came over to the window.

'Nothing on earth would make me use a gym. *Only criminals run*, is my motto. Anyway. I called for a reason. I managed to track down that police officer, Lewis Tate, through an old colleague.'

'Does he live locally?'

'About an hour away,' said Ade. 'But he's willing to talk to you about the Charlie Julings case. However, he has some requests.'

'What kind of requests?'

'He wants to meet in Plymouth.'

'I'm happy to talk to him on the phone.'

'He wants to meet in person. And he wants cash for talking.'

'What does he have to say?'

'He says he worked the Charlie Julings case for four months and saw a lot. He didn't want to elaborate.'

'How much does he want?' sighed Tristan.

'A hundred quid.'

'A hundred?' Tristan looked out of the window at the beach crowded with people. It was unusual to pay people for information, and he was a little annoyed with Ade for getting into a negotiation with this Lewis without calling him first.

'Is money out of the question?' asked Ade.

'I'd need to talk to Kate,' said Tristan. Money was still tight in the agency, and the caravan site was still their primary source of income.

'I think Lewis is hard up. No one likes a bent copper. And he's thinking back to his days on the force when we had our narks who would pass information on to the police for cash,' said Ade.

'But I'm not a police officer. And isn't this the same guy who went down for stealing drugs from police stores?' asked Tristan.

'Yes.'

'How do I know he isn't just going to make a load of crap up?'

'I'll text you his number,' said Ade. 'You two can thrash it out.'

'What would you do, Ade? If you were me.'

'Well. I'd be having a lot more fun if I looked like you.'

'I'm serious.'

Ade sighed.

'Lewis has very little to lose. If you agree to give him money, then make it clear that you only want the truth, even if it seems bland and uninteresting. The most interesting nuggets of information can come from the smallest comment or facial expression.'

Tristan heard a ping on his phone.

'Okay, thanks, Ade. I got the number.' As Tristan ended the call, he saw he also had a message from Joel Mansfield, Charlie's father. Joel had written that he was in Spain on holiday for the next week with his wife and daughters, but he would be happy to meet with Tristan and Kate on his return. Tristan tried Kate's phone, but it was engaged, so he went to have a shower.

Sarah and Leo had returned home, so Tristan's flat was empty. He savoured the quiet when he stepped through the door, and then busied himself making a huge omelette. He had just served it up when there was a ring on the doorbell. Kate was outside.

'I was wondering where you'd got to,' he said when she entered the hallway. 'Would you like some eggs?'

'No. I've just eaten half a bag of chocolate and sweets. I think I'm regretting it,' she said, holding up the carrier bag with the discarded wrappers.

She came into the kitchen, and as Tristan ate, she filled him in on what had happened at her meeting with Jean.

'I still don't know what's going on in her head,' Kate said. 'I think Jean feels guilt that Charlie vanished on her watch and blames herself for Becky's death. She thinks going to the high court to get the death certificate triggered Becky's suicide. But at the same time, she insists that Declan had nothing to do with Charlie going missing.'

'But he pimped her out,' said Tristan. 'He was violent to her for years and had a thing for underage girls.'

'And he went down for GBH,' said Kate. 'But Jean wants us to look at other suspects, and she now thinks Charlie is alive.'

Tristan sighed, and they were quiet for a moment.

'Joel is away on holiday in Spain for a week, and Lewis Tate, the police officer who worked on the case, won't talk to us unless we pay him a hundred quid in cash,' said Tristan gloomily.

'Jean gave me Declan's address, so we should pay him a visit. Also, look at this.'

Kate took the crumpled copy of the *Okehampton Times* from her bag and showed him the photo of Anna Treadwell's house. 'Anna was murdered a couple of weeks after Charlie went missing, and it looks like her house has been abandoned since then. There is no sale in the land registry records. It makes me wonder what the circumstances of her murder were. Was it notorious enough to put people off buying her house? Jean didn't have a good word to say about Anna. She said that a neighbour called social services when she heard a row in the night between Jean and Declan. Charlie was away at the time with Becky and Joel. Jean says that she explained this to Anna, but she still started an investigation into Charlie's welfare.'

'Wouldn't that be normal for a social worker to investigate complaints?' said Tristan.

'Jean seems to think Anna had an unhealthy interest in Charlie.'

'What makes you think there is any link between Anna and Charlie going missing?' asked Tristan.

'I don't know if there is,' said Kate. 'But there's something about this that's making me uncomfortable. I'd like to go and look at Anna Treadwell's house and see if we can talk to any neighbours. I also want to talk to Sadie at the solicitor's again and find out what she knew about this. And phone this police officer Lewis back. You never know, it might be worth a hundred quid to talk to him.'

19

The following day, Kate and Tristan drove to Kirby Cane Walk. It was on the edge of a modern housing development on the outskirts of Okehampton. To Kate's relief, the weather was much cooler, and the sky was a grim grey.

They parked outside number four. The house was concealed behind a vast hedge of evergreens, and a faded For Sale sign was half-buried in the branches. Kate thought the name Kirby Cane Walk had sounded quite jaunty, but in reality, it was a grim little cul-de-sac of six homes. There was an empty patch of land next to number four, and it backed onto a scrubland of trees and undergrowth running behind the houses. Kate and Tristan got out of the car, walked around the tall evergreens, and onto the scrubland. Running along the side of number four was a low fence with a missing panel.

They were just debating going through the gap when they heard a voice.

'Can I help you?'

An older man with a balding head was standing on the pavement, staring at them. Wisps of his remaining hair were dancing in the breeze, and he wore a long brown coat over jeans and crocs. Kate could tell from his trembling voice that he was a little scared of people and that coming out to talk to them had probably taken a lot of effort.

'Sorry. Hi, me and my – ' Kate made a lightning-quick decision, ' – son were just passing the end of the road, and we saw this house is for sale.'

'Yeah. Sorry if we're trespassing,' said Tristan, walking back to the pavement.

'Yes, sorry,' repeated Kate. If in doubt, in England, say sorry. The man's eyebrows rose, and after another apology from them both, they came to join him on the pavement. His shoulders seemed to relax.

'That's okay. We don't see many new people here in the cul-de-sac,' he said, sounding a little lonely and sad. He looked back at the house and sighed. 'Well. It needs a lot of work, and don't tell anyone I said this, but you could probably get it for a steal.'

'Really?' said Kate.

'That's good. Our budget isn't huge, is it, Mum?' said Tristan. Kate glanced at him for a second, worrying that he was laying it on too thick, but the man seemed to take what they were saying at face value.

'So many estate agents have tried to sell the place,' he said, looking at the faded sign. 'This lot, Coveney's, are the seventh or eighth. They're nice. I've even got a key; I got to know Marcia there, and she would ask me to let people in for viewings.'

Kate glanced back at the fading sign, which had almost been consumed by the overgrown hedge.

'Actually... Do you think you could show us around?'

He looked a little uneasy and pulled a face.

'You should really ring the agent. I'm happy to let people in when asked, but I'm not qualified to tell you about the place.

I've lost count of what the sale price is now. Having this here in this state has brought down prices for the rest of us,' he sighed.

Kate nodded sympathetically.

'Of course, we wouldn't want to put you in an awkward position. If I bought it and did it up, it could be a nice home, and I'd be adding value. Listen. We're only in the area for a short time. Would you be able to use your key and let us have a look? You'd really help me out, and I can call the agent if interested. I'm Kate, by the way, Kate Marshall,' she said, smiling and holding out her hand. They shook.

'And I'm Tristan.'

'I'm Gregory Cleever,' he said, shaking Tristan's hand. He squinted at them again. 'Okay. I suppose there's no harm. Can you wait here? I'll get the key.'

He hurried off back inside his house.

'What is our budget, Mum?' asked Tristan with a grin.

'I was thinking on my feet.'

'Can I choose my bedroom?'

'Okay, very funny. He's coming back,' murmured Kate as she saw Gregory hurrying out of his front door and holding up a key.

The front gate was hanging off its hinges, and the front garden was wildly overgrown. The weeds were waist-high on either side of the path leading up to the door. A row of evergreens to the right of the house filled half of the garden.

The windows were covered with white metal grilles, one of which had been spray-painted with something illegible in black. The front door also had a tall grille with a padlock. Piles of rubbish had been blown up against the base of the walls, where weeds were growing out of the mess.

'Who put the grilles up?' asked Tristan as Gregory undid the padlock.

'The council. People were breaking in,' he said.

'Squatters?'

'Yes... and...' He hesitated. 'Yes,' he repeated. The grille swung open with a groan, and he unlocked the front door. When they stepped into the hallway, it was very dark. 'I brought a torch, there's no electricity,' said Gregory, flicking on a small penlight. Kate and Tristan switched on the lights on their phones. The hallway was bare, and there was a scrubbed look about the floors and walls. The smell of strong disinfectant was mixed with mould. Directly to the right was a door to the living room. There was a significant dip in the concrete floor.

'What's that?' asked Kate.

'Subsidence. The evergreens on the west side of the property have gone wild, and their roots have grown into the house's foundations, pulling out all the moisture. We've been trying to get the council to come and cut them, but it's too late now. Whoever buys this would have to shore up the foundations.'

'That's not good,' said Kate. The living room walls were grimy and looked as if they'd been whitewashed. When Kate shone her phone light over the wall above an empty fireplace, she could make out some graffiti in a ghostly pink under the paintwork. Tristan angled his light up to the ceiling and stopped at a large patch of pink spread out around the light fitting. Again it had been painted over but needed another coat to cover it up adequately.

'What's that?' asked Kate, her heart leaping a little. Gregory shone his torch up to the patch of pink. He hesitated.

'The previous owner was... she was... she died, sadly,' he said.

'How?' asked Tristan.

'It was a break-in. Quite a few years ago. Anna, that was the previous owner. She was killed,' he said.

'Is that her blood?'

Gregory sighed.

'Yes. Now you can see why this house has been impossible to sell. What with the subsidence and Anna's death, which has never been solved. It really was a nice house when she was alive.'

His use of words interested Kate.

'She was murdered?'

'Yes,' said Gregory.

'Can we see the upstairs?' asked Tristan.

'Really? You're still interested?'

'We're here now,' said Kate. She saw Gregory's face, and he looked surprised.

'This way,' he said. They followed him back into the hall and started climbing the stairs. It was very dark and cold, and the breeze blew through the grates over the windows with an eerie whistle.

20

At the top of the stairs was a poky landing with a small window. Sunlight shone through the grating, casting a pattern of tiny squares on the bare floorboards. There were three doors leading off the landing, and Kate moved to the door above the living room.

'How long has the electricity been off?' she asked, leaning in to flick the light switch. Nothing happened.

'Years,' said Gregory. Tristan followed Kate inside. The rust-coloured bloodstain was on the floor in the left-hand corner of the room. As Tristan moved his light up, she saw a faded pink column of blood spatter up the wall. 'Do you know they've had people in to clean and paint over that twice now? But something keeps happening. A little while after they cover it, the stain keeps showing through.'

Kate didn't believe in the supernatural, but his soft voice in the darkness gave her the chills.

'Who found Anna's body?'

'I did,' he said quietly. 'I'd been away on holiday with my sister. And when I came back, I noticed a couple of large parcels on the front step, and one was soaked from the rain. So I checked it out. The front door was locked, and all the windows were closed. I broke the window on the downstairs loo, and I found her.' The light from Gregory's torch was bouncing back off the walls, casting his face in long shadows. 'Whoever did it used a hammer. They battered her when she was lying on the floor. There,' he said, indicating the mysterious bloodstains. 'Her body had been lying here for twelve days. I don't know if you can imagine. There were maggots. The stench was awful.'

'Was it... was she sexually assaulted?' asked Kate.

'The police said no.'

'Well, that's a small positive in a horrible situation,' said Kate, realising that she was sounding exactly like a private detective.

'Why was the body left for so long? Didn't anyone else miss her?' asked Tristan.

'I was away. Anna was on holiday from work. We live on a quiet cul-de-sac. I'm her only direct neighbour. There's the patch of land on the other side. No one missed her, it seems.'

Kate's eyes followed the trajectory of the blood from the floor as it arced up the wall.

'Did the police have any idea who did it? And how they broke into the house?' she asked.

'No. Anna had had a couple of scares in the weeks leading up to this.'

'What kind of scares?' asked Tristan.

'One night, she was in the kitchen making her cocoa when the back door handle was tried. She said she saw it move. A week later, she was woken up by a noise in the back garden. She went over to the window.' Gregory indicated the back window with the grate over it. 'There was a person in the back garden, by the back door, all dressed in black.'

'What did she do?'

'She called the police both times. They advised her to get a security light put in. And she did. She also had an alarm put in with those motion sensors downstairs. The works. It cost her a lot of money. But that's what doesn't make any sense. When I found her, all the doors were locked but the alarms were deactivated.'

'Was someone waiting for her, maybe? When she came home from work?' said Kate.

'It's possible. But who would do that? She had very little of value. Anna wasn't a rich woman, and she helped so many people. She was a social worker, and occasionally she fostered children, short-term if they needed somewhere to go.' He shook his head.

'And the police never caught who it was?' asked Tristan.

'No. It didn't really make the news in any big way. Just a bit in the local paper. That surprised me. Perhaps more people are murdered every day than we know.'

'The police found no fingerprints?' asked Kate.

'They found hers because she lived here, and I had to give my prints to rule me out, but I never really came inside the house. We'd chat on the road or in the garden. They did find the murder weapon on the path of scrubland behind the house. It was a claw hammer, wrapped in a plastic bag.'

They were silent, and Gregory indicated the door. Kate was glad to leave the room. The lingering blood spatters and the stained floorboards gave her the creeps. They went back out onto the landing.

'That was the loo. Squatters ripped it out, so you'd have to put something new in,' Gregory said. The bath was full of dust, and the toilet bowl, sink, and taps were missing. They moved through to the second bedroom. This was in better condition than the other rooms. It was empty of furniture, but on the walls there was faded, but still rather beautiful, wallpaper covered in animals. There was also one side piece of a cot, with wooden bars, propped up against the wall. Tristan glanced up at Kate and raised an eyebrow.

'Did she foster many children?' she asked.

'I don't think so. I remember once seeing a police car pull up late at night, and they dropped off a young girl. She was maybe two years old... This wallpaper is nice, isn't it?'

Kate nodded. She looked around the room. She wondered how those children felt, being dropped off at this house tucked at the back of a quiet cul-de-sac.

'Was she married?' asked Tristan.

'No,' said Gregory. There was something about how he said this, as if he had never expected her to be married.

'Children?' asked Kate.

'No. Anna was a bit of a hermit. She always seemed to be working. Kept herself to herself.'

'And the police never thought it was a neighbour who killed her? Was she in dispute with anyone?' asked Tristan.

'Good lord, no. This is a nice quiet street. There's me, old Mrs Grundy, Mr and Mrs Patel who run the post office. They're very well thought of. And another woman on the end has been renting for years. She works abroad a lot, I think.' Gregory looked between Kate and Tristan, and she wondered if he was becoming suspicious of all their questions.

Gregory took them back downstairs and they went along to the kitchen at the back of the ground floor. The back door was boarded up with a metal grille. The kitchen units had been ripped out, so there wasn't much to see. They came back out of the house and into the front garden. Kate was glad of the sunshine and fresh air. Tristan asked to see the back garden, and they walked around the path at the side of the house, but it was overgrown, with chest-high weeds. A line of tall trees backed onto the scrubland at the end of the garden.

'The Coldharbour housing estate is only a mile away, beyond the trees,' said Gregory. He gave a theatrical shudder. 'It's far enough away, but I wonder if it wasn't someone from there who killed her. It's rather rough.'

'Did the police think someone from the estate was involved?' asked Tristan.

'No, but I mentioned it to them. I don't think they bothered to take me seriously.'

'Have you ever had trouble from the people at the estate?'

Kate could see Tristan bristling a little at the vague mention of people on council estates being bad.

'Well... no, but that's not to say we wouldn't have trouble from them,' said Gregory.

'Has anyone from the estate ever decided to walk or drive here?'

It was a deliberately opaque question, but Gregory seemed to consider it seriously.

'I don't know if many of them have cars. Apart from the burned-out ones you see in the local paper. Like I say, it's far away. Thank goodness.'

There was a silence as they looked at the tall weeds swaying in the overgrown garden. Kate gave Tristan a look to warn him not to get into an argument. Gregory finally seemed to notice Tristan's annoyance.

'You're not from the estate? Are you?' he asked.

'No. We're from Ashdean,' said Kate quickly.

'Right. What line of work are you in?'

'Mum runs a caravan site on the coast. I help her,' said Tristan. *Good one*, thought Kate. If they needed to talk to him again, they wouldn't have to bend the truth too much.

'Do you think you'll be phoning the estate agent?' he said. His hopefulness broke her heart. He just looked like a sad man in a tragic, forgotten place.

'I don't think so, but thank you for showing it to us,' said Kate.

She looked back at the house. The murder had interested her, but what was it to do with Charlie? Probably nothing, she thought. But something niggled at her. She thought back to her meeting with Jean. The social worker, Anna, had an interest in Charlie. It was as if she wanted to take him away and keep him for her own. That's what Jean said. *Take him away and keep him for her own.*

21

Kate and Tristan drove into Okehampton and parked in one of the town centre car parks. Dark clouds were gathering at the horizon just as he switched off the engine, and rain started to fall, rattling on the windscreen. Kate undid her seat belt and turned to him.

'What do you think?' she asked.

'Did she have so few people in her life that her body lay undiscovered for twelve days?'

'She'd been on holiday from work, so no one missed her.' She rummaged through her bag and found her notes on the original newspaper article.

'Still. You'd think someone would have phoned and then been worried when there was no answer.'

'Her body was found on July 8th 2007,' said Kate, flipping through her notebook. 'A couple of weeks after Charlie went missing. There's just something about it being a hammer attack. The crazed violence of it. I know that someone committing a robbery would go into a house armed. I've seen the aftermath of hammer attacks. It's usually gang-related violence or sadism. And Gregory said she wasn't sexually assaulted.'

'Would he know that for sure?' asked Tristan.

'I don't know. The article in the newspaper didn't say that Anna was raped.'

'Would they print that?'

'The police might release those details if they were relevant to their investigations,' said Kate, wishing for the thousandth time she had access to the HOLMES police database. 'Anna was a social worker. I don't want to make assumptions, but I'm guessing she wasn't rich. And Kirby Cane Walk is a decent area.'

'But a mile away from a council estate,' said Tristan.

'It really burned you, what Gregory said?'

He nodded. 'I come from a council estate, I've had a lot of stuff like that slung at me. I know there can be plenty of bad apples, but we're not all bad.'

'I agree. But you have to admit if this Coldharbour estate is rough, someone from there could have done it.'

'Gregory said the doors were locked when he found Anna's body, but the alarms were deactivated. Would she install a security system only to let some stranger in from a council estate? And can you tell someone is from a council estate, just by how they look?' said Tristan. 'And are we getting away from our case? What does this have to do with Charlie?'

'There is a connection to Jean,' said Kate. She rummaged in her bag and took out her phone. 'I'm going to call her.' She put the phone on speaker and dialled. Jean answered her phone after a couple of rings. The rain was coming down hard now on the windscreen, and the glass was misted up.

'All right, love?' Jean said. 'I was just thinking about you and how it was going.'

'Jean, I'm just here with Tristan,' said Kate. She briefly told her about their morning at Kirby Cane Walk. 'Did you know that Anna Treadwell was also registered as a foster parent?'

'No, I didn't,' said Jean. 'But that makes more sense to me. She was an odd one. Very robotic and distracted, and she took an unhealthy shine to Charlie. I called it an itchy womb.'

'Itchy womb. You mean that this social worker wanted a child?' said Kate.

'Yes, and not just any old child. Like I said, I think she wanted Charlie. Anyway, what's that social worker got to do with Charlie after all this time? Do you know how many people from rough areas get hassled by social workers?'

'Can you tell us more about Anna Treadwell? How often did she visit you at the flat?' asked Tristan. There was a pause.

'The first time, I was on me own. That was when Becky and Joel were away with Charlie.'

'What did you say to her?'

'She said someone had phoned their hotline to flag a safe-guarding issue for a child at the property. She used some highfa-lutin language like that. She said it was a neighbour, and then I knew it was Helen, from upstairs, who'd made the call. I told her there were no children in my flat when this safeguarding issue happened.'

'Then what happened?' asked Kate.

'She didn't like having the wind taken out of her sails. She said she would come back, which she did, a few days later. I was in the living room with Becky and Charlie, and we was watching *Postman Pat*. It was one of those lovely days. The house was clean, and we were all quiet and happily watching TV. She hammered on the door and was very pushy about coming inside. I let her in, and she went and picked Charlie up off Becky's lap! Without asking or anything like that. I had to stop Becky from hitting her. Charlie started to cry and, I'll always remember it, this Anna woman started to talk to him in a low voice, saying that she would be keeping an eye on him and make sure he wasn't in danger. And that she could take care of him if he wanted her to. It was creepy. I got Charlie back off her because he was so upset, and then we asked her to leave.'

'Did you see Anna Treadwell again?'

'Yes. She came round a few more times over the next couple of weeks. Strange, out-of-hours times, too. Once at 6am on a Sunday morning, another time at 11pm on Friday. She was trying to catch us drunk or being loud, I dunno. And another time she followed us to the supermarket, Becky and me with Charlie. She came up to us in the biscuit aisle and tried to pick Charlie up from the trolley. He didn't like her and started to cry.'

'Did Anna Treadwell ever file an official report at social services?' asked Tristan.

'Gawd knows. Anna said my neighbour, Helen, phoned her again, but I think she was lying. I'd been around and had words with Helen.'

'Do you have her number?' asked Kate.

'Helen's? I'm sure I do, somewhere, but it wouldn't do you any good. She'd dead. She was decapitated in a car accident a few years back, and it couldn't have happened to a nicer person. I know I'm talking out of turn here, but we had nothing but trouble with her as a neighbour. She was mean for sport. I tell you, I've never seen a happier widower than her husband, Alan.'

'Jean, I know this sounds strange, but do you think this Anna Treadwell could have had anything to do with Charlie going missing?' asked Kate. There was a long silence on the end of the phone.

'What? No... No. I'd never put the two things together,' she said.

'You said that Anna came on the scene a few months before Charlie went missing. When exactly?' asked Tristan.

'I suppose it all happened February-March time. I'd have to have a think. Yes, Becky and Joel went to Center Parcs with Charlie in the February because it was cheaper. But no, she was off the scene by then. By the time Charlie went missing, it was June, and Anna was long gone. I always assumed she couldn't get us on anything, so she'd moved on to another kid.'

'Did you report Anna to the social services? Because this sounds very unprofessional,' said Kate. They heard Jean laugh dryly.

'As I said yesterday, you probably think of the authorities differently, but where I come from, they're the last people you phone if you're in trouble. And my flat is on the Coldharbour estate. It's the kind of place the police don't bother coming out to.'

Tristan looked at Kate with his eyes wide. It was the same council estate behind Anna's house.

22

Okehampton was only eight miles from Gidleigh, where Declan Connoly lived, so Kate and Tristan decided to use their time wisely and pay him a visit.

Kate had never been to Gidleigh, which sat on the edge of Dartmoor and was surrounded by woodland. When they drove into the village, the grass out front of a tearoom was busy with people in walking gear sitting, sipping drinks, and eating cake. Tristan peered at his GPS and saw three winding lanes leading off the village green in different directions.

'It looks like he lives off an unmarked road, but I can't see which one we should take,' he said.

'Let's ask him,' said Kate, spotting a postman who was just opening the village postbox.

'Excuse me. We're looking for Zieger Cottage?' she said, winding down the window when Tristan pulled close. 'A man called Declan —'

'Declan Connelly?' said the postman squinting at her as he pulled a bundle of envelopes out of the post box and stuffed them into his bag.

'Yes.'

He gave Kate directions up a lane partly covered by a group of trees beside the church graveyard.

'If you get to a crossroads, you've gone too far,' he said. Kate thanked him, and they drove off past a group of children playing croquet on the empty side of the green. The lane led up steeply from the village, and the views across Dartmoor were stunning. They could see a couple of smallholdings nestled in the valley ahead. As the road banked down again, they found themselves in a tunnel of trees with tall, drystone walls on either side. They came to a gate in the wall and heard a high-pitched whining sound.

Zieger Cottage was a crumbling squat house with roof tiles missing and pebble-dashed walls. It was set back from the road and had a large plot of overgrown land surrounded by drystone walls. A battered white van was parked in front of the house, and its wheels were half-submerged in a wide, churned-up patch of mud. A tow truck was parked a few metres away with a winch cable attached to the hood of the half-sunken van. A hard-faced woman with dark greying hair tied back in a thin ponytail was gathering up a row of wooden planks, forming a walkway out to the van. A wild-haired man with a florid red face and large watery blue eyes was inside the tow truck, revving the engine. They hadn't noticed Kate and Tristan arrive over the noise.

'Is that Declan?' asked Tristan.

'Yeah. I recognise him from the newspaper articles,' said Kate.

They left the car and went to the wide farm gate, watching for a moment as the truck revved and shot forward on the soft earth. The van rocked on the end of the long cable, but its wheels looked stuck fast. Then with a lurch, the line broke, and the truck shot backwards. The man slammed on the brakes.

'Cherry. Cherry!' he yelled. She looked up, and he switched off the engine. He came bowling out of the truck towards her. He was stout and wore dirty shorts and a T-shirt with wellington boots. 'You're supposed to watch the cable!'

'I was watching the fucking cable, Dec!' she shouted back. She threw down the planks of wood and reached into the pockets of her muddy trousers to take out a packet of cigarettes.

'No, you wasn't. You were miles away!'

'I wish I *was* bloody miles away. I need a fag.'

'No, you're gonna walk the plank and re-attach that fucking cable.'

'I'm having a fag!' She put the cigarette in her mouth and took out a long box of matches. As she struck one, Declan reached her. He grabbed the cigarette from her mouth and threw it into the mud. She went to protest, but it was then that they both noticed Kate and Tristan, and Declan did an almost comedic double-take.

'What do you want?' he said.

'Hello, Declan? Can we talk to you for a moment?' asked Kate. He hitched up his shorts and came slopping over to them in his muddy wellies. He raised his chin, and Kate felt a little twinge of anxiety at his posture. He wanted a fight. Cherry still held the box of matches and stared at them with her mouth slightly open.

Kate explained they were private investigators and that Jean had hired them. Cherry joined them all at the gate, and with her mouth still slightly open, she lit two cigarettes, passing one to Declan. When Kate said they were investigating the disappearance of Charlie Julings, he rolled his eyes.

'Jesus Christ. I haven't got time for this,' he said.

'We just want to ask you some questions about the night Charlie went missing—' started Kate.

'Went missing?' said Declan. 'Charlie didn't go missing, Jean didn't keep her eye on him, and he fell into the river or the Quakers. Isn't that what the court ruled in the end?'

'The court granted Jean a declaration of presumed death for Charlie. They didn't rule on his cause of death,' said Tristan, speaking for the first time. Declan took a puff of his cigarette.

'Is this your son?' he said, indicating Tristan with his lit cigarette.

'No. We work together,' said Tristan.

'Ah. Right,' Declan said with a leer.

'We work together in our agency.'

'Work together. Your "agency". You can't have a lot on if you've both got time to come here and ask me stupid questions.'

'And how do we know you are who you say you are?' said Cherry, peering at them. 'You got ID?' Kate found one of their business cards and handed it to her. She looked at it and gave it to Declan.

'The Kate Marshall Detective Agency,' he read. 'Which one of you is Kate?'

Kate rolled her eyes. 'I am.'

'Who's the pretty boy?'

'I'm Tristan Harper. Partner in the agency.' Kate could see Tristan puffing up his chest and squaring up to Declan.

'Can we ask you about your relationship with Jean Julings?' said Kate, wanting to diffuse the situation.

'He ain't got no relationship with Jean Julings,' spat Cherry.

'Yeah. And we're fucking busy here. This van is worth a fortune, even as scrap, and as you can see, it's about to go the same way as Charlie in this little Quaker.'

'Quaker?' asked Kate. 'And what do you mean about Charlie?'

Declan looked at Tristan.

'You sound local. You tell her what a Quaker is, and it's nothing religious.'

'It's boggy land,' said Tristan to Kate. Declan took another drag of his cigarette. 'If you want to know what I think about Charlie, it wasn't the river that got him. It was one of the Quakers near that campsite.'

'Devil's Way,' said Kate.

'Yeah. There are all kinds of nasty Quakers and Feathers... another name for boggy land, around the ground. And if you get sucked into a deep one, you'll never be seen again. That's what I think. The police used sniffer dogs to try and find him, and those dogs led them down to the river. Charlie went down to the water and then stumbled into the bogland.'

'But the river was swollen the night he went missing,' said Kate.

'Then he fell in,' said Declan, shrugging. 'Listen, I liked the little bugger, but I didn't have nothing to do with him going missing. It was an accident.'

'The police found Charlie's blood in your car,' said Tristan.

'He'd cut himself two weeks before when I took him to the park in my car. Becky vouched for me on that. Look. I got drunk that night, and my car ended up in a ditch. The police questioned me, but then they realised I had nothing to do with it. They had no grounds to charge me. The case is closed, and Jean effectively locked it shut by going to court for a declaration of presumed death. They had a funeral. They buried an empty coffin.'

He dropped the cigarette butt and ground it out with his boot.

'Can I ask you about a woman called Anna Treadwell?' asked Kate.

'Who's she?' snapped Cherry, turning on Declan.

'Fuck knows,' said Declan, putting up his hands in surrender. 'Who is she?'

'She was a social worker concerned about Charlie,' said Kate.

'Of all the women I've known, most have kids, and all of them have social services knocking on their doors.'

'I've never had social services banging on my door,' said Cherry.

'You only had one kid. It's the slags who have big litters of bastards that can't cope, and then the social gets involved.'

'And my Todd is a good lad,' said Cherry. 'You hear?' she repeated to Kate.

'Where is the boggy land that you're talking about near Devil's Way?' asked Kate.

'Look at a map!' he said. 'We have to get on.' Without saying anymore, he went back off to the patch of mud. He picked up the planks of wood and started making a path back to the van. Cherry sneered and flicked their business card over the gate. Then she went off to help Declan.

Kate and Tristan returned to the car.

'Boggy land, Quakers and Feathers,' said Kate. 'He thinks Charlie drowned in boggy land.'

'Do you know how many people have drowned in bogland on the moors?' said Tristan.

'I don't have the exact figures, but I'm guessing it's a lot, over the years,' she snapped. Kate took a deep breath. 'Sorry. That wasn't meant for you.'

'It's okay. He's so sure of himself. He's got me believing him,' said Tristan. They looked back at Declan and Cherry arguing over the placement of the wooden planks across the mud to the van.

'Let's talk to that police officer, Lewis, who worked on the case. I'll make an exception, and pay him. I'd like to hear everything that went down during their investigation into Charlie going missing,' said Kate, starting the engine.

23

Kate and Tristan decided to split up the next day. Tristan arranged to meet Lewis Tate in Plymouth, and Kate opted to stay at the office and bring the case details up to date.

Tristan set off at nine and made it in good time for his meeting at eleven. Lewis had chosen a pub in the harbour area called The Ship. Tristan found a parking spot a few minutes away and still arrived early. The pub wasn't open until eleven, so he sat on a bench outside, which looked out directly onto the harbour wall and the sea.

A bleary-eyed young woman with short, bleached-blonde hair was hosing down the harbour path just as a delivery truck arrived.

Lewis Tate appeared a moment later around the side of the truck. Tristan guessed Lewis was in his late forties. He was tall and wiry with a clean-shaven face and ink-black hair down to his shoulders. His face was chalk-white and gaunt, but his features were softened by his striking brown eyes. He wore baggy jeans, white trainers and a red T-shirt with the Versace logo on the front.

'All right, mate, you Tristan?' he asked. He had a swagger to his step and spoke with a trace of a cockney accent.

'Yes. Hello,' said Tristan getting up off the bench. He offered his hand to shake, but Lewis ignored it. He looked him up and down and said, 'You got the cash?'

Tristan hadn't expected him to be so blunt.

'Yes.'

'Can I see it?'

Tristan took the envelope containing five crisp twenty-pound notes from the back pocket of his shorts and handed it over. Lewis checked the contents.

'And you're buying the bevvies?' he added, fixing him with a keen stare.

'Of course.'

His gaunt face broke into a smile, and he slapped Tristan on the back.

'Great. Ask me whatever you want. Let's go inside. I'm choking for a pint.'

A pint, thought Tristan. *It's only eleven o'clock in the morning*. The landlady was just opening the doors when they went inside. It was an old-fashioned boozer with a low ceiling and lots of wood and horse brasses.

Lewis asked for Guinness with two fingers of Jameson's whisky. Tristan was going to order a cappuccino but asked for a pint of Guinness and no whisky. They were the only people in the pub, apart from a florid-looking man who came in with shopping bags and sat at the end of the bar. They took their drinks to a booth in the corner by the window. Lewis downed the whisky in one and then took a long pull on his pint. They made small talk, and then Tristan asked about the circumstances of Lewis leaving the police.

'Everyone was at it, everyone. There were so many officers

dipping into the stash of drugs we seized,' said Lewis. 'I was just stupid enough to get caught. And mind,' he said, holding up his index finger where a sovereign ring was planted up to the knuckle. 'I never used to sell the drugs on, not to adults or kids, not like a lot of the bent coppers. It was just for personal use.' He took another drink of his stout and wiped his top lip on the back of his hand. 'Anyway, I don't miss the police work. It was getting far too political when I left. I do miss the uniform and the badge. And I got so much pussy. You wouldn't believe it.' Tristan nodded. He didn't know how to respond to this.

'You got a girlfriend?'

'No. Single,' said Tristan. A part of him just wanted to say he'd recently had a boyfriend. But he felt that Lewis had assumed they were two straight guys together. He didn't think Lewis was homophobic, but telling him might shift the dynamic of the conversation, and he needed to win Lewis's trust. 'You got a girlfriend?'

'Nah, I've got an ex-wife, though. Expensive she is too. I give her maintenance for our daughter, but I think the bitch just spends it on fags and tequila. I should never have married her. I should have paid attention to the genetics of her family.' Tristan panicked that he was going to say something racist, but Lewis went on, 'When you get serious about a girl, always check out the mother. Cos, nine times out of ten, that's what she'll turn into,' he said, holding up the finger again with the sovereign ring.

'What's her mum like?'

'Let's put it this way. She makes Jabba the Hutt look like a supermodel.'

Tristan laughed. There was silence, and they looked out the window to the harbour walk.

'So, do you enjoy private detective work?' asked Lewis.

'Yeah. It's tough. I've only been doing it a couple of years. And I'm learning all the time on the job.'

Lewis leaned in and started to fiddle with the little sugar sachets in a pot in the middle of the table.

'I've thought of doing it, but I haven't got the patience. And I like a drink. Charlie Julings was my first and only truly "missing" kid case. I was involved in a couple of others where we found the kid a few hours later. He'd just gone wandering off. The other was when a father kidnapped the kid, and we tracked him down the next day to a flat in Scotland.'

He finished his pint and handed Tristan the empty glass.

'I'll have another one, no chaser.'

When Tristan returned from the bar, Lewis had a piece of paper on the table. It was a hand-drawn map of the Devil's Way Tor and the surrounding landscape. Tristan put down the glasses and moved the sugar, salt and pepper out of the way.

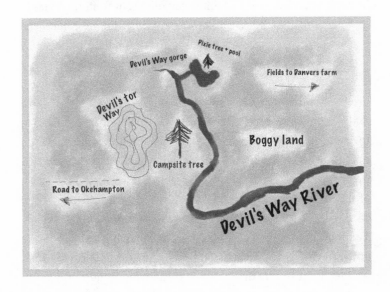

'Okay, so you can see Devil's Way Tor, next to the tree where Charlie Julings tent was pitched underneath. The river runs beside the tree to the gorge, and the Devil's Way sinkhole,' said Lewis, taking a gulp of his fresh pint. 'Have you been there?'

'Yes, a couple of days ago,' said Tristan.

'Our first theory was that Charlie left his tent under the tree and could have gone to the river and fallen in.'

'Why would he have gone to the river when his parents' tent was so close?' asked Tristan. Lewis shrugged.

'Exactly. But with the river theory, the grandmother says that the water was low the day before, they were paddling. But then, during the night, the water level suddenly increased. We checked with the Met Office. There was a big storm further up the river, a few miles away in the mountains.' He indicated the edge of the map. 'The rainwater flooded down from the hills into the Devil's Way river. If Charlie had gone down to the river in the dark, it would have looked very different from the twinkly little stream a few hours earlier. If he'd fallen in, he could have been swept downriver into the gorge and down the sinkhole.'

'There's a grate—'

'—covering the sinkhole, yes, but after the storm, the water level was three feet higher than the grate. The kid could have easily been washed over. Another theory is that if he didn't go to the river, he could have come out of his tent and gone along the road towards Okehampton, but someone would have picked him up or seen him. The road is a dirt track, but it's surrounded a lot of the way by drystone walls. That leaves us with the rest of the land where they were camping. You see this area of boggy land? That's a ten-minute walk along the river, moving away from the gorge in the other direction. It's nasty bog land. If Charlie had wandered off in that direction, he could have come a cropper in the bogland. The search teams went along there and dug around with long sticks, systematically searching the edges of this bog land all along the river. Nothing.'

'Did you use scanners or anything to check the boggy land?' asked Tristan.

'What do you mean *scanners*?'

'Probes or magnetic scanners?'

'You mean ground penetrating radar?'

'Yes,' said Tristan.

'No. We deployed all our search dogs; cadaver and search and rescue. They didn't pick up Charlie's scent leading up in the other direction towards the bogland. But they did detect Charlie's scent along the riverbank close to the Devil's Way gorge.'

'What's this here, the Pixie Tree?' asked Tristan, seeing where a smaller tree surrounded by a pool was drawn on the map.

'Where the river veers off into the gorge, there's a small fork and a narrow distributary runs in the other direction.'

'We didn't see that. It was all overgrown.'

'Okay, this distributary is almost nothing, a small trickle, but it leads down through the undergrowth and forms a pool next to an ancient tree, what they call the Pixie Tree, where offerings are made.'

'Offerings? You mean those trees where people tie on pieces of fabric as offerings of good health or to make wishes?'

Lewis nodded.

'Yeah, it's a lot to do with the pagan religion.'

'Okay. But you said Charlie's scent stopped at the river on the other side? Which led to the theory that he fell into the river.'

'Yeah.'

'What's that?' Tristan added, pointing to an arrow with "fields to Danvers Farm" written underneath.

'Danvers Farm is a smallholding a couple of miles across the moors. We checked it out. The couple who lived there were a little odd. We asked to search the house, and they let us, but they were twitchy. It was a real tip.'

'When did the search happen? Can you remember?' asked Tristan, thinking Ade hadn't mentioned this.

'A day later at most.'

'The 23rd June?'

'Yeah. Charlie went missing in the early hours of 22nd June. And it was the next day. The National Park organised a big outdoor search with volunteers. We called in the dogs, and then we widened the search around the area, and that's when we went to Danvers Farm.'

'Why were the couple odd and twitchy?' asked Tristan.

'I dunno. Instinct told me something was going on there. The wife, in particular, was very shifty, but then again, the husband was quite an imposing bloke. Maybe she was scared of him, or what he would do when we left. They had a young baby. There was pictures up of him on the sideboard, I remember, but they said he was away with the grandparents. Their car also was in a real state.'

'In what way?'

'They were farmers. They had a tractor and an old banger car, which a lot of local farmers keep for going around their land. Their "good" car was in a right state, covered in mud. The guy said that the old banger car had broken down, so they had to use the other one.' Lewis waved it away. 'I dunno. We didn't find anything, and we searched the place from top to bottom, and then just as we finished, the results got radioed back to us from the dogs that they'd traced Charlie's scent to the river, where it stopped. I dunno. There are a lot of weirdos around that area. People who don't get out much. We left the farm and that's when we started to work on the theory that Charlie fell in. Oh, and the grandmother's boyfriend, Declan Connoly, was also a suspect.'

'What do you think happened to Charlie Julings?' asked Tristan.

'I worked a lot with sniffer dogs when I was in the force, both cadaver dogs and drug squad dogs and they're rarely wrong. I think Charlie fell in the river and got sucked down the gorge into the sinkhole, never to be seen again.'

24

Kate slept well for the first time in days and woke up at 9am. She debated going for a swim and got as far as the kitchen door, but at the last minute, she chickened out. The thought of stepping into the breaking waves filled her with fear and dread.

Feeling like a failure, she made some tea and toast and sat in the living room with her laptop. She opened Google and stared at the search bar for a moment, wondering where to start.

The internet always fascinated Kate. It was possible to go into all kinds of weird and fascinating places. She likened it to searching down the back of sofas. You never knew what people had left behind.

She decided to concentrate on discovering more about Anna Treadwell, but it looked like she'd never had any social media, no Facebook or Twitter, or if she did, it had been taken down. An image came up with her name in the Google search, a rather unflattering close-up picture taken from her social worker ID card. Anna had a broad face with a high forehead and a strong chin. Her blue eyes were piercing and set close together. In the

ID photo, her forehead shone from the camera flash, her dark hair was tied back, and several strands had escaped, making a light corona of chestnut brown frizz around her head.

Kate did a reverse image search on the photo, but nothing came back. She then found a small obituary without a picture, which stated that the funeral of Anna Treadwell would take place on October 23rd 2007, at Exeter Cemetery. It must have been a few months after her death until the body was released. The text underneath read:

It is Anna's wish that there are no flowers. Charitable donations can be made via Maureen.Cook@Cranboroughwriters.com

She googled "Maureen Cook Cranborough Writers" and found a rather cheesy website with the words 'Cranborough Writers Group' spelt out in Scrabble tiles. It said the group met once every two weeks at a community centre in Cranborough, a small town close to Okehampton. Kate clicked on details of the group's latest anthology collection. It was called *The Seven*, and it had its own page on the website, advertising a published version of the group's work consisting of seven short stories.

The cover for the anthology looked amateurish. "The Seven" was written in typewriter font against a black background. Below was a line of seven glowing human figures in silhouette, standing in line with their arms outstretched. Underneath the cover image was written:

Seven dark tales to intrigue, move and amaze.

A young mother has to let go...
A secret box in a garden shed opens the door to a terrifying new world...
A long-lost friend appears at the door of an elderly gent and becomes his worst nightmare...
A bungee jumping accident leads back to a man hiding a pocket knife in his sock...
A married gay couple's sleep is disturbed by mysterious bumps in the night...
And many more!
Are you ready to experience THE SEVEN?

Copies of THE SEVEN can be bought via Abble Graphics Ltd RRP £14.99

Kate noted that Anna wasn't one of the seven authors included in the anthology, but she was intrigued that Maureen Cook had been close enough friends with Anna to organise tributes for her funeral. Kate thought back to what Gregory had told them: Anna had no friends.

Kate sent a short neutral message to Maureen's email address, asking if she could speak to her in confidence about a former writing group member.

Kate turned her attention back to Anna. The newspapers didn't give away much about her murder beyond it being a "vicious hammer attack", but she figured this could attract the ghouls. It took a great deal of digging online over the next couple of hours, but she eventually found a Reddit blog where someone had uploaded the crime scene photos.

Kate had seen a lot as a police officer and a private investigator, but the pictures turned her stomach. Anna's body lay on the carpet next to an unmade single bed. The wall and carpet were covered in blood spatter fanning out in all directions. The sheets and blankets were soaked in blood and bunched up at the end of the bed. Anna's left leg was raised and tangled at the end of the sheets. She was lying face up, but her head and face were unrecognisable, such was the brutality of the attack.

Six photos were uploaded on the Reddit blog, and the other images showed the trail of blood spatter and bloody footprints leading from Anna's body to the window and back out of the room. What surprised Kate was that two sets of footprints had been marked up and numbered. As she clicked back through the photos, the two sets were prominent, and their route was marked as coming in and leaving. These weren't accidental footprints. Whoever came in and out didn't skirt around the body, trying to avoid the blood. She made a note to ask Gregory, the neighbour, about this. Did he step in the blood when he found her body?

Anna's bedroom was rather sad, with minimal furniture. In the final photo, the mirror above a vanity table in the corner of the room reflected a crime scene photographer in white overalls. She could clearly see his face when she zoomed in on the image. The mirror was angled so that his face was captured slightly side on, showing his entire face. Kate stared at it for a moment. She dragged the photo onto her computer desktop. She zoomed in on it, cropped the image and then sharpened it so that the picture of the man's face was now in close-up and much clearer. Kate then opened Google Reverse Image, dropped in the file, and pressed search.

It only took a moment for Google to search for similar images using the man's face. A grid of three images appeared: two from Facebook, where the same man was pictured behind a barbecue in his garden, posing with tongs and wearing a stripy apron. In the third, his photo was used in an interview with a forensics magazine.

'Bingo,' said Kate. His name was Bernard Crenshaw. She debated for a moment and then sent him a short message.

25

In the early afternoon, Kate had a message from Tristan that his meeting with Lewis was over, and he'd be heading back to the office. It was a hot day, and her house didn't have air conditioning. Kate felt the heat was sapping her energy; she was still struggling to have any appetite and had to force herself to eat a slice of toast with a thin spread of butter, and she only ate because she had to put something in her stomach when she took her antibiotics.

Just after three, Kate left the house and went next door to their office. The campsite shop was busy with people going in and out. As Kate reached the steps leading up the side of the building to their office on the second floor, two shirtless young surfer guys in board shorts came out of the shop. They were both good-looking and in their twenties with shoulder-length dark hair.

'Hey, how are you doing?' said one of the guys. He had an American accent and seemed to know her.

'Can I help you?' she said. It came out a little more tartly than she'd intended. She'd just wanted to get to the office without someone from the campsite asking her about something.

'I'm Dieter. This is Wolfgang. We found you in the water,' he said. Kate stopped on the stairs, turned to face the young guys for a moment, and then felt her cheeks flush with embarrassment.

There was a ding as the door of the campsite shop opened, and an elderly British couple in walking gear came out of the shop with ice creams. Kate walked down the stairs and waited until they were out of earshot.

'It was you who pulled me out of the water?' she said.

'Yeah. You were in real trouble,' said Wolfgang. His bare legs were covered in a dusting of white sand.

The feeling came back to Kate of being dragged down into the water and turned over and over. The pain as her arm and face scraped along the seabed. And the horrible thought that her life would be over within a few seconds. Kate put her hands over her face. These two beautiful young men had saved her life.

'Hey. Are you okay?' asked Dieter.

'No,' said Kate, unable to stop the tears now. She didn't know what else to say. How do you thank someone who saved your life? She had no memory of what happened. She took her hands away from her face and wiped her eyes. They were silent as they stared at her. 'I'm sorry. I should have come over to speak to you both, to say thank you.'

Out of nowhere, a big sob rose from her chest, and she began crying. The guys looked around, clearly not knowing what to do.

'What's up there?' asked Dieter.

'My office,' said Kate through her tears. They each grabbed an arm and helped her up the stairs to the office. The agency office space had been Myra's living room, and it still had the old 1970s patterned carpet. A row of windows ran the length along the back of the building and looked out over the beach. Dieter and Wolfgang guided Kate to an armchair next to the big table in the middle of the room.

'Get her a glass of water,' said Dieter. He crouched beside Kate as Wolfgang went off to the small kitchen.

'We heard you were in the hospital,' he said. The water groaned in the pipes as Wolfgang filled a glass and returned, handing it to Kate.

'Yeah. But I'm okay. I'll be okay, thanks to you both. Bit of a chest infection.' Kate took the glass in her shaking hands. She took a gulp of water and found a tissue in her pocket to blot her face and nose.

'I don't know what to say to you both, but thank you.'

Wolfgang crossed his arms over his bare chest and smiled.

'We didn't do anything, really. Do you know about rip tides? Do you know how dangerous they are?'

'Yes, and that makes me feel all the more stupid. I've been swimming in the sea first thing every morning for years.'

'Have you been back in the water since?' asked Dieter.

'No.'

'You've got to get back on the horse. We've both been busted up bad by the sea.'

'I fell off a fifty-foot wave in Portugal,' said Wolfgang. 'It's like landing on concrete. I busted two ribs, and my pelvis bone broke and came through the skin.' He pulled down the waistband of his shorts a little to show her a long curving scar above his pubic bone.

The door opened, and Tristan walked in. He didn't seem to know what to say to this odd tableau of the two topless surfers standing over Kate sitting in the armchair, one of them with his shorts pulled down.

'Is everything okay?' said Tristan, looking at Wolfgang and Dieter.

'Yes,' said Kate, wiping her face and getting up. 'These are the guys who pulled me out of the water.'

Wolfgang pulled up his waistband. Tristan's demeanour changed, and they all shook hands.

'I've seen you around,' said Dieter to Tristan. 'Sweet tattoos.'

'Thanks,' said Tristan.

'Wolfgang was just telling me that he fell off a wave in Portugal,' said Kate.

'Yeah. I was in the hospital for a month. But I went back in the water, and you need to get back in there,' he said.

Kate nodded.

'How long are you both staying? I meant to tell you, I'm going to comp your week. You won't have to pay,' she said.

'We're going back tomorrow,' said Dieter. There was another awkward beat.

'Do you guys want coffee?' asked Tristan. Dieter stretched his arms above his head.

'It's our last day, and we wanted to catch some surf before we left,' he said. Wolfgang nodded.

'Absolutely. You two, please go and have fun, and thank you again,' said Kate.

The two guys went off, and Tristan watched them from the door before closing it.

'That was mortifying,' said Kate, crossing to the kitchen to put the kettle on.

'Those were the guys who rescued you?'

'Yes.'

'Did they give you mouth to mouth?'

'I don't know.'

'I think that's something you'd want to remember if they

did,' he said. Kate laughed. She was feeling much better, but a part of her felt shabby and embarrassed that she hadn't sought them out to say thank you. She made a pot of tea, and they sat down to discuss the day's events.

'I feel like you've done better than me,' said Kate, looking at the map from Lewis. 'This is the first time we've heard a direct theory from the police and how their investigation progressed. Do you think this Lewis guy is reliable?'

'For the first half an hour of our meeting, I thought he was a bit of a twerp, and then when he started talking, I could see that he had been a dedicated police officer.'

'Until he stole drugs,' said Kate. 'And how many pints did he drink during your meeting?'

'Three, with whisky chasers. But he did tell us about a visit to the couple on the nearby smallholding, Danvers Farm, who were acting weirdly.'

'From his perspective as a drunk and a drug addict?'

'He did say that their car was in a right state. Muddy.'

'They lived on a farm. Farms are muddy. And what was their motive or link to Charlie?'

'Theirs was the closest dwelling to Devil's Way Tor. Lewis said that they searched the farmhouse and buildings and they found nothing.'

'Let's focus back on the link to the social worker, Anna Treadwell. The fact she lived so close to the Coldharbour estate where Charlie lived. And also what Jean said about her fixation with him.'

'What would be a motive for killing Anna? She didn't have any money, that we know of.'

'Isn't that an assumption?' asked Kate. 'She bought a house in an okay area.'

'You know about my past,' said Tristan. 'After my mum died

and dad was AWOL, Sarah took on the role of parent. She was only sixteen, and we had an endless parade of social workers knocking on the door. I was fourteen, and at one point, I came close to being shipped off to a children's home for a couple of years. Sarah had to fight to be my full-time guardian. Anyway, my point is that all those social workers came to see us; men, women, old and young, and none of them had the look of being rich. I think there are good and bad social workers, but none of them goes into it for the money.'

Kate got up and went to the window. She watched two families on two sides of the beach. In both places, the fathers were larking about with the kids, and the mothers were packing up the picnic baskets and organising everything. She thought back to her early years with Jake, and how the social workers she contacted were hostile to her, quite rightly, it turned out.

'Okay, regarding Anna. Her neighbour said someone was on her property twice before she died. Someone tried the handle late at night, and she saw someone in the garden in the middle of the night a few days later. Why? If they weren't after her money, what were they after?'

'There could have been a vengeful father whose kids had been taken away from him or the mother. And she could have had an antagonistic personality. What if she did the same to other parents as she did with Charlie?'

Kate came and sat back down.

'Jean said that Anna became obsessed with Charlie. She said to him that they would soon be together.'

'Do you really think she abducted Charlie?' asked Tristan. 'Why would she abduct him if she already had the power to take him away from Jean and Becky? And she was a registered foster carer. If she wanted to, she could have had him removed from Becky's care.'

'I know. Whatever happened to Charlie, he was taken from here.'

Kate looked back at the map on the table, with Lewis's writing on it, indicating the boggy land and the Pixie Tree leading off the tributary, where the police dogs had detected Charlie's scent. 'Right now, we're waiting for Joel to return from his holiday, and I don't know when these two people I emailed today will get back to me. We have this map and an idea of what the police did as part of their investigations. I'd like to go back to Devil's Way. Do you think Ade would be up for coming with us? He was one of the first police officers on the scene. It could help us to have his perspective. I just need to see it all again.'

26

The mercury was already tipping twenty-eight degrees Celsius when they set off for Devil's Way on Monday morning.

Kate was driving, and the air conditioning in her car had packed up so they had the windows wide open. Ade was sitting in the back, wagging a paper fan like an overheated señorita.

'Sorry about the heat,' she said, eyeing him in the mirror. His long hair, which he always blow-dried straight, was starting to curl up and frizz. And he was wearing some kind of long dress robe or kaftan with bright blue and green stripes.

'I bought this from a souk when I went down the Nile,' he said, seeing Kate studying his attire. 'Very cooling. And this fan is from the pound shop in Ashdean.'

'Did you like Egypt?' asked Tristan.

'I did. The landscape and people were so beautiful... The sense of being part of history, seeing the Pyramids. And I didn't get the shits at all. Not once. Saying that, I washed everything with Palmolive hand soap, even lettuce,' he said, fanning himself furiously as they bumped their way along the track. Tristan looked sideways at Kate, and they exchanged smiles.

'I've been over my notes from my police pocket book, and I've got them with me,' he said, patting a tote bag beside him. 'Do you want me to run through what I can remember that day I got the call about Charlie being missing?'

'Yes. Where were you coming from on that day?' said Kate.

'I was on the night shift in Okehampton, and we got the call at 4am. I can remember my heart sinking when I heard. I only had two hours left till clocking off.'

'It's around ten minutes from Okehampton town centre to where we are now,' said Kate as they passed a fallen tree on the moor beside the road. Ade flicked his fan closed and tapped it on the back of Kate's seat.

'Stop the car!'

Kate hit the brakes, and they jolted to a stop. Tristan rubbed his neck and looked back at Ade. 'Sorry, Tris. I've just realised it's here where we found the bloke in the ditch in his car.'

They all got out. The heat was beating down on the dusty track. Pale grass lined the road on each side, and they could hear the crickets chirping. There was a large tree, which was broken in half. A few long-dead leaves clung to the branches, and the grass grew out of the trunk's split. Next to it was a deep ditch.

'What bloke?' asked Kate.

'Whatshisname, Declan,' said Ade.

'Who you found in the ditch in his car on the way to the Devil's Way.'

'Yes. The car was on its side. I think there was water in the ditch back then. The car was lying on the right side, which indicated he'd been driving away from the Devil's Tor when he came off the road. At first, we thought he was dead. He was sitting in the driver's seat, kind of lying against the inside of the door. It was still quite dark. I jumped down into the ditch with a torch to check if he was okay.'

'What time was this?' asked Tristan.

'I think it was around quarter past four in the morning. Yes, we got the call at four, and it took us ten or fifteen minutes to get here.'

'And Declan was fine?' asked Tristan.

'Yes. Pissed as a fart, but unhurt. He seemed quite annoyed at me for waking him up.'

Kate looked back up the road towards the Devil's Way. The Tor wasn't visible from this point.

'What was he doing here at this time? Jean told us Declan left around 10pm when she got rid of him,' she said.

'Declan told us he'd been on his way to The Feathers, a local pub, for a lock-in. At this point, we didn't know he was involved with Charlie Julings's family, and another squad car arrived, so we left them with him.'

Kate looked at the ditch and then turned back, shielding her eyes from the hot sun. The Devil's Tor was a couple of miles away, and the track was straight as it banked down towards it.

'What was he doing here five hours after he left Jean? Unless he came off the road and spent a few hours here asleep,' said Kate.

'Jean said he was completely blotto. He'd drunk almost a whole bottle of whisky,' said Tristan, flapping his T-shirt in the heat. Kate pondered for a moment, and they returned to the car and carried on. The heat was rippling off the track when they saw the Devil's Tor rising out of the moors. Ade peered out of the window.

'I'd forgotten how tall it is. It must be six or seven storeys high,' he said, squinting up at the massive rock formation. Kate parked the car at the base of the Tor, under a rocky outcrop with shade.

'What exactly did you see when you first arrived?' asked Kate.

Ade used the fan as a visor to cover his eyes. He looked out at the field with the vast ancient tree. They could just see a glimpse of the river twinkling in the grass to the left-hand corner of the Tor.

'There was a blue car parked here, just about where we're standing, and a tent was pitched next to it... And next to that, Jean and Becky were fighting in the grass. My colleague pulled them apart, and the other bloke helped. Charlie's father—'

'Joel,' said Kate.

'Yes. Joel. He didn't seem surprised that they were fighting. Like it happened often.'

'What else?'

'There was the tree... I couldn't see anything else.'

'Was it dark?' asked Tristan. 'The other tent was pitched under the tree.'

'We couldn't see the other tent.'

Kate looked at Tristan.

'Everyone has said that both tents were pitched,' said Kate. Tristan took out his phone and found the photo from that day, of the search teams and Ade surrounding Becky Juling's car at the bottom of the Tor.

'Look at me. Face like a beef tomato and no style,' said Ade, squinting at the screen. 'Look, can you see the grass growing in the middle between the tree and the Tor? You can't tell in this picture, but it was very tall. I'd say it was waist-high on me. And because of that, Jean and Charlie's tent wasn't visible under the tree when you stood here.'

They walked over to the tree, across what was now a short mossy scrub. Kate, Tristan and Ade stopped under the shade of the immense trunk, and it suddenly felt ten degrees cooler.

There was a very light breeze, but the tree creaked loudly as the air moved between the massive branches.

'Was there long grass under the tree?' asked Kate.

'I don't think so,' said Ade, breathless and leaning on the tree with one hand, fanning himself with the other.

'Can you remember how far the long grass extended across this patch of land?'

'It was wide. I think it went down to the river on the other side of the Tor.'

Kate and Tristan crouched down on the ground, facing the Tor.

'We've been questioning how Charlie could have wandered off at night when the two tents were pitched so close together, but we didn't know about the grass,' said Kate.

'Imagine if you're only knee-height. You come out of this tent and stumble into long, adult waist-high grass. And it's dark, too. It would be easy to get lost and wander off in the wrong direction,' said Tristan.

'He was only three, so his mum, dad, and gran probably still picked him up and carried him around. During the day, he was up on an adult's hip and saw that the two tents were close together,' said Kate.

'So he comes out of the tent, scared that he's alone. He hears Jean's voice with Declan, and he heads towards her, but she's on the other side of the Tor, and he gets lost in the long grass, and that's how he ends up wandering alongside the river,' said Tristan.

'Did the police have this theory about Charlie getting lost in the long grass?' asked Kate, looking at Ade leaning with his back against the tree.

'No. I don't think so.'

'Why not?'

He thought about it and pulled the folder with his notes out of the tote bag. He spent a moment flicking through.

'It all happened so fast. We arrived on the scene and organised a search. A big search party was arranged that morning. I think the National Park authority got a hundred people to come here who helped with the search. And that was in the afternoon. You have to remember that this was what we focused on. No one was talking about abduction or Charlie being dead. We all thought he'd wandered off in the night and we'd find him again. On top of the search team who came here, there were quite a lot of press and fifteen or twenty police officers, police cars, four or five big vans. I even remember a couple of coaches from the National Park. All of these people and this movement between the two tents quickly flattened out all the grass.' Ade fanned himself for a moment, looking between Kate and Tristan. 'Well, bugger me. I'd never thought of that. By the time Charlie Julings was being talked about as an abduction, the grass was all flat.'

27

They walked from under the tree down to the river at the side of the Tor. The dry heat felt heavy as the sun rose higher in the sky.

Their discovery, that the grass had been longer between the tents, lent credence to the theory that Charlie had wandered off and lost his bearings. The only problem was, if he had fallen in the river, how would they prove it?

As they passed the Tor, they carried on through the cluster of boulders at the base. The cool breeze coming off the river and the sound of the running water were soothing as they stood on the edge of the mossy banks.

'I'm sorry, chaps, I absolutely have to cool off,' Ade said, pulling off his trainers and socks. 'Grab my arm,' he added to Tristan. 'I don't want to go arse over tit.' He held out his hand, and Tristan helped him down the bank and onto a half-submerged flat rock twinkling in the sun as the water lapped over it.

Tristan slipped off his flip-flops and waded in after Ade. Kate wasn't going to follow, but she was sweating, and their reactions to the cold water convinced her to change her mind. She slipped off her sandals and waded in after them.

'Does the water level look even lower than when we were here the other day?' she asked Tristan.

'It does.'

'I remember this as a raging muddy torrent when we came down that day,' said Ade. He stepped off the rock into the water, lifting his kaftan slightly. The water only came up to his calves, and he was tall.

'Lewis told me the same thing,' said Tristan. 'He said that earlier in the evening, there had been a storm up in the mountains, where there's a tributary to the Devil's Way river.'

Ade raised an eyebrow at the mention of Lewis.

'I always remember him as being a poor excuse for a police officer, quite sloppy and arrogant,' he said.

'He gave me this map,' said Tristan, holding it up. 'And he was on the case longer than you.'

'But I was amongst the first responders,' said Ade haughtily. 'Lewis only came along later that afternoon.'

'But he stayed on the case longer than you did. You said you were only on it for the first day.'

'And lest we forget,' said Ade grandly, pointing his fan at Tristan, 'Lewis is a bent copper, and not in a good way. Selling drugs his colleagues risked their lives to seize! He's no better than Declan.'

Tristan opened his mouth to say something else.

'And we're grateful for your help,' said Kate, shooting Tristan a look to back off. She wanted Ade on their side, and she could see that he was temperamental.

'Sorry. You're right. And you have all your pocketbook notes, which Lewis wasn't able to give us,' said Tristan.

'Thank you,' said Ade, holding out his arm. 'Now help me out. I can feel myself pruning.'

Tristan helped Ade and then Kate out of the water, and they all carried on along the river bank towards the gorge. They stopped when they reached the point where the river turned sharply to the left. Kate shielded her eyes with her hand and looked across the moors. It was a hazy day, but she could just make out the Danvers Farm Lewis mentioned in the distance. Ade stopped and put up his hand.

'Hang on a minute. Where's the bridge? There was a bridge here,' he said, having to shout above the sound of the roaring water in the gorge. 'A small wooden footbridge.'

'What? No one mentioned a bridge,' said Kate.

'Well, there was one. It was rather rickety and old, where these stones are.' He indicated a line of stepping stones across the water to the other side. 'When we arrived the water was so high, right up underneath the bridge and washing over it.'

'Did Lewis mention a bridge?' said Kate.

'No,' said Tristan.

'But he drew you a map?'

'He didn't mention a bridge.'

'Well, *I'm* not a thieving drunk ex-copper, and I remember there was a bridge here,' said Ade.

Carefully, they crossed the river, stepping easily over the row of stepping stones to the other side. The last time they visited, Kate hadn't noticed there was a small stream which flowed off from the main river to the right and down a grassy bank. They followed it for a hundred metres or so. As the roaring of the gorge faded behind them, the bushes grew thicker. Flies buzzed in the heat. Tristan had to part the dense undergrowth so they could keep following the water, and the ground was muddy. On the other side of a row of bushes, they emerged into a small clearing where the stream fed into a sizeable stagnant pond. It smelt of standing water, and flies and mosquitoes buzzed above it.

'It's so muddy—' Ade started to say, and his voice trailed off.

On the opposite side of the pond was a vast, ancient tree. It sat squat and low on the muddy banks and seemed to spread across the edge of the pool. Scores of its thin branches were growing down into the water. Along the length of every branch, of which there were many, pieces of coloured material had been tied. Some were faded and ragged, and others looked newer. There were even rags tied on the very tips of branches and half-submerged in the stagnant water, the fabric wet and edged with algae. The tree had barely any leaves and looked like it was sinking under the weight of it all.

'Oh my word,' said Ade. 'What is this?'

'It's called the Pixie Tree,' said Tristan. 'It was on Lewis's map.' Kate glanced at him and saw he shared her feeling of unease. There was something imposing about the tree.

Despite the heat and the bright sun, there was a feeling of sickness in the air beside this fetid pool. It was cloying in the heat, and it frightened Kate.

28

They moved closer to the Pixie Tree, skirting around the soft mud at the pond's edge. The bushes and undergrowth were tall all around the water, and Kate peered down to try and see how deep the water was, but the light didn't penetrate the gloom and algae.

Tristan had his mobile phone and was reading from an article he'd found.

'These rags tied on are called "clouties". They're left as gestures of acknowledgement and respect for the spirits of the land and sometimes as prayers requesting general blessings or specific aid from those same spirits,' he said.

Kate looked at the hundreds and hundreds which hung on every branch. Up close, the tree was overwhelming and must have been thirty to forty metres wide.

'The piece of rag is first dipped in the water, pressed against the troubled part of the body, if the sufferer is there at the time, and tied to the tree. The cloth then absorbs the illness and carries it harmlessly back to the elements as it slowly weathers over time and disintegrates.'

When he heard this, Ade took a step back from the water's edge, and Kate felt the same squeamishness. Tristan went on, 'The tying of these "clouties" is a quiet, private act of communion between human beings and the local spirits of the land... I've seen other trees around Dartmoor like this, and they're all covered in these pieces of material.' He looked up at them. 'Lewis said that this was where the police search dogs tracked Charlie's scent on the day he went missing. But I don't understand how he got here if the river had swelled so large with water.'

'The bridge,' said Kate. 'Charlie could have walked across. Ade, did the bridge have rails?'

'Yes. It wasn't just a plank of wood. It was enclosed with a high rail, but the water was so high, it was running over the bridge when we arrived.'

'We need to find out if this pool was dredged or searched by the police.'

'Would scent dogs have been able to detect Charlie, if water was running over the bridge? Wouldn't it have washed the scent away?' asked Tristan.

'I don't know,' said Ade. Kate looked back at the dank pool where the mosquitoes were hovering. The crickets seemed louder here. They jumped when they heard a cracking in the undergrowth. A wild-looking elderly lady, hunched almost double, came pushing through a gap in the undergrowth. She was wearing a ripped and filthy shell suit. Her bare feet were caked with mud, and her face was burnt by the sun. She was rail-thin, with a gnarled hand leaning atop a stick.

She grimaced at them, and Kate saw she had a few blackened teeth remaining.

'Hello,' said Tristan. She gave him the once-over but ignored them all and moved through the muddy banks to the tree. She put her bag down and staked her stick into the mud so it stood on its own. When she turned to the tree, Kate saw the old lady was wearing a red Spider-Man-branded children's backpack. It stood out for its newness against the grimy back of her ripped clothes. She shrugged it off and, wheezing, unzipped it and took out a piece of material. She carefully dipped it into a bloom of green algae at the edge of the pool, then slowly removed her shell suit jacket. Underneath, the woman wore a grimy, black, sleeveless vest, and Kate was shocked to see her twisted, hunched-over spine. Her bones bulged up through her skin in odd shapes. She bent over to retrieve the piece of rag from the water, and pressed it against her back.

Kate suddenly felt like they were intruding on a private moment.

'Come on, we should go,' she said, tilting her head away from the tree. Ade and Tristan nodded, and they started walking back towards the stream. As the undergrowth cracked around them, the elderly lady glanced over her hunched back with a malevolent stare and then moved to the tree to tie the rag on a piece of branch.

They walked back up the trickle of the stream, and then as they emerged from the bushes and trees by the gorge, the roar of the water and a slight breeze brought them back to reality. They crossed the stepping stones and stood on the opposite bank of the river.

'I didn't like it there. It felt like we were under some kind of spell,' said Tristan, shivering. 'And I don't believe in magic.'

Ade nodded. He stepped out of his shoes again and into the river's cool water.

'Where did that lady come from?' asked Kate, looking around at the thick undergrowth. Tristan pulled the ordnance survey map out of his pocket and unfolded a couple of the flaps.

'There's a thick band of trees and undergrowth which go back, according to this scale, for five hundred metres or so, and then it's open moorland.'

Kate moved around to look at the map.

'I wonder where she came from. Does she live nearby, does she have a car?' she asked. 'Come on, let's go back and talk to her. She might live locally. She didn't look like she had a car.'

'I'll stay here,' said Ade, waving them away with his fan. Kate and Tristan retraced their steps, but when they reached the pond again, the elderly lady was nowhere to be seen. Kate went to the spot in the undergrowth from where she'd emerged and pulled back the thin branch of a tree. She stepped into the dim gloom of a densely packed forest of trees and weeds. The ground was very soft underfoot, and Kate saw footprints in the mud. She pushed further into the undergrowth. It was only possible to see a few feet in front of her, and at points, she couldn't move through the knots of weeds, tree branches and twisted roots.

'Kate, don't go too deep. You might get lost,' she heard Tristan saying behind her. She carried on for a few more minutes, flailing about. The sweat trickled down her back, and the flies and midges bit her exposed skin.

Where had the old lady gone? The still undergrowth was silent. Kate stopped and shuddered, looking down at her sandals, caked with mud. She looked back and saw Tristan's feet had sunk into the earth, and he was struggling to retrieve one of his flip-flops.

'We can look this up online,' said Tristan. 'We're going to vanish in the mud if we're not careful.'

Kate looked back into the shady depths of the undergrowth.

'Let's go back and find Ade,' she said.

29

They walked back to where Ade was waiting on the broad, smooth rock above the gorge. He was sweating profusely in the hot sun.

'Do you want to come with us into the gorge?' asked Kate.

'Yes. It's in the shade,' Ade said, heaving himself to his feet. They took the footpath down into the gorge, which was much cooler, surrounded by the damp mossy walls.

Their last visit had been at dusk, and she could see better in the light. Kate noticed the water level was lower than the previous week, and she estimated that the narrow rocky path next to the river was around two or three metres above the water rushing past below. They came to the tall grille at the bottom where the path ended, and the water continued to rush through. Kate put her hand out onto the cold metal. It was thick and sturdy, and the rusted padlock was wet from the water running down through the fronds of moss above.

On the other side of the grille, the gorge's walls made a smooth wide semicircle, like the cross-section of a deep well in front of them. The water poured into this large basin with a gush of foam and then formed a natural whirlpool which grew in intensity in the middle, whirling with force like the plughole in a vast sink, and then the water just disappeared.

'It's quite overwhelming to look at,' said Ade, raising his voice above the roar of the water. 'One reason they call it Devil's Way is that the whirlpool runs anti-clockwise.'

The 'plughole' where the water was vanishing was half a metre wide.

'A three-year-old would easily fit down there, and even a full-sized adult,' shouted Tristan, following her train of thought.

'When you and your team came to look at the river, it was swollen by several metres?' asked Kate. Ade nodded. 'What about this footpath here?'

'We couldn't get down it. We had to stay up top. The water was raging down here, covering the footpath,' said Ade.

'If Charlie fell into the gorge, could he have been washed over the grille into that hole?'

'Yes. But only if he floated. He could have been sucked underwater and stuck against the grate. But that didn't happen. The water level dropped after a few hours, and there was no body.'

Tristan and Ade turned to go back up, and Kate had a sudden image of being dragged under the water. She gripped the grate and closed her eyes for a moment. Her hands were shaking. She took deep breaths until the panic passed, then followed the guys back up the footpath.

The sun was still scorching hot when they came out of the shade of the gorge. Ade asked to be excused and returned to the car because the heat was getting to him. Kate and Tristan decided to walk along the riverbank in the other direction. As they set off under the relentless glare of the beating sun, Kate wished she'd brought a hat with her.

They had to climb up a steep bank of rock, where they followed the river for another ten minutes. They passed the large tree at a distance and, after a couple of minutes, came to a small waterfall. Kate stopped for a moment and leant forward. There was sweat dripping off her nose, and she felt faint.

'Are you okay?' asked Tristan.

'I'm sweating and drinking nothing,' she said. She eyed the crystal-clear water gushing down over the rocks. 'Do you think this is safe to drink?'

'I think so,' said Tristan. He squatted down, scooped up some water, and drank out of his hand. Kate knelt beside him, ladling up handfuls of the sweet, freezing, cold water and drank. It tasted good. Tristan moved downstream, stepped into the current, stripped off his T-shirt and dunked it in the water.

'That's better,' he said, wringing it out and putting it back on. Kate leant forward and submerged her head. The water was so cold it jarred her teeth. She wrung out her hair and sat back on the bank.

'Are you sure you're okay?' asked Tristan.

'I don't know. I suddenly feel the weight of responsibility for finding Charlie, and if he did fall into the river, we could never prove it.'

'I meant, are you okay in the heat? You look really pale.'

'I'm fine,' she said. 'Let's keep going.'

He got up and started to climb the steep slope up the side of the waterfall. The heat was getting to her, and Kate struggled to keep up. She slipped a couple of times, and Tristan reached out to grab her arm. For the first time in ages, Kate felt the age gap between them.

When Tristan put out his hand to catch her at the top of the slope, it only annoyed her even more. They carried on walking as the river began to widen and move past at a much slower pace. Devil's Way Tor was now a hazy blob on the horizon.

Kate's hair was almost dry when they reached the point where the river spread out on an extensive open patch of flat boggy ground, with undulating fields of moss and short grass reaching out to the hills in the far distance. She stopped to catch her breath. The bright sunshine made her squint, and it was suddenly far too dazzling. She closed her eyes and felt another wave of dizziness. When she opened them, she saw Tristan had walked across the grass for a couple of metres, and she watched as he jumped up and down. The grassy surface around him rippled, and as he landed, it shifted like a giant water-bed.

'It's the weirdest thing. It feels firm, but it's all moving, as a big block,' he said, looking back at her and grinning.

'Are you crazy? That's bogland,' shouted Kate, afraid for him and annoyed at his immaturity. She'd heard stories of people getting out of their depth in boggy land on Dartmoor and drowning. He jumped up again, this time higher, and as he landed, the grass seemed to sink into a depression and then right itself. The gorse and scrub surrounding it rippled outwards. Her headache was now pounding behind her eyes.

'Lewis told me the police search teams got as far as this and searched the boggy land for Charlie's body, but the dogs didn't detect a scent. The river is wider here. We don't know how much higher the water level was here, on the night Charlie went missing.'

He jumped up and down again, the ground rippling under him like a large saggy trampoline.

'Tristan. Stop! If you get pulled under, I'm not coming in after you.'

He walked back to her, picking his way over the rolling grass until he joined her on the firmer ground. 'I had a horrible vision of you sinking into the bog and me having to tell Sarah you're missing. And she isn't my biggest fan.'

'Okay, go easy,' he said. There was an awkward silence, and they both looked out on the boggy land. A group of birds took off into the sun, cawing as they crossed the sky.

'Do you really think that a three-year-old would come all this way in the middle of the night?' asked Kate. 'We've been walking for almost half an hour. It doesn't add up. He'd have had to climb that steep slope back by the waterfall, and when he finally reached this point, he'd have had to start out across the moors. He might have got lost in the long grass outside the tent and stumbled about for a bit, but why would he turn and walk all this way in the other direction?'

'What if he was sleepwalking?' asked Tristan. Kate's headache was intensifying like a needle in her eye. She shook her head, which set off even more pain. Tristan looked at her.

'People, children, do sleepwalk. And Charlie left the tent in the middle of the night.'

'I can't go back to Jean and tell her that all we've come up with is that Charlie might have gone off sleepwalking,' Kate snapped.

'I'm not saying we present it to Jean.' Tristan sighed and shook his head with frustration. 'Perhaps you should have something to drink—'

'What's that supposed to mean?' said Kate, her anger and the pain in her head mingling. He stared at her.

'I meant another drink of water. We're probably both dehydrated. What did you think I meant?'

'Nothing. Nothing. You're right.'

'Did you think I was talking about alcohol?'

Kate rubbed her eyes. She just wanted this conversation to be over. She wanted to be lying down in a dark room.

'Just forget it. It's the heat.'

'Okay. But just for the record, I would never...'

'I know. Fine,' said Kate.

They stood there in awkward silence. This was the first time she'd argued with Tristan, and it felt horrible. He shielded his eyes and looked back across the expanse of moorland. Far in the distance he could see the hazy blur of Danvers farm.

'When Lewis mentioned his visit to the Danvers farm close to the gorge, he said the farmer and his wife were acting jittery. What if they saw something? That's something more concrete than my sleepwalking theory.'

Kate closed her eyes against the sun, and took a deep breath.

'Yes. That's something we should look into.'

'Come on, let's go back to the car,' said Tristan, moving off. They walked back in stony silence, sweltering in the midday heat. They stopped to drink at the waterfall, and she saw Tristan wanted to help her down the slope, but she sat down on her haunches and skidded down so she wouldn't trip. She was now feeling awful. The cold water had been refreshing, but she'd drunk so much that it sloshed around in her stomach and made her nauseous.

She was relieved when they drew close to the Devil's Way Tor and the car. Kate could see Ade sitting on the bumper under one of her umbrellas from the boot. Tristan was a few feet ahead when she suddenly went ice-cold and felt dizzy, like she was going to faint. As she sank down on her haunches in the grass, Ade noticed her, got off the car bumper and came rushing over. Tristan turned back as Kate crumpled, her stomach lurched, and she threw up on the grass.

30

'Sorry if that's cold,' said Dr John Boucher, Kate's GP. She was lying on the examination table in his office as he listened to her chest with his stethoscope. She winced at the feeling of the cold metal on her breast bone.

'Thank you for seeing me so fast,' she said.

'It seems this afternoon is unusually quiet in the surgery.'

His office in Ashdean was quiet and calm, and he had an Axminster carpet on the floor under his desk, which softened the room. She watched his face as the clock ticked in the silence.

'Breathe in. Good. And out.' He listened for a moment longer and then took the stethoscope out of his ears and hooked it over his shoulders. 'You can put your shirt back on.'

John slid his chair back to the desk. Kate sat up and pulled on the T-shirt, still damp with sweat. Tristan had given her one of his sports rehydration drinks to sip as he drove them back to Ashdean, and she was already feeling better.

'I think I just got dehydrated in this heat,' she said. 'I was out on the moors all day and forgot to drink.'

'You've only just been discharged from hospital. You have an upper respiratory tract infection. It's a side-effect of the seawater on your lungs. How's your breathing?'

'My chest feels heavy,' said Kate. He consulted his notes again.

'You were discharged from hospital—'

'A week ago.'

He raised an eyebrow. 'And you are back at work?' Kate nodded. 'You should be signed off sick.'

'I need to work. I have a new case.'

He looked up from his notes.

'What about your AA meetings? You missed the last two.'

John was a fellow AA member, and they'd been going to the same Thursday night meeting at the Kingdom Hall in Ashdean for the past few years. He had also been Kate's friend Myra's doctor.

'I was in hospital,' said Kate, hearing the flimsiness of her excuse.

She watched as he paged through her medical file. This was the first time she'd visited John as her GP in a few years. Seeing him with his doctor's coat on felt a little odd. He sighed and peered over his glasses at the computer screen.

'Okay. I'm going to put you on a different course of antibiotics. The Erythromycin could be the reason for your stomach problems and lack of appetite.'

'Yes. I've lost a bit of weight and didn't have that much extra to begin with.'

'This new course is a lot kinder on the tum.' He typed away, and the printer whirred and spat out the prescription. He signed it and went to hand it to her. Kate got up. He put the prescription back on his desk. 'Don't stop coming to meetings. It's hard, I know. So many times I want to stay home, but if you start skipping them, it's not good.'

'I know all of this. I know it,' said Kate.

He looked at his watch. 'I have ten minutes until my next patient. Would you like to have a meeting?'

Kate was surprised. 'Now?'

'Yes. Our consultation is over. I sponsor a couple of guys, and we sometimes do emergency meetings.' He didn't wait for her to answer. 'Hi, I'm John. I'm an alcoholic and drug addict. It's been seventeen years since I last used.'

Kate looked at the signed prescription sitting on his desk. She wanted to grab it and leave, but she sat back down on the edge of the table. Kate and Myra had had one-on-one AA meetings in the past, and she'd heard John talk about his struggles with alcohol and prescription drugs.

'Okay,' she said. 'Hi. I'm Kate, and I'm an alcoholic. It's been thirteen years since my last drink.'

John nodded.

'That's impressive. How do you feel about that?' he asked.

'I wonder if it's worth it right now.'

'Okay. Why?'

'Alcohol hasn't been on my mind since the accident. Actually, that's not true. I was so close to making myself a hot toddy, for *medicinal purposes*. Is it written in my medical file about my accident?'

He shook his head.

'I'm not here as your GP, Kate.'

She nodded, took another sip of the energy drink and tried to organise her thoughts.

'I swim every morning in the sea. I started sea swimming to combat depression, and I love it. Particularly in the winter, the cold water and the positive feeling afterwards. Last week I went down to the beach the same way I do every day, but I wasn't paying attention and blundered into a riptide. I almost drowned and was pulled out by a couple of surfers. It's mortifying. And now... I'm afraid to get back in the water.' Kate felt tears in her eyes and wiped them away. 'Of course, I can't go back in the sea whilst I feel like this. I have this infection—'

John nodded and listened.

'—swimming in the sea is part of my routine. It is my routine. I sort of hang the rest of my day off it, if that makes sense. It clears my mind. It makes me feel good about being alive. I started just when I got sober and moved here. I moved here to stay sober and alive, so I could regain custody of my son, Jake... But he's grown up now. He's in America studying at university, off by himself, which is a good thing. I lost custody of him when he was six. He went to live with my mum in Whitstable when I... wasn't capable, and by the time I got well, he was almost eight and had friends at school in Whitstable, and they had a dog, he had his own room, and he'd just got through a period of night terrors which I think stemmed from me. He was happy there with my mum and dad. I didn't want to break that. I spent so long working on being sober so he could be with me for the school holidays and Christmas, and when he was sixteen, he came to live with me full-time, which was great, but those two years went by so quickly. And now he's gone again, studying in California. He was meant to come back for the summer, but he's staying there and I probably won't see him until Christmas.'

Kate wiped her eyes with the back of her hand.

'When I was in hospital, I met this woman whose grandson went missing, and we've ended up taking on her case, and this one, it's really haunting me. It's haunting me that the more we learn about the little boy, Charlie, the less we know. It's complicated, and it's pushing my buttons. There was a social worker who got involved, and it reminded me of that time when social

workers got involved with me and my fitness to look after Jake...
I always thought I'd made it right with Jake, but now I'm
worried I didn't have enough of a chance, and I keep thinking
about Charlie. I want to make it right, but I don't know how. I'm
scared that this one won't be solved. We'll never find out what
happened to him.'

Kate finished, and sighed. It felt good to talk to someone
who just listened, and that was what AA meetings were about.
Listening.

'I can't solve any of your problems, Kate,' said John. 'But you
do know that having a drink won't help any of it.'

'I don't want a drink.'

'Good, but don't let this all overwhelm you, so you end up
wanting to drink.'

'Thank you.'

'Oh, and putting my doctor hat on again, I can recommend
paddling,' he said, handing her the prescription. 'Even if you
can't swim, you can paddle. It might help you get back on the
horse.'

31

It was late in the afternoon after they dropped Kate at the doctor's surgery. Ade and Tristan went to The Blue Boar pub, which was nearby on Ashdean high street. They were starving, so they each ordered a curry and a pint of lager which they quickly demolished.

'I feel like Kate is annoyed with me,' said Tristan.

'I think she's still run down from her accident,' said Ade, delicately wiping the last of his naan bread around the remnants of curry sauce. 'She looked very peaky, poor thing. You have to be so careful about getting dehydrated.'

'You weren't there when we were on the moors. I was stupid.'

'What did you do?' said Ade.

'I was jumping up and down on the bogland.'

'Which is just what a stupid teenager would do. Have you seen how many people come a cropper on Dartmoor bogland? It's dangerous.'

'I stayed near the edge.'

'Spoken like a true teenager.'

Tristan sighed and watched Ade, still wiping at the plate with the piece of naan.

'You're going to wipe the pattern off that plate. Why don't you just order another curry?'

'No. I can't eat any more,' said Ade, pushing the plate away.

'I've just watched you eat all my naan bread as well as your own.'

'I'm telling you, Tris. Prawn bhuna is my Kryptonite. I once ate four in one sitting. Saying that, there was barely enough to fill a gnat's hat,' he added, throwing a dirty look over to the bar, where Len, the perpetually miserable landlord, was polishing glasses.

Tristan stared moodily at the last of his lager.

'We're in business together. And I just feel like Kate's shutting me out of things. She did all of this internet research the other day, and she was supposed to share it all with me, and she hasn't.' He picked up his phone. 'And I said to her, text me when you're done and if everything is okay. Nothing.'

'She might still be at the doctor's surgery, and she's a complicated woman, Tris. Think of everything she's been through in her life. She must have trust issues. Is she seeing anyone?'

'I don't know. Kate never talks about that side of her life. I don't think she is.'

'And it's still early days with your business. You're transitioning from being Kate's research assistant at the university to being her equal partner in the agency. Think about it for a minute. You both went out today on the moors to try and retrace Charlie's steps. This tiny little boy could have wandered out and got lost on the moors or strayed into the bogland. Did you really need to jump up and down on it like you were on a trampoline?'

'No,' said Tristan, feeling uncomfortable.

'Exactly. That's the thing to remember, you are private detectives. You've pledged to do your duty and right wrongs. And don't forget, Kate was a police officer in London. She might have lost colleagues in the line of duty. She has probably seen colleagues die. I know I did.'

Tristan rubbed his face with his hands.

'God, I'm an idiot,' he said.

'Don't beat yourself up. We all make silly mistakes. In fact, I'm about to make one now.' He turned to the bar and shouted, 'Len, give us another prawn bhuna, three poppadoms, and a naan bread.' He turned back to Tristan. 'What? I told you the portions were tiny.'

'Do you want mango chutney?' shouted Len.

'Yes, but next time you can make sure this ramekin is filled up to the brim!' Ade held the empty mango chutney ramekin in the air. Len muttered something and disappeared through the door behind the bar. 'I've seen him at the cash and carry buying that mango chutney in a huge catering jar. The least he can do is give you a proper portion.'

'Maybe I'm too immature. Maybe I'm not ready yet for all this,' Tristan said.

'You did those private detective training courses?'

'A month at an old polytechnic. Police officers train for years,' said Tristan with a sigh.

'Now stop this,' said Ade. 'Do you know how many people would kill for your opportunity? It will be a pretty poor showing if you quit and throw in the towel, over what? A silly row. You started off as a cleaner at the university, and it was Kate who saw something in you. Now pull yourself together. Do you want another pint?'

Tristan checked his phone.

'Kate's just texted me. She says she's going to take a couple of days off, and she'll ring me. That's it.'

'See? That's good. I think she just needs a rest. Time to recuperate. She got very peaky on the moor... Is that a yes for another pint?'

'Go on then,' said Tristan. Ade picked up his bag and went up to the bar. Tristan stared gloomily at the jukebox with its spinning lights. Another text message came through, and for a moment he hoped it was Kate with something more personal, but it was from his sister, Sarah, asking if she and Leo could stay another night at the flat. Apparently, their house was still stinking from the paint.

Ade came back a few minutes later with their drinks.

'Thanks for coming with us today,' said Tristan.

'No problem. It felt good to be detecting.' He took a sip of his beer.

'What do you think happened to Charlie?'

'To be honest, I've no idea. The logical thing would be that Charlie fell in the river, but after fifteen years on the force, logic sometimes goes out of the window. You wouldn't believe some of the cases I worked on and the weird and messed up things that happened.'

It was 9pm when Tristan left the pub and set off home, and he felt a bit better after a few drinks with Ade. It wasn't until he was in the kitchen turning on the tap that he remembered the text from Sarah. The water squealed through the pipes. He waited for the sound of Leo's screaming, but thankfully, the house remained silent. He crept upstairs to his room, the stairs creaking. A coloured light was playing across the ceiling of the landing, and when he rounded the corner of the stairs, the door to the spare room was open. Sarah was lying flat out on the bed, fast asleep with her mouth wide open. Leo was sitting up beside her, holding a plastic brick. He looked at Tristan for a moment, wide-eyed and cute, and then went to shove the brick into Sarah's open mouth.

'No, no, no,' whispered Tristan, hurrying over and scooping him up off the bed. He took the brick from Leo's tiny hand and put it back in the toy box. Sarah shifted and carried on snoring. He covered her with a blanket and carried Leo to his room.

'Here we go. Why don't you cuddle up with me for a bit, and we'll get you off to sleep,' said Tristan. He put Leo down against the pillows on his bed and then quickly got ready for bed. He slid in beside Leo, who looked at him with wide blue eyes. Leo reached out and poked at the eagle tattoo on Tristan's chest.

'Why can't you sleep?' said Tristan. He got comfortable with Leo lying in the crook of his arm.

Tristan pulled up Google Maps on his phone and looked at the Devil's Way gorge. He swiped with his fingers and if he zoomed in very close, he could just make out the blurred branches of the Pixie Tree and the coloured rags festooning its branches. He thought back to the elderly lady with the withered and twisted back bones. He zoomed out and saw that the whole area was covered in thick undergrowth and trees, spreading out for a mile or so towards the road leading up to the Devil's Tor and the open moorland. As Tristan zoomed out further, he saw a pin in the map with the name DANVERS FARM, and some contact information. Leo was now asleep on his left shoulder and snoring lightly. Tristan's eyes began to droop, and he fell into a troubled sleep where he was trying to find Leo amongst thick undergrowth. He burst into the clearing and the old lady with the twisted and hunched back was cradling him in her arms.

32

A week passed, and Kate worked hard at getting well. She was impressed that Tristan had stepped up and taken responsibility for the agency and the caravan park. He'd sent her a couple of messages during the week, checking in, and he also said he'd been in contact with Exeter prison to request a visiting order for Declan Connoly, but apart from that, he let her be. When she woke up on Monday, it was the first morning she felt back to her old self. Almost. She lay in bed for a moment and knew that she had to try and swim.

Kate emerged from the dunes with her heart racing in her chest. The sand grew wet and solid as she made her way to the water's edge. The beach was empty, and the waves seemed huge, although she was used to bigger. The first wave crashed down a few metres from where she stopped to pull on her goggles, and the surf surged up to her knees. Kate put her hands down and felt the pull as the water dropped away, leaving her on the wet, shifting sand, with a few strands of green seaweed between her fingers. She took a deep breath. It was just water.

John's words came back to her. *You can just paddle.* Her

throat was suddenly dry, and she swallowed and looked around. The beach was completely empty. Was this a good thing? What if she got into trouble again? No, this was ridiculous. She was a strong swimmer. Kate took a step and then two more. Another wave crashed in, bigger than the last, and it surged up and around her hips, jostling her on her feet. Kate gritted her teeth and engaged her arms and hips, pressing her weight into the sand as she walked against the water. And then, another wave came barrelling towards her, and she dove into it. The water enveloped her, and Kate swam off, kicking out vigorously. She felt sleek and fast, like an arrow cutting through the surf under the breaking waves. Kate could see down to where the sand rapidly fell away to a rocky gloom. The roar of the water came and went as she broke the surface every four strokes to breathe. Kate swam, her body surging toward the horizon, and she felt the freedom she'd craved over the past couple of weeks. She was far out, moving against the swells of water as they rolled toward the shore. Kate slowed and allowed herself to float on her back, rising and falling with the waves. She felt the warm fingers of the sun's rays as it broke the horizon, and she suddenly felt her zest for life return. Kate looked back at her home and the office sitting on top of the rocky cliff. Cold and warm currents moved on either side of her. This was her life, the life she wanted to lead, and it was hard won. There wasn't another moment to waste on insecurities or sadness.

Kate gave two strong kicks and started to swim back. The sun was warm on her hair, and as the shore came closer, she rode the growing swells, feeling her heart pumping and the zing on her skin from the salt water. A wave rose up behind her, and she caught it as it broke, her feet wheeling under her, pulling along the sandy bottom, feeling the exhilaration of riding a wave until the sand was gritty and firm under her feet, and she was safe again on dry land.

When he arrived at the office, Tristan was surprised to see Kate at her desk. She was drinking coffee and looked more like her old self again. Her hair was still wet, and her cheeks were flushed pink from the sea.

'Morning, how are you doing?' he asked. He still felt embarrassed after their disagreement.

'Much better. Sleep, antibiotics, lots of cheese on toast, a swim and an AA meeting all seem to have done the trick.'

'Is this you finally divulging your beauty secrets?' he asked. Kate laughed.

'Yes. I also owe you an apology.'

'You don't.'

'No. I do. I was ill and feeling weird, and I shouldn't have taken it out on you. You are my colleague, and I hope, my friend.'

'Of course. I felt like I was being immature with the whole bouncing on the bogland. We were working.'

'Tris. It's fine. Shall we agree to move on?'

'Yes,' he said, feeling huge relief.

'Good. Now. I'll make you a nice coffee, and you can fill me in on what's been happening.'

'It was a quiet week for the Charlie Julings case. But two caravans were left in a bad state when we did the changeover. Two windows smashed, a broken bed frame, and someone tried to flush a nappy down one of the toilets.'

'Yuck.'

'That's all sorted, and then last night we had a flurry of

emails. Joel is back from his holiday and wants to meet tomorrow afternoon.'

'Ok, good. Thank you for stepping in and dealing with everything.'

'No problem, that's what we're in business for,' said Tristan, feeling a sense of pride from the praise. 'We also heard from Maureen Cook, the lady who runs the writing group who was friends with Anna Treadwell. She would be happy to meet this afternoon.' Tristan hesitated, not knowing if Kate was now back at work fully. 'I can go on my own.'

'No, don't do that. We'll both go and meet her,' said Kate.

'Okay. We also had a message from a man called Bernard Crenshaw.'

'Yes! I've been messaging him this week. I didn't get the chance to tell you about the crime scene photos I found last week. I discovered that Bernard was the crime scene photographer because he'd caught himself in one of the pictures.'

Tristan listened as Kate filled him in on the crime scene photos she'd found on Reddit, and she pulled them up on her iPad. He swiped through them and felt sick when he saw the close-up shot of Anna's destroyed head and neck. There was also a photo of the clawhammer that they'd found in the garden.

'I sent Bernard a few Facebook messages. I thought he was ignoring me. I also included our website. Maybe that did the trick.'

'What do you want to ask him about?'

'You can see in the crime scene photos that the contents of her handbag or a bag are strewn across the floor. There's an old mobile phone and a thick notebook that looks filled with papers. There's a big elastic band around it to keep everything inside.'

'Are you thinking he saw the contents?'

'No. When that room became a crime scene, everything in it

became evidence. I need to find a way in, a way to find out if those things, her notebook, which could contain information about her work in the months leading up to her death, and phone are still being stored by the police,' said Kate.

'Could someone have come forward to claim Anna's belongings? It's almost ten years since she was murdered,' said Tristan.

'It should still be an open case. The police haven't caught who did it, so the evidence would still be held by the police.' Kate had the business emails open, and she saw the reply from Bernard.

'He says he's around all this week, and he's in Taunton. How about now?'

'Absolutely,' said Tristan.

'Okay, let's go to Taunton and then this afternoon, we can pay a visit to Maureen Cook,' said Kate.

Tristan grabbed his bag and keys, happy that things were okay with Kate again.

33

Bernard Crenshaw offered to meet them in a coffee shop opposite his house in Taunton. Kate had only given him the information that she was a private detective working on a historical murder case that might interest him. His replies had been short and blunt.

They arrived at the coffee shop just before ten and ordered lattes. They'd only just found a spot in a couple of chairs in the window when Kate saw the front door of a terraced house opposite open, and Bernard came out wearing shorts and a thin woollen jumper.

'He doesn't know what we look like,' said Tristan.

'And we don't have a phone number for him,' said Kate.

The coffee shop was quite busy, and Bernard joined the queue and perused the drinks menu on the wall above. He was quite a sprightly older gentleman, in his early sixties, but thin. Bernard placed his order but didn't look up and around the coffee shop or take out his phone. He waited at the end of the counter with his back to them.

'I'll go and talk to him,' said Kate. She often wondered if it was easier in a place like America to introduce yourself as a private detective, where people took the concept of a PI seriously. In the UK, social contact with a stranger was much more nuanced. In fact, it was all about nuance. Bernard would make a snap judgement about her based on class, sex, if she was guarded or friendly, sexually desirable or past it. Kate knew she needed to pitch this right.

Kate smoothed her blouse and got up from the table, hooking her handbag over her shoulder. When she approached him, she saw he wasn't engrossed in his phone like the other customers waiting for their coffees. He was staring out of the window, deep in thought.

'Hello, Mr Crenshaw?' she said, smiling. He was tall, and he wore bifocal glasses. Kate noted he had to dip his chin down to his chest to peer at her through the top of the lenses. 'I'm Kate Marshall. I'm a private detective... ex-Met police officer. I was a detective inspector. We've been messaging.'

'How do you do?' he said, offering his hand. They shook. His coffee order was called, and he took the cup from the barista. He went over to the milk and sugar station, and Kate followed.

'And what can I do for you?' he said, picking up a sugar sachet and one of the little wooden stirrers.

'I'm working for a woman whose grandson went missing.'

'I don't deal with missing persons,' he said, tipping in the sugar and stirring his coffee vigorously.

'But you did attend the murder scene of the social worker investigating the family.'

He hesitated and put the lid back on his cup, and Kate knew she had his interest.

'I'm not police. I'm a forensic photographer. I can't show you any photos. Whatever it is.'

'You don't need to. I found the photos you took of the crime scene posted online.'

He turned to her and looked irritated.

'Really? Bloody hell. Who was it?'

'I don't know who put them online. It was a Reddit blog.'

'No, the victim. Who was it? And where?'

Kate kept her voice low, trying not to be too graphic with her explanation as customers milled around them. He listened for a moment and seemed quite impressed.

'You have an agency in Ashdean?'

'Yes.'

'I think I've heard of you...' The penny seemed to drop, and he looked down at her through his bifocals again. 'Yes. The Nine Elms Cannibal? That's you?'

'It is,' said Kate. She could tell by the shock that crossed his face that he knew her backstory.

'I'm happy to talk to you, but I'm unsure what I can help with,' he said.

'If you can remember anything at all, it would be beneficial. My associate is over here,' she said, indicating Tristan. 'Could we sit down for a moment?' she asked, pointing to the armchairs in the corner.

'That's not everything from that particular crime scene,' said Bernard when he was sitting opposite Kate and Tristan. He was holding Kate's iPad with the crime scene photos she found on Reddit. 'I photographed the journey her assailants took out of the house. Whoever did it carried the claw hammer down the stairs, leaving a trail of blood, bone, and brain. And of course, footprints.'

'Do you think two people carried out the attack and murder?' asked Tristan.

'Yes. There were two sets of footprints. If I remember correctly, we thought it could have been a male and a female. There was a larger print, which was found to be a man's size trainer. The other print we lifted came from a lady's branded trainer, which I never thought could be so specific.'

'The neighbour told us they found fingerprints,' said Kate. 'He said he voluntarily gave prints to rule himself out of the investigations.'

'I don't remember that.' Bernard sat back and crossed his arms, putting his chin on his chest, thinking about what to say next. 'This one did stick with me. The brutality. And it was a strange house. I remember the police officers at the scene were searching for children. There was a children's bedroom filled with toys and nappies and a cot with a mobile above it. They were worried that the woman's children had also been attacked, but there were none. And then, during the post-mortem, they checked to see if she was pregnant, but she wasn't.'

'She was an approved foster carer,' said Kate. Bernard narrowed his eyes.

'She wasn't, though,' he said. 'Anna Treadwell had been refused clearance twice to be a foster carer. That's what stuck in my memory.'

Kate was shocked.

'Do you know why she was refused?' she asked. Bernard shook his head.

'No. And this is more of a personal observation. That house was at the end of the cul-de-sac. It was in such a lonely, strange position. It gave me the shivers.' He shrugged. 'That's just my opinion.'

'Do you remember much about the neighbour?' asked Tristan.

'Not really. A bit of a loner. He was shaken up. He'd found the body, and he was a puker. We had to deal with that at the scene, which adds another layer of unpleasantness.'

Kate saw Tristan wrinkle up his nose and push the rest of his coffee away.

'Was there anything else you can remember?' she asked.

He thought for a moment.

'Well, yes. The police at the scene wondered if Anna knew her attacker, or, I should say, attackers. It appeared like she'd let them in. The house was locked up, and they'd even set the alarm on their way out. The alarm was armed when the neighbour broke in.'

They were silent for a moment, deep in thought. Tristan looked at Kate as the silence stretched out.

'It would really help our investigation if we could, potentially, access the evidence gathered at the scene,' she said. Bernard sat up his chair.

'Okay,' he said, looking between Kate and Tristan. 'Has your agency been hired for any private contract work by HM government departments?'

'Yes!' said Tristan, enthusiastically. 'Yes,' he said again, a little less high-pitched.

'We've done some work with the Devon and Cornwall NHS trust,' said Kate. 'Checking out people they suspect of abusing disability benefits. We've also done work for Exeter council, checking out an employee they suspected of fraud.'

'Okay. Good, good. So you and your associate have had all the background checks, CRB, credit, criminal records?'

Kate glanced at Tristan not to say anything. He hadn't had these checks.

'Yes,' she said.

'Okay then. This is my colleague in Exeter police,' Bernard said, grabbing Kate's notepad and pen. He wrote out a name, email address, and phone number. His writing was fluid and precise. 'If you can wait until later this afternoon. I want to give her a call first and tell her what you would like. I can't guarantee anything of course, that would be her call.'

'Thank you,' said Kate glancing at the name, grateful to have landed the public authority contracts in the past, which might have felt run-of-the-mill, but the police and authorities had increasingly started to work with private detective agencies and outsource work. He pushed the notebook back across the table.

'Kate, you are ex-Met police, and what about you, Tristan?'

Tristan hesitated.

'He's taken some training courses, and I've been training him. He also worked as my research assistant for four years.'

'Great,' he said, slapping his legs with an air of finality and getting up.

'Thanks again,' said Tristan as they all shook hands.

'Don't thank me quite yet. I can't promise they'll even let you near the evidence store, but this case is cold, and top brass might see this as an opportunity to take the credit if you find anything.'

'I just want to look at the victim's personal effects. Anything I find out will be handed over.'

He put his hands up.

'You don't have to convince me. I'm just telling you how it is,' he said.

34

'Do either of you have allergies to nuts or shellfish?' asked Maureen Cook, holding out a silver three-tiered tray with small triangular-shaped sandwiches.

'No,' said Kate. She took a couple of cucumber sandwiches and placed them on the doily on her porcelain plate. Tristan shook his head and took a smoked salmon sandwich.

'Don't be shy, a strapping lad like you,' said Maureen, holding the tray closer to Tristan. He smiled and took another couple of the neatly cut triangles. 'Oh. I've forgotten the milk jug,' she added, and she went off to the kitchen.

Kate looked at Tristan, who seemed equally bewildered. Maureen Cook lived in a thatched cottage on the outskirts of Cranborough. It was very warm inside, and the chintzy living room had six glass-fronted cabinets, all filled with china tea sets and porcelain figurines. It was the only private house that Kate had been in, barring an embassy, with a photo of the Queen on the wall.

When Maureen had invited them for a cup of tea, Kate and Tristan had assumed it meant just that. They had rushed over from their meeting with Bernard in Taunton, buying petrol station sandwiches, having no idea that Maureen would prepare a lavish high tea.

'Here we are,' said Maureen when she returned with a willow pattern jug.

'This is very generous of you, Mrs Cook,' said Kate, sitting up and putting her plate on the table.

'Please, call me Maureen.' She was a large lady in her late fifties who seemed to have overdone it with the fake tan. She was almost orange, and her bright blue beady eyes and the blue eye shadow on her hooded lids clashed with her skin. She'd been smiling since they arrived, but her apparent bonhomie didn't quite reach her eyes. She had a Margaret Thatcher-style bouffant of red hair and wore a blue silk dress covered in a pattern of tiny pink flowers.

'Thank you, Maureen,' said Kate. Tristan nodded through a mouthful of smoked salmon sandwich.

'Not at all,' she said, waving the thanks away with a sizeable orange hand. She sat down heavily in the easy chair opposite and poured the tea. 'Your email was very interesting. I haven't heard or seen Anna's name mentioned in years. Such a tragedy.'

'Were you close?' asked Kate.

Maureen seemed to have to think about that for a moment.

'Yes. Anna was a member of Cranborough Writers. We met once a fortnight here.'

'Met? Is the group not still active?'

Maureen's smile faltered.

'No. The group disbanded. There was a coup. Six years ago.'

'A coup, in a writers' group?' asked Tristan. Maureen nodded and bit her bottom lip.

'I was betrayed by the very people I thought were friends. I own a photostat copier.'

'A photocopier?' Kate asked, clarifying.

'Yes. That's what I said, dear. I've always provided photostat copies for the village; the programmes for local school plays, and the church newsletter. I also used to produce the Cranborough Writers annual short story anthology.'

'On your photocopier?' asked Kate.

'Yes, I have a professional office-grade photostat copier,' said Maureen. She paused for dramatic effect and Kate wondered where she was going with this. 'I would always provide these services at cost. I never made a profit. Then a couple of ungrateful upstarts with a graphic design studio in the next village took it upon themselves to solicit business from the church and the local fete. They also offered to print our anthology. My position became untenable, so I left the group.'

Kate could see that Maureen liked to organise. She was one of those people who sought power and worth from being in charge.

'Is the group still running without you?' asked Tristan.

'No. That's the irony. It fell apart within a few months. I was the linchpin.'

'How did Anna come to join the group?' asked Kate, steering the conversation back.

'I first met her at one of our summer fetes. I was working on the organising committee and ran the cake stall. Anna was on her own that day and seemed rather mournful and alone. I told her about our writers group. At the time, we had a few single male members, and I thought another woman might balance things out.'

'Did Anna like creative writing?' asked Tristan. Maureen waved this away as if liking creative writing wasn't too important for a creative writing group.

'Not at first, but everyone has a story in them, I like to think.

You know, it's often the ones with interesting jobs who write interesting stories. That's what made me extend the invitation to Anna to join when she mentioned she was a social worker.'

Maureen leant forward and pawed at the tray of sandwiches, which were slightly out of reach. Kate pushed the tray closer, and she palmed four of the wholemeal salmon sandwiches and stuffed one in her mouth whole.

'Yum. I love a good high tea,' she mumbled, chewing.

'How long did Anna attend the creative writing group?' asked Kate.

'Hmmm,' said Maureen, chewing. She took a slurp of tea and swallowed. A dribble of tea ran down her chin, and she wiped it with the back of her hand. 'Six months. Maybe longer. She didn't always show up every fortnight, but she always phoned to apologise for her absence.'

Maureen popped another sandwich in her mouth.

'Don't stand on ceremony,' she said, spraying spittle and crumbs across the table. 'Have more.' Kate felt the spray of crumbs land wetly on her face, and she fought the urge to gag. She dabbed at her mouth with her napkin.

'What reasons did Anna give for not coming to meetings?' asked Kate, thrown off her stride.

'Work, of course!' said Maureen, swallowing another swig of tea. 'Anna had a very stressful job in social services. And I took my hat off to her. You see some of the mothers these days. Awful. Smoking. Swearing. Acting like prostitutes. When did it become fashionable to have a bastard baby?'

Kate froze with her cup in mid-air, and Tristan choked on his sandwich. Maureen glanced over at him.

'I'm sorry, dear, to use that word, but I think the moment we stopped calling them bastards was the moment it became okay to have a child out of wedlock.' She folded her arms and sat back in the chair. 'There we go, I've said my piece. That's why I had a lot of respect for Anna, going into those situations where the parents maltreated their children.'

'Not all single mothers maltreat their children,' said Tristan. Maureen chuckled and put her hand to her mouth as an aside to Kate.

'Listen to the youngster, always so liberal. You'll change your tune as you get older,' she said, turning to Tristan. 'Have you got a girlfriend?'

'No. I did have a boyfriend.'

Maureen's face froze in a manic smile, and then she recovered.

'Lovely. More tea?'

'No, thank you,' said Tristan putting his cup down. 'Did Anna ever talk about her work?'

'No, dear, she only ever spoke in vague, nebulose language.'

'Nebulous?' repeated Tristan.

'Yes. Anna couldn't talk in detail about taking children away from bad mothers, etcetera. It all had to be kept confidential.'

'How did you hear about her death?'

Maureen clutched her hand to her chest and shook her head.

'It was awful. *Awful!* I was concerned when she didn't show up to a meeting or call me. And then I read about it in the newspaper, like everyone else. Battered to death with a claw hammer. What a terrible way to go... I hope I die in my sleep, or maybe a brain aneurysm. I've read that's very quick. You can drop dead in two seconds.'

'How did you come to organise the flowers for her funeral?' asked Kate.

'I enquired about who was arranging the funeral, and then the undertaker told me no one was! How awful, I thought. Anna had no family, and she seemed to have no close friends. Her neighbour was apparently friendly with her, but he was a bit wet, to be honest. So I stepped up and organised things and printed the order of service.'

'Did many people go to her funeral?' asked Tristan.

'We all attended from the writers group. That was before they all betrayed me. Her neighbour was there, and I think a couple of her work colleagues. It took them some time to release her body, so the funeral wasn't until months later.'

'Did Anna ever confide in you that she felt in danger?' asked Kate.

'No. Anna was a very spiky, determined person, but I think I was breaking down her barriers, and sometimes she would stay after the group met, and we'd have a drink together.'

'What kind of things did she write for the group?'

'She never wrote anything.'

'In six months, she never wrote anything?' repeated Tristan.

'No, and that was fine. She would often join in with critiquing other people's work. Sometimes she could be harsh, but she always made interesting points.' Maureen poured them each a fresh cup of tea. 'Anyway, what does this have to do with your investigation? You mentioned on the phone that you are looking for a missing child?'

Kate briefly outlined the case and Anna's link to Charlie.

'I see. Anna was concerned with the welfare of the young boy?'

'According to Charlie's grandmother, there was some confusion over that.'

'Was there?' said Maureen, raising an eyebrow. 'And the family comes from the Coldharbour estate? Not much good comes out of there.'

Kate ignored this comment.

'Did Anna ever mention anything to do with Charlie Julings?'

'Of course not! As I said, she didn't ever talk about her work.'

Kate and Tristan stayed chatting for a while longer, but Kate felt that Maureen didn't have much to offer in the way of information about Anna. On their way out, Kate noticed a display of framed photos in the hallway. There were nine or ten, and they all showed Maureen in glittering evening dresses, posing with various dashing young men in captain's uniforms.

'That's my cruise collection,' said Maureen, following Kate's gaze. 'That's my yearly treat. I'm off on a cruise to the Caribbean tomorrow. I'm heading down to Southampton tonight, and I've got some super new luggage.' She opened the door to a small office packed with folders on bookshelves and a vast office photocopier. There were a couple of smart leather suitcases with "M.C." monogrammed in gold letters on the side.

'That's my new luggage. I had it made bespoke from an offer in the back of the *Daily Mail*,' she said proudly.

'Who are you going with?' asked Tristan.

'Oh. Just by myself, for a bit of "me" time,' said Maureen, her smile faltering for a moment. They stared back at the photos. In every one, Maureen was on her own at the various captain's tables. 'Yes, and it's my favourite ship again. The *Duchess of the Ocean*. Beautiful.'

Kate felt she'd consumed too many calories as they left, but they'd learned very little new information about Anna Treadwell.

35

Tristan shifted awkwardly in the car seat as he tapped the office address into his GPS.

'I ate too much,' he said.

'Me too,' said Kate, staring out at Maureen's thatched cottage.

'What did you think of her?' asked Tristan.

'I think she's lonely, and loneliness can be a disease that makes you weak and vulnerable.'

Tristan nodded and looked back at the GPS.

'You know, it wouldn't be too much of a detour to swing past Danvers Farm,' he said, pointing to the map. 'If we just come off the motorway here, it's a couple of miles in.'

'Okay, let's do that,' said Kate. It wasn't top of her list to see the farm, but it would save making a deliberate trip on another day.

It ended up being a longer journey than they wanted. They got lost a couple of times, and the GPS didn't seem prepared for the winding unmarked roads. Finally, Kate saw it when they passed a wooden farm gate on a long stretch of a tree-lined lane.

'That was it,' she said. Tristan backed up to the gate where a small sign said 'DANVERS FARM EGGS 4 SALE'. There was a small concrete yard and a large barn, but the rest of the land was surrounded by trees.

'Do we ring the bell and tell them we're private detectives?' asked Tristan.

'Yes, but I was thinking I do need to buy some eggs. It would be a good excuse to engage the owners in conversation,' said Kate.

Tristan nodded. They parked the car by the road and went to the gate. A small doorbell was attached to the wood. Tristan rang it, and a woman rounded the corner a few moments later. She was what Kate would term apple-cheeked, and she had long dark hair in a bun on top of her head. She wore a long woollen high-necked dress, and was probably no older than her late forties.

'Hello, do you want eggs?' she asked brusquely.

'Er. Yes. A dozen, please,' said Kate.

'Come in,' she said, opening the gate. They followed her up the wide driveway. It curved to the left, and a narrow concrete path wove through an arcade of trees. They could see glimpses of the road to the left and to the right, as the pathway fell away on a steep slope leading down to undergrowth.

A group of cats of different colours lay around the path, and then the trees parted, and they were in the courtyard of a small cottage with a blue slate roof. The yard was filled with over-grown plant pots, and on top of a large drain lid were six or seven mismatched bowls with remnants of drying cat food.

There was a small shed to the right of the front door, and the woman went to it and unlocked it with a key attached to her neck with a long piece of string. Inside it was packed with egg boxes. She put two in an old plastic bag and handed them to Kate. Then she took out a cash box.

'That'll be four pounds,' she said. Kate handed over a note, and the woman tucked it into the cash box. She was locking up the shed when a young girl came out of the front door. She was skinny and looked to be nine or ten.

'Mum. Jack hit me,' she said matter-of-factly. She was holding a bag of frozen peas against her eye. She saw Kate and Tristan and nodded. 'Hello.'

'I didn't mean to throw it at her,' said a boy's voice from inside. A tall young lad who might have been thirteen or fourteen came to the door. He had long brown hair down to his shoulders and wore a red Adidas tracksuit with filthy bare feet. 'She asked me for the remote, and I threw it to her.'

'Why are you both telling me this? I have to do the animals,' said the woman.

The girl gave a look of resignation which belied her years and pushed past the boy. He staggered back into the doorframe.

'Did you see that?' he said indignantly, holding his arm. His voice was breaking, and it had a piping tootle.

'Jack, are you going to help me with the animals?' said the woman. 'Because that's all I care about with your father being away.'

The boy thought about it and then disappeared back inside.

'When they were younger, they used to think everything I said and did was wonderful. And now, I'm an annoying old mum,' said the woman. She indicated they should follow.

'Can I ask you about something?' said Kate as they started back.

The woman stopped and turned, mild irritation crossing her face.

'What?'

'We're actually private detectives. My name is Kate Marshall and this is my partner, Tristan Harper. We're working on a case of a small boy, who went missing nearby, at Devil's Way,' she said, pointing across the moor. The woman seemed to study them properly for the first time.

'Private detectives, is that a thing round here?'

'Yes,' said Kate. 'Can you help us?'

'Yes, I remember hearing about it. Charlie Julings was the young boy,' said the woman impatiently. 'But why have you come here?'

'You have the closest house to Devil's Way where he disappeared. We wanted to ask you about the local area and to try and find out if you saw anything that day?' said Kate.

'No. We didn't live here then. It was before our time. We took over the farm in 2008.'

'When, in 2008?'

'January.'

'Do you know why the previous owners left?' asked Tristan.

'Previous tenants. We're tenants. This farm is Crown Land. We rent from the Crown. Now, if there's nothing else, I'm busy. I need to feed all my animals. The woman who usually helps me is away, and so is my husband.'

'What's your name?' asked Kate.

The woman hesitated and pursed her lips; she didn't seem to enjoy being questioned like this.

'Mrs Dawn Grey.'

'Do you know the whereabouts of the previous tenants?'

'No. I don't. I think they run another farm somewhere up north, but that's all I know.'

Kate looked around at the land. Now she knew that the previous tenants had left, she was disappointed but her interest was heightened. 'Do you mind if we take a look at the landscape across to Devil's Way?'

'Fine,' she said impatiently. 'You'll get the best view from up by the edge of the small wood. Follow the farm buildings up to the top of the yard. Just close any gates when you're done,' she said.

'Thank you,' said Kate to her back as she hurried off. Kate and Tristan started off up the path past some outbuildings. They came to a broad concrete platform, and they could hear cows mooing inside a huge shed, and a strong smell of manure wafted over them. They passed another shed filled with hay bales and emerged through the farm buildings onto a wide rocky path which led up a grassy platform with trees. They stopped and looked at the moor rolling out in all directions. It was a breathtaking view. Kate could see very clearly, in miniature, the Devil's Way Tor and a silvery thread of the river glinting in the sun. The fields across the two miles towards it were flat, and pockets of haze gathered in patches stretching out to the Tor. They stared for a moment.

'Okay. What now?' asked Tristan with a grin. Kate glanced sideways at him and laughed.

'I know. I feel a bit stupid. What are we doing? This woman wasn't even living here when Charlie went missing.'

She glanced around and saw that, to the left, there was a small copse of trees beyond the farm buildings. It was slightly higher than the rest of the land. Kate set off the short distance, and Tristan followed. When they reached the edge of the copse, they stopped. This slightly elevated point afforded them a better view with more detail. They could see the dirt track road which led back to Okehampton.

'Look how huge that patch of gorse and woodland is around

the Pixie Tree,' said Tristan. 'I was looking at it on Google Maps. We don't know if the police searched that area.'

'We should ask Ade, Lewis, or someone, how overgrown it all was back then. Eleven years is a long time, and it could have been much smaller,' said Kate. 'It's a good point. We should ask.'

'If they organised a huge search party, they probably did check,' said Tristan. The sun was now hot. Kate stepped into the shade of the trees and immediately felt cooler.

Tristan followed, and they walked a little way into the copse. In places, the sun shone through high branches, dappling the woodland floor, and Kate could feel dead leaves underfoot. They came to a cluster of three boulders. One was big enough to climb up and sit on, and the other two were smaller.

'Hey, look at this,' said Tristan. He was standing by the thick trunk of an oak tree. In the centre of the bark, around head height, there was a strange deformity in the wood, a foot high, which was in the perfect shape of an ear.

'I like to call it the listening tree,' said a voice.

'Jesus!' said Kate, turning to see the young boy, still barefoot, wearing the red tracksuit. He moved out from behind a tree.

'Have you been there the whole time?' asked Tristan, who looked equally shaken up by the intrusion.

'Maybe,' said the boy with a grin. He had a big gap in his front teeth and large brown eyes. He was handsome in an odd, geeky way, thought Kate. Or he would be when he was older.

'Was this carved into the wood?' asked Kate, pointing to the ear.

'Nope,' said the boy, seeming bored and detached. 'It grew that way. Cool, isn't it? It reminds me of those mice in that online video, with the ears growing out of their backs.' He took out a roll-up cigarette from his pocket and a lighter. Cupping his hands, he lit up. Kate could smell right away that it was marijuana.

'How old are you?' she said.

'I'll be fourteen next year,' he said, exhaling thick white smoke between his teeth.

'Does your mother know you smoke weed?'

He shrugged.

'I haven't told her. I could tell her that I came up here, and he put his hands down my trackies,' he said, indicating Tristan, 'and you just watched.' He grinned. 'But I won't.'

Kate looked at Tristan, who shook his head and rolled his eyes. She noticed a pile of cigarette butts at the base of the large boulder, which was probably the kid's smoking spot.

'Okay, we'll leave you to it,' she said. She glanced at the perfect ear in the tree trunk, and they set off back to the car.

'Today seemed to start so well,' said Kate when they were driving back to Ashdean. She checked her phone. 'And that Bernard guy didn't call.'

'He might not have got through to his colleague in the police,' said Tristan.

Kate looked out of the window, and she had that familiar prickle on her tongue and in her throat, the need for a drink.

'Can you drop me in Ashdean?' said Kate. 'I'm going to go to a meeting.'

36

Kate arrived home just after six and made herself some cheese on toast. She took it with a glass of iced tea to the living room window and sat in her favourite chair, watching the last of the tourists leaving the beach as the sun sank on the horizon. She thought back to their meeting with Bernard. He'd seemed genuine. She hoped he wasn't now going to ghost them.

When Kate finished her food, she poured another glass of iced tea and got her notebook out of her bag and tried to organise her thoughts. She placed Anna Treadwell to one side and reviewed her notes from the day.

The previous tenants of Danvers Farm had left, when? Late in 2007? Charlie went missing 21st June 2007. Kate opened her laptop and googled "Danvers Farm". When they went to the Exeter records office, the farm hadn't been on their radar, so they hadn't looked for it. After a short search through local news listings, Kate found a small article dated January 5th 2007:

South Zeal farmer arrested on suspicion of attempted GBH after car flips

A South Zeal man remains in police custody after he was arrested following a crash on Danvers Road. The incident happened just before 6pm on Thursday when his car overturned on the main road. The man, and a woman who was travelling with him, escaped the car unharmed.

Danvers Road was blocked for hours, and police arrested the man at the scene.

A spokesperson said: "Police were called at about 5.50pm yesterday (January 4th) to reports of a road traffic collision in Danvers Road, near Danvers Farm, in which a car was on its roof. The occupants of the car, a man and a woman, both managed to exit the overturned vehicle safely."

Kate carried on her Google search and found a court report from March 21st 2007:

South Zeal farmer handed suspended sentence

Steve Hartley (31), a farmer from South Zeal, appeared in Exeter Magistrates' Court and was handed a three-month suspended sentence for dangerous driving. Hartley of Danvers Farm was arrested on January 4th for flipping his car on Danvers Road outside his farm.

An 18-year-old woman named as Jennifer Kibbin was in the car with Hartley at the time. The couple initially told police that Jennifer Kibbin was Steve Hartley's wife, Libby, who was at home with the couple's two-year-old son.

Jennifer Kibbin of Poole Road, Exeter, had been charged with providing a false name and address, but this charge was dropped. Libby Hartley (30) attended Exeter Magistrates Court to support her husband.

Underneath the article text was a picture taken of Steve Hartley walking down the steps of Exeter Magistrates' Court. He was a tall, broad, handsome man with a square jaw and brown hair parted neatly to one side. His wife, Libby, was petite and elfin beside him. She had a heart-shaped face, and her black hair was cropped short. She wore a dark blue cardigan over a long flower-print dress with a Peter Pan collar. With her doe eyes, downcast from the camera, she had the martyred look of Princess Diana about her. She was cradling a small boy on her hip, who had a mop of brown hair, and he was wearing denim dungarees. Underneath the picture, the caption read:

Steve Hartley was accompanied in court by his wife, Libby Hartley, and their two-year-old son, David.

Kate sat back in her chair for a moment. Steve Hartley had been caught in a car with this eighteen-year-old Jennifer, and they'd tried to say that she was Steve's wife, Libby.

Libby had stood by him, or so it seemed to say in the local paper. Kate did some more googling to see if she could find out any more information about Jennifer Kibbin but there was nothing. She wondered when the Hartley's left Danvers Farm.

When Kate googled "Steve and Libby Hartley farmer", she

found that they were now working on another farm in Shropshire on the Welsh borders. Shropshire wasn't as 'up north' as Dawn Grey thought. There were no photos, but the farm had a Facebook page that advertised hay for sale, and also stabled horses. There was a short description: "*Hill Brook is a family-run farm; Steve and Libby Hartley live with their two children, David and Daisy.*"

The page only had eighty likes and hadn't been updated for three years. Kate felt like she'd reached a dead end. She wondered why they had given up Danvers Farm and moved away. Perhaps it was due to Steve's public affair? The car crash had made the local paper along with the fact that Jennifer Kibbin, the teenage girl with him, tried to pass herself off as Libby. People in small rural areas love to gossip. Maybe that's why they upped sticks and left the area.

Kate turned her attention back to her notebook and rechecked her phone, debating if she should call Bernard. She tapped her fingers on the table. No, she wouldn't chase him until tomorrow.

Bernard had told them Anna had been denied a licence to foster children. Was that unusual? Maybe not. She had been a single woman, living alone with a demanding job. Is that why they turned her down? And what about Anna's friendship with Maureen?

Kate put the notebook away, took out her iPad to look at the crime scene photos again, and saw that she still had the page open to Maureen Cook's Writers Group. She went to swipe and minimise the page, but she pressed on the link to the group's anthology, which took her to an Amazon ebook product page. Kate noticed that Maureen's short story 'A Little Light Extinguished', was listed first in the collection, and something about the title piqued her interest. She clicked on the link to download the free sample, and the first few sentences grabbed her:

I've lost count of the days since we lost our boy. My lack of sleep is unbearable. I've lost count of the days since... since... I can't bear to write it, but I must.

It seemed so unlike the woman Kate and Tristan met that afternoon. Did Maureen have children? She hadn't mentioned anything. Kate went back and started to read the whole story...

37

'A Little Light Extinguished' by Maureen Cook

I've lost count of the days since we lost our boy. My lack of sleep is unbearable. I've lost count of the days since... since... I can't bear to write it, but I must.

My little boy had been scared in the house. I knew it. His bed is in the back room, further from where we sleep than I would like, but the mould is so bad in the room next to ours. And in the summer months, the walls run with condensation and the moment I try and scrub the black mould away, it comes back. The spores lie in wait for when my back is turned and bloom through the plaster and wallpaper.

So I put him in the other room to save his little lungs.

His face had been flushed for a couple of days, and he was running a fever, but... I'm scared to take him to the doctor. That social worker has it in for me, and I know that if I take him to the doctor, it will be seen as my neglect. BUT I DON'T NEGLECT. I DIDN'T. I LOVE. THAT'S WHAT I DO.

LOVE.

I brought him into our bed on the third day. He was delirious. I managed to keep it from Dan, who was distracted due to the harvest.

I had him with me when Dan came to bed at midnight. He seemed a little better, his breathing was less shallow, and he even cried out a few times. That should have been good, shouldn't it? Crying out. It's only when they're quiet that you should worry.

Dan kissed us both on the head, and he fell into a deep sleep the moment his head hit the pillow. I lay awake in the dark, listening to the boy's breathing. I kept talking to him, asking, 'tell Mummy how you feel?'

One moment he said 'hot', and the next, he said 'cold' in his little voice. That voice. It was on my mind to call the doctor, but I just kept thinking of that bitch who had it in for me... I've read about those children's homes and some of those foster parents.

Children go missing.

They get "lost" in the system, and there's no recourse for a bad mother, is there? They can just take him if they want, and I'd never see him again, and they wouldn't have to tell me where he was or what they did with him...

So I kept him wrapped up, but not too much. I got up in the night to wet a washcloth which I kept on his forehead... Dan's alarm went off at four, and when we checked on the boy, he seemed better. His face wasn't as flushed, and his temperature had gone down. I cried with relief... Dan went off to do his rounds.

And that's when I allowed myself to drift off. And the Devil always gets you when you least expect it.

What happened next is a blur. Like I'm looking at it through dark smoky glass. I woke up, and the boy wasn't beside me. I put my hand out, and then I felt how I was lying oddly. Like a pillow was under me, but it felt harder.

His little body was under me. I'd rolled on top of him in my sleep. I pulled him out, and his blond hair glinted in the light, but his face and lips were blue. I tried to blow in his mouth and pressed on his chest, but he was limp and cold.

I was really calm. I put the boy back in his cot and tried to work out what to do. He was dead.

I don't know how long. I just sat there for a long time, and then I got overwhelmed with panic. I left the room and walked around the house. It was so quiet, and I stood in the hallway leading down to the boy's bedroom. And for a moment, I thought it was all fake, and I dreamed it. I held my breath to try and hear any sounds that he might be making. Those little snuffly sighs when he sleeps, but there's nothing. Not even the clock is ticking. The battery is flat.

It's getting hot inside, and I haven't closed any of the curtains in the rest of the rooms. I can smell something... It's something that I don't want to acknowledge. And I hear the sound of a fly buzzing.

I grip the wall and go down the long dim corridor to the reddish glow at the end. The curtains are red in the boy's room. I hate that colour and wanted to change it, but Dan said no. They're perfectly good curtains, and why do we need to spend our money on things we don't need?

When I reach the door, I see flies hovering above the boy's cot. And then, when I get close, a fly crawls over his left eye. I shoo it away, and when I look closer, I see it's laid its filthy eggs in the crease between his eyelids.

I take out a tissue to wipe it away, but his skin isn't firm anymore, and the eyelid turns inside out horribly, making me squeamish. His eye underneath half-stares back at me through the slit.

I see the cross above the door frame. The dark wood of Jesus on the cross tells me what I have to do.

I didn't take my medication this morning. And I haven't taken it for a couple of weeks now. Dan doesn't know. He doesn't understand how bad it makes me feel, and now without it, my mind is crisp and clear, like a diamond. Dan texts me to say he has to go see the boss in Exeter, and he'll be back late. My mind gets clearer as if it's fate.

I take the boy and wash him, then I find a clean sheet and wrap him carefully to keep him away from the filthy flies. I put the tiny bundle back in the cot and open the curtains and the windows to let his spirit free. Then I remember he was inside our bedroom when he died, so I go through there and open the windows too. A breeze flows in, and the room stops feeling stuffy and trapped.

Go free, I say in a whisper, go free.

I wait until the sun sets and the tall trees' shadows are long. I take the boy in the bundle and wrap him in a beautiful blanket, which I can't remember who I got it from. I strap it to my chest in the papoose and pack a spade in a backpack. I try not to notice it shifting across my shoulders as I walk up the yard. I go up to the forest at the top end of the land. The bit Dan told me will never be farmed.

I don't see anyone. At the top of the yard, I climb over the gate. All the way there, I tell him how much I love him and how sorry I am, but there's something about how he feels strapped to my chest. He's gone, and what's left is just a husk, a shell.

I look up and see the most beautiful setting sun, low and golden, and I think about how I let him out of the window, and I know that he flew up to the sky towards the sun, and he's trapped in that golden piece of the horizon between the sky and the ground.

The woods are cool and quiet, and it's almost dark in there. I know the spot I want. The boulders next to the tree with the ear in its trunk. I manage to shift one of the boulders, the smallest one. It takes all my might, and at one point, I feel a muscle snap in my side, but I carry on. I dig a deep hole, clearing away the pine needles and weeds and chopping through roots.

I stand back, sweaty and out of breath. And just then, a ray of the setting sun comes like a laser through the trees, and I feel it hot on my skin, dazzling my eyes.

It's a sign. It's the boy, still trapped between the horizon and the ground. I put his husk deep in the hole, say a short prayer, and then start filling the soil back in.

It takes me longer than I think, and by the time I've got it all packed down and the surrounding brush and scrub clear of the wet soil, it's dark.

I roll the boulder back over the hole, brush it with my hands, and then it's done. I hope he's free now and no longer trapped between the sky and the setting sun.

I come back to the farmhouse, sit here, write this, and then it's darkness. Darkness and nothing. I need to find a way for the boy to forgive me.

THE END

38

Kate sat for a long time after she finished reading. Was this short story a strange coincidence? How many trees had the shape of an ear growing in the centre of the trunk? She reread it. It was haunting and real. Did Maureen write this?

Kate bought the ebook version of the anthology, and read through the rest of the short stories. They all dealt with different themes; comedy, drama, romance and even sci-fi, but none of them came close to being so good. This short story stuck out in the anthology and made the rest of the stories seem phoney and amateurish. Maureen captured the raw emotion and fear of a woman with psychological problems who'd had this terrible life-changing experience.

A link in the back of the ebook version said the anthology had been typeset by a company called Abble Graphics, based in Exeter. Kate tried to call Maureen, but her phone number went to voicemail. She debated leaving a message but then hung up. She needed to think.

She called Tristan, and when he answered, she could hear Leo screaming in the background.

'Is this a bad time?' she asked anxiously.

'No. It's perfect timing, hang on,' said Tristan. She heard him leave the flat and walk out onto the promenade. 'Leo screams and screams and screams. I think Sarah came close to shoving a pillow over his face today... And if I complain about him again, I think she'll shove a pillow over *my* face...' He then picked up on Kate's silence. 'Are you okay?'

'Something peculiar just happened,' she said. Kate told him about the contents of Maureen's short story, and the description of the child being buried by the tree with the shape of the ear growing in the bark.

'That's the description of the wood at Danvers Farm,' said Tristan, his voice shaking.

'I know. I just tried to call Maureen, but she's not answering. I need you to read the story.'

'Hang on. I'll grab my Kindle and download a copy and read it. I'll call you back.'

'Okay, call me as soon as you've read it,' said Kate. She hung up, went to the kitchen, poured herself a glass of iced tea, and came out of the back door. It was now past 9pm, all was quiet, and the campsite shop was closed. Kate took her phone and her drink and walked down the cliff to a spot in the sand dunes where there were two ancient rusting deckchairs. She dusted the sand off one and sat down. Far down the beach, there was a group of people around a fire they'd lit on the sand. Kate felt cocooned in the dunes. She used to come down here with Myra, and even though her friend had died a few years ago, she hadn't moved the other chair.

Tristan rang back a few minutes later.

'I read it. Jesus. It made the hairs stand up on the back of my neck,' he said. 'And the description is exactly where we were today; the tree, the three boulders. The shape of the ear growing out of the trunk.'

'But what do you think Maureen has to do with it?' asked Kate.

'I don't know. Does she have a connection to the farm? Has she been there?'

Kate hesitated.

'It's very good for a short story. It's the work of someone who can write. Do you believe that Maureen wrote it?' There was a long pause on the end of the phone.

'I don't know. We only met her for a couple of hours. What if it's real? I mean, autobiographical?'

'Do you think she had a child, rolled on it in her sleep, and then buried it in the woods?' asked Kate. 'I don't think that fits in with her life, organising local fetes and holidaying on cruise ships.'

'It's often the ones like her who judge everyone else and then have the dark secrets,' said Tristan.

'Good point. Maureen had a lot to say about bad mothers and bastard babies. That could be her deflecting her own experience. The guilt and shame. If she did write it, how did Danvers Farm become her inspiration?'

'What if she grew up on that farm, and it's based on the experience of her own mother?' said Tristan. 'She could be telling her mother's story or another woman's story.'

Kate looked down at the sand and scrunched it between her toes.

'We've been banging our heads against the wall with this case. There seems to be nothing to go on, and then this happens. It's such a weird coincidence,' Kate said.

'Charlie was abducted. This is a short story about a boy who was buried. Where is the coincidence?'

'I meant the co-incidence that we meet Maureen, visit the farm, and then read this short story all in a matter of a day. Even if it's not to do with Charlie, it's weird. Although, I feel like we're so close to something that could link to Charlie.'

'Okay. But what can we do about it?'

She hesitated.

'I'm just going to say this out loud—'

'—you want to go back there and dig?' said Tristan.

'No —'

'— Good,' he said, sounding relieved.

'I meant no, not exactly.'

'You think there's a real body buried there?'

'Didn't you say that guy, Lewis, was talking about methane probes and how he worked with forensics when he was in the police?'

'He was.'

'What if... What if we could borrow equipment to detect a body?'

There was a long silence on the end of the phone, and the wind caught Kate's hair, blowing it across her face.

'Shouldn't we contact the police?' said Tristan.

'And say what? We've read a short story about a child being buried, which features in a real place and based on that alone, we think you should mobilise a search team and obtain warrants to search the property?'

'When you put it like that—'

'We're still waiting to hear back from Bernard Crenshaw about gaining access to the Anna Treadwell crime scene arte-facts. Think how I had to persuade him of our credibility. If we go to the police with this, we'll be laughed out the door, and we'd never be able to ask them for anything again.'

Kate could feel her frustration mounting.

'Which is precisely why we should think about this for a moment. We should talk to Maureen,' said Tristan.

'She's said she was leaving for Southampton tonight, for her cruise. Do you think she's going to tell me over the phone that yes, the story is real, and yes she buried the body of a dead child?'

'What if we go back to Danvers Farm and asked for access to the wood?'

'And what if they say no? If they have anything to do with this, they would be alerted to it...' Kate sighed. 'I know I sound crazy, but you must admit there's something here?'

'Yes.'

'Lewis told you that when they searched Danvers Farm a couple of days after Charlie went missing, the old tenants were acting weird, particularly the wife. He also said their "good" car was beaten up and muddy, as if it had been driven on rough ground. Lewis said that, didn't he?'

'Yes,' said Tristan, still sounding unsure.

'And this is the nearest house to Devil's Way. Where Charlie—'

'—went missing, yes.'

Kate felt her frustration bubbling over.

'Why aren't you with me on this, Tris? Where is your curiosity?'

'I am with you, always. But what we have here is a short story, just that.'

'No. What we have is a lot of questions. What if there is a body buried there? And Maureen knows about it, and she wrote this short story? What if there are other bodies buried on that farmland? We've been investigating Charlie's disappearance for a couple of weeks now, and we have nothing. This could be something.'

'You think if there's a kid buried there, that it's Charlie? The woman in the story accidentally killed her child. Charlie was three when he vanished.'

'Tristan,' said Kate, feeling exasperated.

'Shouldn't we call the police?' said Tristan.

'No! I spent years in the force, having to follow the rules, and look where it got me... I've worked hard to build up this agency, and now we're in a position to do what we want. What if us taking this risk leads to a huge breakthrough?'

'It would be trespassing.'

'And?'

Tristan was silent again on the end of the phone. Kate heard a yell on the beach and saw that a wave had rolled in and extinguished the fire. The young kids around it shrieked with laughter, and she could see the steam rising into the moonlight. 'Tris. I understand how you feel. I'm not asking you to do anything I wouldn't do myself. I'm sorry if I've been pushy. Let's sleep on it and talk about it again tomorrow morning.'

Tristan didn't sound too enthusiastic when they ended the call, but Kate felt nervous excitement when she came off the phone. There was something about the experiences she'd had over the past couple of weeks that had renewed the rebel inside her.

As long as it didn't hurt anyone, she relished the thought of breaking the rules.

39

Kate woke from a night of disturbed sleep and went for her swim. When she came back up the cliff from the beach, she heard a car door slamming out front. A van was parked in the driveway with DB Gas and Plumbing written on the side.

'Can I help you?' asked Kate, wrapping herself in the towel. When she came around to the back of the van, she saw Tristan with a tall, gangly guy with long black hair, wearing cut-off denim shorts and a faded Pink Floyd T-shirt.

'Oh, it's you. Hi, Tris,' she said.

'Kate, this is Lewis Tate,' he said. Lewis held out his hand, and they shook.

'Nice to meet you. What's this all about?' she asked as Lewis opened the van's back doors, and Tristan helped him lift down a small box on wheels with a handle.

'I'm here to help with your plumbing emergency,' said Lewis. He slipped an elastic band off his wrist and tied his long hair back.

'Do we have a plumbing emergency?'

'That's what Tristan told me. He said you want to put in a

jacuzzi for your campsite guests, but you need to check there's nothing important buried where you want to dig,' he said, giving her a wink. Kate looked at Tristan.

'I called him last night after we spoke,' said Tristan.

'And you told him about the—'

'Hey, hey, hey,' said Lewis. He put up his hand and glanced behind him. The nearest person was twenty metres away, an older man at the bottom of the campsite hill, walking to the toilet block with a towel over his shoulder. 'All I need to know is that you asked to borrow this GPR unit to check for pipes in the ground where you want to put in your jacuzzi.'

'Right,' said Kate, catching on. 'Are you a plumber?'

'No. My mate is, and he's on holiday. So this gear is available to hire.'

'And can you come with us when we need to do the scan?' asked Kate.

''Fraid not,' Lewis said. 'I'm here to demonstrate how you use it.'

'I thought we'd use the dunes on the other side of the house,' said Tristan.

'Sweet,' said Lewis. He got up into the van and retrieved a backpack. Tristan took Kate to one side.

'Listen. You were right last night. We need to take risks. Lewis was keen to help.'

'And Lewis is charging a fee of four hundred quid, and he needs the gear back tomorrow morning,' said Lewis, closing the van's doors. Tristan looked at Kate and raised his eyebrows.

'Tomorrow morning. That means we need to investigate our jacuzzi placement tonight?' she said, slightly panicked at the thought.

'You can have it for another day, but that will cost another four hundred quid,' said Lewis. 'Plus petrol to Plymouth and back.'

Kate looked at the gear and tried to conjure back the feelings of confidence she had the previous evening.

'No. That's okay. Let me make us some tea, and you can show us how it all works.'

———

They set up on the other side of the house, in the middle of the dunes. Lewis was very twitchy about Kate and Tristan discussing what they wanted to do, and he insisted on talking about using the ground penetrating radar to check for plumbing. He set to work with a spade and quickly dug two holes, spaced a few metres apart.

'Can I ask you something about the Devil's Way?' said Kate. Lewis looked up from digging.

'Yes?' he replied cautiously.

'It's about the river near the gorge. There used to be a small wooden footbridge there?'

Lewis stopped digging for a moment and leant on his spade, he pursed his lips and thought for a moment. He wiped his forehead.

'Jeez. Yeah, there was a bridge,' he said, reacting as if he'd forgotten this detail.

'Why didn't you mention this when we met before?' asked Tristan.

'I'd forgotten... Yeah. The footbridge. The water was very high. It was splashing over the walkway, making the wood wet... It's the booze,' he added in a mournful voice. 'It makes things... Patchy in my head.'

'You said that the scent dogs tracked Charlie's scent but it stopped at the river?' said Kate.

'That's right.'

'Is it possible that Charlie crossed the bridge, but because of the water level and the water running over it, the dogs weren't able to detect him crossing?'

Lewis dragged the spade through a pile of sand and blew out his cheeks.

'It's possible, but the dogs are usually able to detect the slightest scent.'

'But there's a chance the water running over the bridge could have thrown the dogs off?'

'Yeah,' said Lewis. He was squinting and looked like he was struggling to remember.

'Did the dogs pick up his scent on the other side of the river?'

Lewis had to think about this.

'No. I don't think so. All I remember is that the dogs stopped at the edge of the river,' he said. Kate looked at Tristan and he raised his eyebrows.

'Okay. Thank you,' she said. Lewis stared to dig again, and there was an awkward silence.

When the holes were finished, one had a depth of one metre, and the other, two metres. Lewis produced an iPad and two objects from his backpack: a length of copper piping and a Tiny Tears doll wrapped in a blanket. He buried them both, and Kate helped fill the holes. When it was all smoothed over, Lewis set up the radar.

Kate went over to the box on wheels. It was small but heavy. Lewis showed them how to switch the unit on, which was connected to an app on the iPad.

'Okay. This is the view we have of the sand right now,' said

Lewis, showing them a graph on the iPad screen. Along the top, the distance was marked out in metres, and then down the left-hand side, it showed the depth marked out in half metres. The land was represented by colours, starting with green at the deepest and then morphing into yellow and orange and then red near the surface. 'What do you know about ground penetrating radar?'

'Nothing,' said Tristan.

'I know a little, but remind me,' said Kate as they huddled around the screen.

'Okay, so, ground penetrating radar or GPR consists of an electromagnetic sender,' he said, pointing to the unit on wheels, 'and a receiver.' He held up the iPad. 'The sender emits high-frequency radio pulses down into the ground. It does this continually, and if the frequency reflects on any objects in the soil, they show up on this screen.'

'How deep can it detect things?' asked Kate.

'The depth of GPR penetration depends on the kind of ground it's on. Right now, we're on sand, and sand will return a very clear image. But GPR will penetrate concrete, fresh water, seawater, rock, ice and asphalt differently due to their electro-magnetic make-up. Clay or clay soil is particularly shitty. When my mate has to look for pipes buried in clay, the penetration depth is only a couple of metres or less. Here, you take the iPad.' He handed it to Kate.

She looked back at where they'd been digging in the sand. It was already hot, and the damp sand they'd churned up was already dry.

'Tristan, if you roll the GPR slowly over the stuff we've buried, I'll show Kate.'

Kate watched as Tristan pushed the unit towards the first hole where the length of copper piping was buried. The coloured bands on the iPad screen warped and bent, showing a thin outline of the object.

'Remember, sand is an excellent conductor, so you can see the thin pipe clearly,' said Lewis. 'Tris, come and look.'

Tristan joined them to peer at the screen and nodded, then moved back to the GPR and pushed it along the sand to the second hole. The Tiny Tears doll had been buried deeper. As he moved closer with the GPR, Kate saw the coloured bands shift, and then they bulged out to reflect the size of the doll buried in the blanket.

'The material of the blanket reflects the radio pulses,' said Lewis as they stared at the round bulge at a depth of two metres.

Kate suddenly felt sick at the thought of what they were planning. Tristan joined them to look at the screen again.

'The doll shows up bigger than the thin length of pipe,' he said.

They were silent for a moment.

'But obviously, you're just looking for pipes in the ground, and if anyone asks me, that's what I loaned you the equipment for,' said Lewis.

'Pipes in the ground,' repeated Kate.

'Yes. Pipes in the ground,' said Tristan. Lewis looked at them both, and he looked uncomfortable.

'Listen. Guys. I was a good copper, but I was drinking a lot more and drugging back then. I've got things under control now,' he said insistently. 'I have.'

Later, when Lewis was packing up his van, and Tristan had gone to the office to get some cash, Kate handed him a piece of paper with her phone number. He looked at it and then raised an eyebrow.

'I'm not asking you out!' she said. 'I'm in recovery, in Alcoholics Anonymous. That's my number, if you ever need to talk.'

Lewis looked at the piece of paper again. He went to say something, but Tristan appeared with the money. Lewis quickly pocketed the paper.

'Here you go,' said Tristan handing him an envelope.

'Thanks,' said Lewis. 'And remember. I loaned you that equipment to look at pipes in the ground.'

'We'll get the equipment back to you tomorrow,' said Tristan.

As they watched Lewis drive away, Kate wondered if he would ever need her number, or if he would just carry on drinking.

40

As the day progressed and the sun sank in the sky, Kate had severe reservations about what they planned to do, and when they set off for Dartmoor at 11pm, it felt too real and reckless.

The GPR unit folded up and fitted into a large backpack, which Tristan offered to carry. It was a warm night, but they wore walking shoes, black jeans, and dark, long-sleeved T-shirts.

Kate felt okay on the short stretch of floodlit motorway between Ashdean and Exmoor, amongst the other traffic and the bright lights, but when they came off the Exeter junction and started down the unlit country roads, she felt exposed.

The map showed that Danvers Farm was a couple of square miles wide, and they parked in a small lay-by a few hundred metres from the main gate.

One of their extensive discussions that afternoon was: did the farm have CCTV? Kate had to assume they did have it in their yard and the fields immediately surrounding the house, but she didn't think so in the area next to the road, which led into the woodland.

When they parked, Tristan switched off the car engine. They

sat in the darkness for a minute, listening to the sound of their breathing. Only a tiny amount of light pollution emanated from Exeter, far off across the moors and below the skyline, and Kate could only see the outline of Tristan's profile. Their midnight trespass suddenly felt like a reckless whim.

'Are you sure you want to do this?' asked Kate.

'Not really, but you've made me curious enough not to want to bail,' said Tristan. 'What if they have dogs?' he added.

'There won't be dogs out loose on their land. There are too many sheep all over Dartmoor, and we're crossing a field that the farm doesn't have directly connected to their house. There's the woodland in between.'

'You sound sure,' said Tristan.

'Do I? Good,' said Kate. A set of headlights burst around the corner, dazzling them.

'Shit,' said Kate. Tristan went to duck down, but she put out her hand to stop him. 'No. Act normal.'

'How do we act normal, sitting in a dark lay-by at midnight?'

Kate leant over and put her head on his shoulder.

'Let them think we're here for sex, and we've been caught,' said Kate. Tristan winced and stared at Kate as she sat up again, and adjusted her top. The lights seemed to advance on them slowly, growing brighter and making Kate's retinas ache, and then the car was gone, thankfully, without stopping.

'That's blinded me,' said Tristan.

'Come on, we need to move,' said Kate, opening her car door.

Tristan followed her, and they retrieved the GPR unit from the back seat. He shrugged on the backpack. Kate had a smaller bag with the iPad, gloves, and a couple of crowbars if they needed to move boulders. They hadn't brought shovels. Kate hadn't wanted to contemplate digging anything up.

The drystone wall of Danvers Farm began a few metres from

where they'd parked. They'd both brought tiny black-light torches with them, which emitted a meagre purple glow. The light from them was barely sufficient, and when they climbed up on the drystone wall, Kate was suddenly terrified when she couldn't see the ground on the other side.

They switched off their torches. Kate figured that a glow on the road might not be questioned, but if someone from the farm saw a faint light moving across their field, it might make them come and investigate.

Tristan took off the backpack, balancing it on the wall, and he jumped down first.

'It's not a big drop, only waist-high on me,' he said in a low voice. They could see the farmhouse on the top of the slope beyond the woodland, and two lights were burning in the upstairs windows. Kate slid over the wall and landed on the other side.

They kept along the boundary wall as they crossed the field. Kate was relieved when they reached the edge of the woodland, and the farmhouse was obscured by the black mass of trees.

They stopped. Kate felt out of breath, and she was sweating in the warm night. She heard a thud and a quiet groan.

'Tris? Are you okay?' she asked. She moved closer to the line of trees, switched on her black-light, and almost stumbled over Tristan lying on the ground.

'I tripped on a tree root, watch out,' he said. He was still wearing the backpack, and it must have landed on him when he went down, thought Kate. She helped him up, and they stepped into the line of trees and started walking into the wood. The next few minutes were terrifying. Kate thought Tristan's idea to bring a compass was rash, but amongst the thick trees and the almost pitch black, they quickly lost their bearings. She held onto the backpack as he moved slowly, keeping them headed north.

There were so many noises in the dark, the crackling of bracken and twigs underfoot and strange rustles in the darkness. Kate was glad to have Tristan and the bulk of the backpack to cling onto. Finally, they emerged out the other side of the wood. The horizon was glowing, and they couldn't see the Devil's Way, but the light pollution seemed brighter after their walk through the pitch black.

The farm buildings seemed much closer on the other side than Kate remembered. It took another twenty minutes of walking up and down the tree line to find the boulders and the ear tree. When they finally found it, they were hot and bothered, and Kate's nerves were hanging out.

She switched on her black-light and shone it over the ear growing out of the wood. It looked grotesque in the half-light and had the shine of real skin and cartilage. Tristan shrugged off the backpack and placed it on the ground. He took out the GPR box. They hadn't brought the handle. When Tristan switched it on, two tiny red lights on the side blinked on and lit up their surroundings with an eerie glow.

'That's bright,' said Tristan. Kate felt around inside her bag and took out the iPad. The screen light activated, and it seemed to blaze out in their surroundings, lighting up the woodland and the canopy of branches above. She quickly turned it and pressed the screen to her chest, plunging them back into darkness.

'We're so close to the edge,' said Kate. She could see through the branches to the farm buildings from where they stood.

'Let's get this over with,' said Tristan. They'd reread the short story a few times during the day, writing down everything they could to find the precise point where the woman could have buried her child. The story stated it was under the smallest boulder between the two larger ones. They each took a crowbar from Kate's bag and tried to prise up the boulder, so they could roll it to one side. When Kate shone the black-light on the spot, it was precisely as described in the story.

It felt like it was fixed to the spot with concrete, and for a moment, as they heaved and sweated, Kate thought it wasn't going to budge. Then the boulder rolled over and moved a few feet down the ground sloping away.

'How did the woman in the story move this on her own?' said Kate. Tristan didn't answer. He lifted the GPR unit onto the ground next to the depression made by the boulder. She could see the sweat on his face, and it was dripping down his nose.

'Can you check if it's connecting to the iPad?' he said. Kate crouched behind the largest boulder and, clutching the iPad to her chest, she turned the screen brightness right down. Then she opened the app. Tristan came round to join her. Even turned down to a dim glow, the iPad screen still seemed so bright, and their shadows were cast on the canopy of the trees above like two huge giants.

The bands of colours were more uneven than they'd been when they were on the beach, and Kate could already see there was some distortion at the edge of the screen.

'It's connecting,' said Kate in a low voice. Tristan moved off around the boulder and gripped the GPR unit. As he rolled it forward, Kate saw the bands of colour bulge and distort. Was she reading this right? There was something under the ground buried at a depth of two metres.

'What can you see—' Tristan started to say, and then there was a crackle of undergrowth and a hissing sound. She heard Tristan scream, and then the air around her seemed to fill with a cloud of noxious gas, and she couldn't breathe; her eyes were streaming and as she tried to stand up, she knew that they had been pepper-sprayed.

'Tristan?' she said, groping around on the grass. Her elbow hit the large boulder. She heard Tristan stagger around and then the spray hit her again. Her eyes were closed but she took in a gulp and threw up.

'Who are you?' screamed a voice. It was the voice of a child, a young boy.

'We're not here to hurt you,' Kate heard Tristan say. She heard the hiss of the spray again and she instinctively put up her hands to cover her face.

'Stop it!' she tried to say. She had lost her bearings completely and she staggered forward and tripped on something. She fell hard on her front, her head hit a rock and she blacked out.

41

Kate was sitting on a long bench by the back door of the farmhouse kitchen. Her head was throbbing, and she could feel a large bruise under her hair. The kitchen was lit by a single light over the table and chairs in the centre, which gave the room a cave-like appearance.

A paramedic was leaning over Tristan, who was slumped on a chair at the kitchen table. His face was swollen and red. Dawn Grey, the landlady of the farm who they'd met earlier, was standing next to the paramedic wearing a dressing gown. She dipped a cloth into a bowl, wrung it out and dabbed at Tristan's swollen face.

'It's alright, this is only mild soapy water,' she said with concern in her voice.

The paramedic gently tipped Tristan's head back and Kate winced when she saw his face was so swollen that his eyes were just small slits. When Dawn pressed the cloth on his skin, he grimaced.

'It's okay, love. This will cool everything down. Try not to touch your skin,' she said, holding his arm with her free hand.

'Can you hold this for me?' she said, putting his hands onto the cloth. He held it and gritted his teeth.

Kate looked over at Jack, the red Adidas tracksuit boy. He was standing in front of the fridge next to a door leading into the rest of the house. He looked very pale and scared. She felt so angry, but she didn't know if it was with herself or this stupid kid. She'd escaped the worse of the pepper spray, but Tristan had received it full in the face. The paramedic moved over to Kate, wearing latex gloves, and examined her face.

'You seem better off than your friend,' she said. She knelt down and examined Kate's head, gently parting her hair. Kate looked around the room. It was a cosy farmhouse kitchen with Willow Pattern plates on a Welsh dresser, and the fridge was covered with children's pictures curling up at the edges. The paramedic knelt down, and shone a pen torch in her eyes. 'You seemed to have dodged the mace, but we should get you checked out at hospital, you may have concussion.'

Kate had no desire to go back to hospital. The back door opened, and two police officers came into the kitchen. She felt her stomach flip, and guilt came over her again. Tristan had his head on the table, pressing the damp cloth against his skin.

One of the police officers was a portly man in his late fifties with a grey beard. He was accompanied by a young lad who couldn't have been more than nineteen. He had peachy smooth skin and jet-black hair. They both wore yellow high-visibility jackets over their uniforms and were sweating. One of their radios beeped, and a voice came blasting through. He reached up and turned it down.

'We've checked the rest of the property. There's no one else we can find,' said the older officer. 'There's a blue Citroën parked out on a lay-by close to the boundary of your property.'

Tristan sat up and looked at the police officers. His eyes were red, but Kate saw he could now open them a bit more.

'That's my car. We're private detectives,' said Kate, putting up her hand.

'Are you now? Well, I'm a detective chief inspector. Detective Chief Inspector Ken Harris,' he replied. 'This is my colleague Detective Duncan West.' He stood over Kate and looked down at her coldly. 'Why were you trespassing on the property?'

'We are private detectives—'

He shook his head and cut her off.

'No, no, no. You are private citizens. And you were trespassing.'

'Using pepper spray as a civilian is illegal,' said Kate, looking over at Jack. She knew she had to defend herself and Tristan right away before the police decided what to do next, and she could sense they were confused by the situation.

'Yes, we are aware of that,' said Harris, following her gaze to Jack.

'I didn't know that Jack had mace,' said Dawn.

'And what's your name, ma'am?' asked Harris.

'I'm Dawn Grey,' she said. She didn't look happy. She wrung out another flannel in the bowl of soapy water and handed it to Tristan, taking the used cloth back to the sink. Tristan dabbed at his burning face. Harris seemed to note that Dawn was helping the two trespassers.

'Jack. How old are you?'

'Thirteen,' he said swallowing and shifting on his feet. He was trembling.

'Why do you have mace?' he asked.

'My dad is away. I was looking after me mum and sister,' he said. 'I saw a light in the woods. I thought it was junkies!'

'What do you mean, junkies? We don't get junkies here,' said

Dawn.

'I didn't know it was them,' said Jack, indicating Kate and Tristan. 'They'd been here the other day to buy eggs!' He now sounded terrified, and his teenage voice cracked. Harris put up his hands.

'Jack. Have you got the pepper spray?'

The boy shifted on his feet.

'Yes.'

'Can I have it?' Harris said, holding out his hand.

'What's going to happen to him?' asked Dawn, stepping between her son and the police officer. Harris kept his hand out, and when Jack retrieved a small can from his pocket he moved around her to take it.

'Where is it from?' asked Harris.

'I got it online,' said Jack. Harris looked around at everyone in the small kitchen and shook his head.

'On this occasion, I will just give you a strong verbal warning that possessing and using mace is illegal. Do you understand, Jack? We'll draw a line under it if you promise never to buy or use this again.' Jack nodded. He put his trembling hands in his pockets. 'Do you understand why it's illegal? Look at what it did to these two people.'

'I know. But they were on our land!' said Jack. Dawn folded her arms and eyeballed her son to shut up.

'Yes. And you could have just called the police rather than taking the law into your own hands. Now, do you understand what I've said?' said Harris.

There was a pause, and Jack nodded.

'Jack does understand, don't you?' said Dawn fixing him with a stare. 'Jack.'

'Yeah. I understand,' he said looking at the floor.

Harris turned to Kate and Tristan.

'And why were you trespassing on their land in the middle of the night?'

'We're private detectives, and...'

'Yes, you keep saying that—'

'And we believe there is a body buried in the woods. The body of a small boy,' said Kate.

'What?' asked Dawn, looking between Kate, Tristan, and the police officers.

Harris put up his hand to silence her. He opened his mouth and hesitated.

'What?' he repeated. Kate explained, and when she got to the bit about the ground penetrating radar, she broke off and turned to Jack.

'What happened to our equipment and the iPad? We were in the woods for a while before the police arrived.'

'I have the iPad,' said Duncan, taking it out of his jacket. He went to hand it to Kate, but Harris gave him a look and grabbed it.

'What other equipment do you have?'

'Ground penetrating radar,' said Tristan, speaking for the first time, the flannel still pressed to his temple.

'Ground penetrating radar?' repeated Harris.

'We hired it from a plumbing company,' said Kate. Dawn was still holding one of the flannels in her hand, looking between them as they spoke.

'How can you possibly think a body is buried on our land?' she said, her voice shrill.

'If I can have the iPad, I can show you,' said Kate.

'You dug up a body and took a picture of it?' said Dawn. Harris took a renewed interest in the iPad and turned it over in his hands.

'None of you knows the pin code, so you need me to unlock

it,' said Kate.

Harris handed her the iPad. She opened it and found the app with the screenshots from the ground penetrating radar that they'd taken.

'Where on my land?' asked Dawn, confused at the image with the coloured lines.

'In the woods. Where the tree looks like it has an ear on the trunk,' said Tristan. 'Next to the boulders.'

Kate watched Harris studying the image.

'You see there,' she said, pointing to the bulging lines of colour on the image. 'This is where we believe it could be buried.'

'It? What do you mean *it*?' shrilled Dawn. 'This is my land. I have a right to know. And what are you going to do about these two people who trespassed? Surely there must be recourse for that!'

Harris considered this and handed the iPad back to Kate.

'That image could be anything,' he said. Kate explained the investigation they were working on and how the farm linked tenuously to the case and the short story.

She also explained that she was the Kate Marshall who had broken the Nine Elms Cannibal murder case. She didn't like to talk about it, but she thought it could be a good Get Out of Jail Free card in this instance. It seemed to work.

'Hang on, hang on,' said Harris. 'You're Kate Marshall, the ex-Met police officer who found the Nine Elms Cannibal?'

'And this is my partner in the agency, Tristan Harper.' She rummaged in her pocket, found their business card, and handed it to Harris. His attitude seemed to change; he seemed slightly in awe, as if he didn't know what to say next.

'What are you talking about?' asked Dawn. The kitchen door opened, and the young girl Kate and Tristan had seen on their last visit poked her head around it with bleary eyes. They widened when she saw everyone.

'Mum, what's going on?' she said. Dawn looked at everyone crammed into her tiny kitchen and moved over to her daughter.

'It's okay, love. Everything is fine. Let's go back to bed. Jack, you can come with me too.' He looked like he didn't want to move. 'Jack. Now, please… I'll be back in a moment,' she added to Harris. When they'd left, Duncan took the iPad and looked through the GRP scans.

'Peter Conway tried to kill you, didn't he?' said Harris.

'Yes.'

'And is it true that you were in your flat looking at the evidence, and you had this lightbulb moment where it all fell into place?' Kate was pleased to see the change in him, but this wasn't the time to do a Ted Talk.

'I appreciate the questions, and I'd be happy to talk about that case. But would you be willing to bring in a small forensics team and check this out?'

'This could be anything,' said Duncan, holding up the distorted lines of colour on the iPad screen. He didn't seem as impressed with Kate as Harris.

'I can explain in more detail, but so much of what we've been investigating links back to this farm. It could be a tree root or an old bicycle, but I feel we had probable cause to check it out. It might actually be a body. Another lightbulb moment, if you like.'

Harris was silent for a moment. He scratched his chin and then looked back at Kate and Tristan.

'Probable cause. Lightbulb moment,' he said, nodding. He reached for his radio and called into the control team.

'Can you send a forensics team out to Danvers Farm in South Zeal? Right away.'

42

Harris and Duncan left the kitchen, and told Kate and Tristan to stay where they were whilst they sealed off the area around the woods. There was a strange lull when they were left alone.

'Are you okay?' Kate asked, moving over to Tristan. He pulled the cloth away from his face and peered up at her. The redness had gone down, and his eyes looked less bloodshot.

'I'm sorry, Tris,' she said, feeling the guilt again.

'It's not your fault. This soap feels sticky,' he said, going up to the sink and gently splashing his face with water.

'How's your head?' he asked.

'Fine. Just a bit sore... I'm not going to the bloody hospital, though,' she added when she saw his concern. Dawn came back into the room.

'Are your kids okay?' asked Kate.

'Shaken up,' she said. 'Both of them are shaken up.'

'I'm sorry about this.'

Dawn eyed Kate for a moment.

'Do you really think a body is buried on our land?' she said, quietly. Kate looked outside the kitchen window and saw the sky was turning a deep blue. It would soon be light.

'Honestly, I hope not.'

Dawn went to the fridge and took out a bottle of milk.

'Why didn't you come to talk to me about this the other day?'

'Would you have believed us if we came to ask you to look on your land for a dead body?' said Kate. Dawn switched on the kettle.

'Are you going to press charges against Jack?' she said, watching Tristan splashing his face with water. She took a clean cotton tea towel from a drawer and handed it to him. Tristan took it and pressed it against his face lightly.

'No,' said Kate.

'Do you want some tea?'

Kate nodded. Dawn worked in silence for a moment, taking out mugs and sugar. Kate looked out of the window impatiently, wanting to be down the yard with the police.

'How much do you know about the previous tenants? Steve and Libby Hartley?' she asked.

'I told you, nothing,' said Dawn. 'I know that they left abruptly. When we took over the farm, there was still stuff of theirs here; bedding, some clothes, and ornaments. They even left food in the pantry.'

'When did you take over the lease?'

'Early in January 2008.'

'How long had the farm been vacant?'

Dawn hesitated with the teapot in her hands and had to think.

'At least five, six months,' she said. Kate looked at Tristan.

'They left in July 2007?' said Kate.

'Around that time, I think so. The land was a mess. The Crown Estate brought in another cooperative of farmers to do the harvest that year, but there were a lot of things overgrown. I heard from the locals that Libby Hartley was having mental health problems. And Steve Hartley had a problem with drinking. Earlier that year, he'd flipped his car over on the road outside when he had a young girl in the passenger seat that he was having an affair with. I don't think they were in a happy marriage.'

'We read about it in the local paper,' said Tristan.

'The rumour is that Jennifer Kibbin, that's the girl Steve was with that day, was pregnant with his baby,' said Dawn. 'It's never been substantiated.'

Kate looked at Tristan. An unwanted baby. And Steve and Libby left the farm so soon after Charlie went missing. She turned to look out of the window, thinking about the woods. Dawn followed her gaze.

'You don't think...' She put the tea caddy down with a clatter and went very pale. 'You don't think that the... the... whoever it is buried on my land is a baby?'

'We don't know,' said Kate, wanting to reassure Dawn but also having the same thought. 'Have you ever met a social worker called Anna Treadwell?' she asked, changing the subject.

'No. Why would I have anything to do with a social worker? My children are happy and loved,' said Dawn. She looked scared now, and haggard. 'My husband is coming back later today. You can talk to him.'

'Where has he been?'

'The Norfolk Show, it's a farm show.'

Dawn wiped her eyes and left the room. It was now light outside. Kate could see the stray cats circling around their bowls and dishes on the drain lid in the yard. After a moment, Kate saw Detective Chief Inspector Harris appear through the gate, and a moment later there was a knock at the back door. Dawn returned with a packet of biscuits and opened the door.

'Kate and Tristan, would you like to come with me?' said Harris. 'And would you like to come with us, Mrs Grey?'

'No. I'm going to stay here with the children,' she said.

'Are you okay, Tris?' said Kate. His face was looking much better. He nodded and looked like he wanted to escape the kitchen.

The sun was now up but behind grey clouds. They followed Harris through the trees and the farm buildings. When they came out into the fields, they saw a forensics van parked close to the edge of the woodland. Kate and Tristan were given white Tyvek suits to wear and coveralls for their shoes. Harris pulled on the protective gear with them.

A path of tarpaulin had been laid from the van into the woodland, and two bright floodlights had been set up next to the boulders.

Kate felt horrible dread and adrenalin when she saw a group of three forensics officers working to clear away a section of the leaves and pine needles around the flattened earth under the boulder.

'It feels real now,' said Tristan, echoing her sentiment. They stood for a long time, just watching from a distance. It was slow work because they had to bag up the soil layers and take live samples of the worms and insects underneath the boulder. As the minutes ticked by, Kate hoped that they would find nothing. The thought of finding a child's body buried here filled her with horror, and she wanted to be proved wrong. The sky was grey, and the temperature dropped, making Kate feel glad about the forensics suits. A few minutes later, it started to rain, and a tarpaulin cover was quickly erected above the ground so the forensics officers could continue to dig.

Tristan and Kate were given an umbrella, and they stood in silence, listening to the rhythmic sound of spades scraping the soil and the rain clattering on the tarpaulin. The ear protruding from the tree trunk glistened in the floodlights and Kate thought again how the soft wood looked like human skin. The sound of the rain intensified and started hammering down, and the clouds grew thick, casting the woodland clearing in a light mist. The smell of the rain on the soil and plants cut through the chilly morning.

The forensics officers started digging deeper, and Kate noticed they were using the GPR images they'd scanned in the night.

'We have something,' came a voice, suddenly breaking through the silence. Tristan and Kate moved closer to the hole. It was around a metre and a half deep, and roots from the surrounding trees poked through the edges. Two forensics officers were working in the hole under the bright floodlights, and their white coveralls were caked in the peaty soil.

Kate watched as they switched out their spades for coarse brushes and started to work more carefully, scraping away the soil. *What is it? Tell us what it is!* a voice shouted in her head.

A few minutes later, a forensics officer lifted a huge, muddy mass out of the hole. As he gently laid the bundle down, a new tarpaulin was placed underneath. The fresh soil clumps fell away, and they started to work with their brushes to expose a faint pattern. Kate could see the contours of a heavy fibre blanket.

The dread started to trickle into her stomach, and a terrible silence spread over the team as they began to gently unroll the blanket. A tiny blackened bundle was inside. A light was brought closer, and they saw the shape of an arm, a small sunken face with eye sockets, a nose, chin and teeth.

'No, no, please no,' Kate heard Tristan say beside her. She reached out and grabbed his hand.

'It's a small child,' said one of the forensics officers, sitting back on his heels on the tarpaulin. The small, decomposed body lay remarkably intact, lying within the folds of the blanket, and there were still wisps of hair stuck to the dome of the child's skull.

'What if it's Charlie?' asked Tristan quietly beside her.

43

The discovery of the body changed everything. A murder investigation was opened, and Detective Chief Inspector Harris asked Kate and Tristan to make a formal statement.

'So. Let me get this straight in my head,' he said when they were talking to him in one of the police support vehicles. 'You stumbled across a short story in an anthology, which led you to decide to search for a body?'

'Yes, it was when we discovered the link to Charlie Julings's disappearance. When he went missing, the police searched this farm, and said the previous tenants were acting strangely. We then discovered that a social worker called Anna Treadwell had been concerned about Charlie's welfare in the weeks leading up to him going missing. Anna Treadwell was then murdered. We found a link between Anna and a local woman, Maureen Cook, who ran a writing group of which Anna was a member. The writing group released an anthology, and one of the short stories, authored by Maureen Cook, was about a woman burying her child under a boulder in a wood which has a tree trunk with the shape of an ear protruding from the bark,' said Kate.

Harris scratched his head and looked over at Duncan, who had been making notes.

'And this Maureen Cook, what does she do now?' he asked.

'We think she's retired.'

'And what's her connection to Danvers Farm?'

'We don't know,' said Tristan.

'What led you to this short story?' asked Harris.

'I looked through it, trying to find if Anna Treadwell, the murdered social worker had written anything. She hadn't.'

'Then why did you pick out the story written by Maureen Cook?' he said, unable to hide his confusion and exasperation.

'It was the ear, the growth on the side of the tree opposite where the body was buried. The exact same ear is described on the tree in Maureen Cook's short story.'

'And that's how we arrived here,' said Kate. There was a knock on the van door, and a police officer poked her head around.

'Guv, the Chief Superintendent is on the phone. He wants a full update,' she said.

Harris's face drained of colour. He looked down at the signed statement from Kate and Tristan.

'I'll need to take a DNA sample from both of you, so we can rule you out of the crime scene,' he said. 'And don't go anywhere far. I'll need to talk to you again.'

Kate and Tristan left the farm through the front gate, escorted by a uniform police officer, who lifted a line of police tape for them to pass underneath. It was just after 8am.

The area out front was filled with police cars and police response vans, and the road was closed off in both directions.

They walked back down to Tristan's car, parked just beyond the police cordon where a local news van was pulling up. *Oh no*, thought Kate.

'Let's get out of here,' she said, pulling up her hood. Tristan did the same.

'Can you drive?' asked Tristan. 'My eyes are still a bit blurry from the mace.'

He passed Kate the keys, and she unlocked the car. The doors of the news van slid open, and a woman who Kate recognised as one of the local from-the-scene news reporters hurried across to them.

'Have you just come from the farm?' she asked as Kate opened the driver's door. Kate shook her head. The news reporter looked past her and saw Tristan's swollen face. 'How are you involved with the murder investigation?'

'We're not,' said Kate.

The news reporter didn't know who she was, which was good.

'We're hearing rumours that a child's body has been discovered? And that it could be the body of Charlie Julings, the three-year-old boy who vanished eleven years ago at Devil's—'

Kate cut her off by closing her door. She activated the central locking and turned on the engine, then put the car in gear and reversed at speed down the road, executing a three-point turn that almost led them into a ditch. She only relaxed as they drove away, and the TV news van started to recede in the rear-view mirror.

She turned to Tristan. He was quiet and staring ahead.

'You okay?'

He shook his head,

'That little body in the blanket. Do you think it's Charlie Julings? I couldn't even see if it was a boy or a girl. How does that news reporter know? We've literally just seen it happen,' he said.

'It must be a leak. A police officer on the payroll of the news. There's chaos back there with all those people.'

'Could they have heard on the radio?'

'It's virtually impossible to listen to police radio. It's now digital and encrypted, but these journalists...' Kate didn't want to start ranting about her experiences with underhand and devious members of the press. She could see that Tristan was severely shaken.

'But the short story. How was the story right?' Tristan said, looking at Kate.

'I don't know. And we need to work that out, but we must first get in contact with Jean. If the local news is already asking questions and has Charlie's disappearance on their radar, I don't want her to find out when she switches on the TV.'

'And Joel,' said Tristan. 'He got back from his holiday last night, and we haven't even had the chance to talk to him about the investigation.'

They passed a convoy of three police cars speeding in the other direction with lights and sirens blazing.

They were closer to Tristan's flat. When they arrived, Tristan's brother-in-law, Gary, and Sarah were sitting in the living room with cups of tea, watching the early morning news. Leo was dozing on Gary's lap. They looked surprised to see Kate with Tristan.

'Tris. I thought you'd gone to work,' said Sarah. Then she saw his face, put her tea down on the coffee table and stood up. 'Look at the state of you! What happened?' She peered at him.

'I got maced,' he said.

'Maced?' she said, turning to Kate. 'You mean pepper spray?'

'We both got maced. I missed most of it,' said Kate. Gary was still wearing his bedclothes, just a pair of briefs and a T-shirt, and he realised and pulled a blanket over his legs. 'Hi, Gary.'

'Hello, excuse me if I don't get up,' he said.

'Mace? Tristan?' said Sarah, watching as he reached for the TV remote and switched to the ITV morning news. She folded her arms. 'Were you protesting about something?'

'There should be a local news bulletin in five minutes,' said Tristan to Kate.

'Tris, you're soaking wet! And filthy!' said Sarah. 'What's going on?'

'I need to get changed,' he said. Tristan disappeared upstairs, and Kate was left standing awkwardly with Sarah and Gary. Kate kept her eye on the TV and saw an advert for teabags. It was a shock to be amongst domestic normality after their night of horrors.

'Do you want to sit down?' asked Gary, going to get up.

'No, Gary. Kate can have a seat at the table,' said Sarah, indicating one of the dining chairs in the corner.

'Yeah. I'll just perch here,' said Kate, sitting on the edge of one of them. Sarah took Leo from Gary, and he sleepily cuddled up to her shoulder. She jiggling him on her shoulder and staring at Kate, waiting for an explanation, but she couldn't bring herself to talk about what they'd just seen.

'So... How's business at the agency?' asked Gary, sensing the awkwardness. He adjusted the blanket covering his lap.

'Good, thank you,' said Kate. They watched an advertisement for toilet cleaner in silence. The floorboards creaked above, and Kate hoped Tristan was only getting changed and not having a shower.

The advert finished, and suddenly the ITV local news headlines were playing. The stretch of road outside Danvers Farm appeared on the screen.

'In breaking news this morning, police have uncovered the body of a young child on farmland on the edge of Dartmoor,' said the voice-over.

'Tristan!' shouted Kate, leaping up, moving to the doorway and shouting up the stairs. 'It's the first item on the news!'

There was a clattering as Tristan came running down the stairs and into the living room, pulling on a T-shirt. Leo woke up and gave a blood-curdling scream.

Kate and Tristan moved closer to the TV screen. The news anchor went live to the same reporter they'd just seen on the road outside Danvers Farm half an hour before. She was standing in front of a police cordon flapping in the breeze where two uniformed police officers were stationed. Tristan turned up the volume.

'Unconfirmed reports are coming in that the body of a small child has been found wrapped in a blanket and buried in a shallow grave in woodland on the property,' the reporter said to the camera. The screen cut to a wide-angle shot of the farm-house, where a small stretcher was being carried to a black van. 'The police were apparently acting on a tip-off from a private detective working on another case in the area. We'll have more updates soon.'

Sarah and Gary were trying to quiet down Leo, but they stopped when they heard the part about the private detective.

'Tristan, do you have something to do with this?' asked Sarah, passing the screaming Leo over to Gary. He immediately stopped crying.

'I can't talk about it,' he said. Sarah came close and put her hand under his chin. 'And you were maced? Were you tres-passing?'

'Sarah. We're fine,' said Kate.

'I'm talking to my brother if you don't mind,' said Sarah,

folding her arms. She looked back at the TV, where there was now a story about the water mains being dug up in an Exeter car park. 'I'm still waiting for an explanation, Tristan.'

He turned to her.

'Sarah. You're always welcome to stay here, but please don't talk to Kate like that. We can't discuss this. We've got important work to do. And the last time I checked, this was my flat.'

Sarah opened and closed her mouth and then went into the kitchen.

'Sorry, Gary, it's not a good time,' said Tristan.

Gary nodded, gathered up the blanket to cover his modesty, and carried Leo into the kitchen, closing the door. Tristan turned back to Kate.

'I don't know if Jean and Joel have a police liaison officer after all this time, but they shouldn't hear this from the TV news.'

'Agreed. We might have to be the ones who break the news. Let's get cleaned up and arrange to meet them,' said Kate.

44

Joel Mansfield ran a pub on the edge of a village called Belstone, on the south side of Dartmoor. It was a giant granite building perched at the top of a narrow road which seemed to fall away to the open moors where sheep grazed in the hot sunshine. When Kate and Tristan arrived, the tables outside the pub were already busy with people drinking under umbrellas. When they went inside, the bar was calm and quiet. The air was musty and smelt of beer, and the ghost of cigarettes smoked many years ago.

A couple of young women were working behind the bar, and their oversized T-shirts were rolled up at the sleeves. There was a television on the wall, but it was switched off. Kate recognised Joel from the newspaper photos, but he was now much heavier set, with a tan, and his dark hair was thinning on top. He was in the middle of changing a beer barrel. He heaved it in place with a clink, then caught his breath when he saw them.

Kate went to say hello, but he cut her off.

'The yard round the back is quiet, and there's shade. Let's talk there. Do you want a drink?' he said. They both asked for coffee – they'd been awake all night – but Kate still felt like she was running on adrenalin. Joel told one of the young girls to bring them coffee, and then he opened the hatch in the bar. Kate and Tristan followed him to a small garden-cum-yard which looked straight out onto a graveyard for the church opposite. It was cool in the shade, and they sat at an old picnic table.

Joel lit up a cigarette.

'What do you think the chances are... that it's Charlie?' he said, his voice dropping an octave and becoming hoarse. Kate saw how the grief and pain moved across his face over the loss of his son.

'We don't know. The police will need to do DNA tests,' said Kate.

'It didn't look like him? Because of all that time buried in the ground?'

Kate didn't know how to answer that. She shook her head.

'Have the police been in contact?' she said.

'Nope. I've only heard from you.' He flicked ash onto the ground. 'You know, I wanted to hire a private detective. I thought about it, but you guys charge the earth,' he said, sitting back and folding his arms. 'How can Jean afford to pay you?' His voice became hostile as he mentioned her name.

'Savings, I think,' said Kate.

There was a cool breeze in the courtyard, sheltered under the branches of the tall oak trees. The long grass shifted between the stones of the graveyard opposite. One of the young girls brought out three small coffee cups on a tray. Joel sat back, rubbing his face. The girl saw the tension, and after placing the cups in front of them, she hurried off.

'Savings... Saved from what is the question...' he muttered. 'Why did you decide to dig at that farm?'

Kate explained the link with the short story, Maureen Cook and the social worker, Anna.

'Did you ever have contact with Anna Treadwell?' asked Kate. Joel shook his head and lit up another cigarette.

'No. I can remember Jean and Becky bitching about her. But then again, there seemed to be a different woman every week who'd crossed them.'

'What do you mean?'

'They loved to bitch, and gossip, and tear people down. There was Jean's neighbour in the flat above her. Friends of Becky's who'd slighted her. My sister, mother, and the woman who worked in the shop down the road. And, of course, there was Declan. Jesus, Declan was always a hot topic. What had he done this time?' he said. 'My point is that someone had always pissed them off, and they never seemed to do anything about it. They never talked to the person who'd upset them. They'd just get caught up in this negative bitch-fest between themselves.'

'But Anna Treadwell was different. She was a social worker. Were you ever worried she would pursue a case to remove Charlie from your care?' asked Kate.

He shook his head.

'I think they rubbed her up the wrong way, and she took a bit of pleasure in making them sweat,' he said.

'Are you and Jean in contact?' asked Tristan. Joel looked at the glowing tip of his cigarette through exhausted eyes.

'We weren't, but I rang her. She's coming over.' Joel glanced at his watch. 'She should be here soon. The one thing about Jean, as much as we disliked each other, I know she loved Charlie, and Charlie loved her. That week when we went camping at Devil's Way, he was so excited to sleep in a tent with her.' He smiled at the memory. 'And kids can't fake liking people, not when they're that little... Jean would let him eat sweets before bed. That drove Becky mad. Becky always blamed Jean for all the fillings she had in her teeth. I used to think that Jean messed up so much in her life that she took looking after Charlie seriously.'

'Do you mind telling us what happened when Charlie went missing?' asked Tristan.

'We left Jean with Charlie at Devil's Way. I'd got a last-minute gig that day, and it was good money. It was twenty miles away on the outskirts of Newton Abbot. It was a pretty big festival on farmland overlooking the sea. Me and Becky got some food, watched a couple of the other bands, then I did my set at 3pm and came offstage half an hour later. We stayed for a few drinks after, much longer than I thought we would. But there were some promoters there, and I felt pressured to socialise with them, which could have led to more work... We set off back to Devil's Way at six, stopped to buy some food, and got back about seven-thirty.'

'Did Jean have a mobile phone? Was Becky in contact with her?' asked Kate. He nodded.

'Jean encouraged us to stay later. She said her and Charlie were having a whale of a time swimming and playing. When we got back, we made a fire and had a barbecue.'

'Did you know that Declan Connoly came to visit that night?'

He nodded.

'And I know that Jean tried to get rid of him. I wish she'd come and told me. I'd have stuck my boot up his backside and kicked him far away.'

'What time did Jean raise the alarm that Charlie was missing?'

'Don't you know all of this already?'

Kate smiled.

'Sorry. We're not trying to catch you out. It's just that sometimes, people can recount things that other people have forgotten.'

'Becky went to check on him at ten-fifteen. That's when she saw he was missing. Jean came back, and we started looking. I thought at first they were being over-dramatic, but as the time wore on, and we couldn't find him, it dawned on me that this was...' He took a deep breath. 'Serious. Then at four in the morning, we called the police.'

A woman came into the small garden with two young girls, who looked to be five or six. They were wearing pink shorts and T-shirts and carrying Barbie-branded swimming towels.

'Joel. We're off,' said the woman, hesitating.

'Come,' he said. The woman looked between Kate and Tristan. The two girls hung back at the door. 'This is my wife, Kelly, and that's Justine and Ruby,' he added. He stretched out his arms, and the two girls came to him, climbing up on his lap.

Kate and Tristan introduced themselves.

'It's nice to meet you,' said Kelly. She turned to Joel. 'Are you sure we should go to the lido?'

'Yeah. Keep things normal,' said Joel, planting a kiss on the cheek of each girl. He hugged them tightly, and they smiled but kept curious eyes on Kate and Tristan.

'You be good. And I'll see you later,' Joel said.

'Girls, you get in the car,' said Kelly, handing Ruby the car keys. They ran off, and Kelly waited until they were out of earshot.

'What's happening with the farm?' she asked.

'We don't know. Kate and Tristan have been telling me about their investigation. We still haven't heard anything.' He looked at his watch. 'Jean will be here in a minute,' he added to Kelly. She nodded.

'I don't want to be here for that. Call me as soon as you hear anything,' she said. 'It's very nice to meet you,' she added to Kate and Tristan.

'Has Kelly met Jean?' asked Kate.

'A few times, when we first got together, I tried to stay in contact with Jean, for Becky's sake... But Jean saw her as a threat. Myself and Becky broke up about four years after Charlie went missing. And I got together with Kelly a few months after that. It was a period of turmoil, as you can imagine. Becky was deep into drugs and booze.'

'What did you think about Jean applying to have Charlie declared deceased?' asked Kate.

Joel hesitated and then put his hand over his mouth. He gave a sob and closed his eyes.

'Sorry,' he said. He scrabbled for his cigarettes and lit another with a shaking hand. 'I never understood why Jean gave up on Charlie. I thought about petitioning for her to stop, but then Becky wanted to have a funeral, and I thought it might give her closure... It didn't. I think that's what sent her over the edge. I know this sounds terrible, but a part of me wants it to be him. This boy you found. I've given up on the idea that he's still alive. People who take kids that young take them for a reason and keep them alive... They keep them alive for a reason if you know what I mean.'

Kate nodded. Joel went on, 'If that little boy is Charlie, I can put him to rest.' He broke down.

Kate found a packet of tissues in her pocket and handed them to him. One of the young girls from behind the bar appeared in the doorway of the courtyard.

'Boss, there are some people here to see you,' she said. Then she saw Joel crying and vanished back inside.

45

Jean was waiting inside with Sadie Dexter, sitting in the corner of the empty bar. Jean was wearing a sleeveless, baggy floral print dress. Her skinny arms looked pasty, and she had a gold watch hanging off her wrist. Sadie was wearing an army print kaftan and peering at the screen of her phone with glasses perched on the end of her nose.

Joel entered the bar in front of Kate and Tristan, and there was an awkward moment as Jean looked up from where she was sitting. He hesitated. Kate thought he might tell Jean to leave, then he went to her, and they embraced.

'It's him, I know it's him, and they've found him,' Jean said, her voice muffled against Joel's shirt. He broke down entirely and sank down in the seat next to her. As Kate watched this, she felt sympathy for Jean's pain but was confused. In the past, Jean had applied for a death certificate because she thought Charlie was dead, and then she hired them as private detectives because she felt strongly that he was alive, but now she was convinced that the body was his. Kate shook off the thought. She was being unkind. She couldn't fathom the roller coaster of emotions Jean must be feeling.

Joel and Jean continued to hug, and Sadie squeezed out from behind the chair and came over to Kate and Tristan, pulling a chunk of the kaftan material from her arse crack.

'Maybe we should give them a minute,' she said, indicating the door. Kate and Tristan followed her into the sunshine outside the pub.

'How is she?' asked Tristan.

'Jean is a complete mess. Thank you for phoning her,' said Sadie. 'She would have found out from the news, which would have been bad. She's only just been discharged from The Lawns, and she's back at her flat, rattling around on her own.'

'Have the police been in touch with her yet?' asked Kate.

'Nope. Nothing. There was a family liaison officer who worked with Jean, a woman called Pat. I tried to call her this morning because Jean still had her number in her address book, but she's retired and gone to live in Spain. Did you think it was Charlie? When you found the body?'

'It was impossible to tell,' said Kate. Sadie pulled a face, which Kate thought was meant to signify horror, but with her vast thick-lensed glasses, she looked like she was gurning.

'You found it at that farm? So close to Devil's Way. You know, I remember seeing a news report from back then where they showed it all on the map, and I thought that farm. *That farm.* It was so close as the crow flies. Could it have been someone who took Charlie and then killed him and—' She stopped herself, clearly not wanting to continue. Her phone rang. 'Oh, this is Steve, checking in on what's happening. If you'll excuse me.' She answered the call and went off around the corner.

Kate was struggling to get the image of the small blanket

caked with mud out of her head. The pub door opened suddenly, and Jean came bursting out, a look of panic on her face.

'Where's Sadie?' she asked. She saw Sadie down the road talking on her mobile phone, and she waved at her to come back. Joel emerged from the door behind her, talking on his phone. 'I just had a call from the police, a Detective Chief Inspector Harris...' added Jean. She was trembling. 'He wants me and Joel to come to the police station in Exeter and give them a DNA sample. He said the body is that of a little boy, who they think was three years old when he died. They want to test our DNA to rule out if it's Charlie.'

Joel came off the phone.

'I can't get through to Kelly,' he said. He looked equally pale and shaken up. Sadie had now come back from her phone call and joined them.

'Sadie. We need to get over to Exeter,' said Jean. 'They want to take our DNA. How do they even do that?'

'They take a little blood,' said Sadie, her eyes huge and wide behind her glasses.

'Oh God. I'm going to be sick,' said Jean, gripping her friend's arm. 'What if it's him? How quickly will they know?'

They all looked to Kate. She thought about the wizened little bundle. If the body did belong to Charlie, it would have been in the ground for eleven years, and extracting DNA might take a little longer than drawing blood. Kate looked at their pale, scared faces.

'It might take a few days,' she said.

'Oh, it's him. I know it is... Do you think they'll ask us to look at the body? And see if we can identify it? I can't do that!' said Jean. Joel looked horrified at the thought of this.

'No. The police won't ask you to do that,' said Kate.

'Now just calm down, Jean,' said Sadie, taking her hand.

'We'll take it one step at a time. Steve is going to meet us at the police station.'

'Okay. I'll phone you and let you know what happens,' said Jean to Kate and Tristan. They all hurried to Sadie's ancient blue Montego. Joel helped Jean into the passenger seat, and he was hardly in the back seat and still closing the door when Sadie drove off with a squeal of rubber on the tarmac.

There was a sense of anti-climax as the car vanished around the corner. The police were now in charge.

'What should we do?' asked Tristan. Kate looked out at the sunny moorland view. What should they do?

'Let's try and contact Maureen Cook again, and I'd like us to talk to the guys at Abble Graphics. They are the ones who typeset and printed the anthology. It's the story and the link to Anna Treadwell we need to concentrate on.'

46

'Maureen Cook. There's an unpopular name,' said Alfie Abble of Abble Graphics.

He was a balding man with mischievous brown eyes. He looked to be in his early sixties and wore an elegant green suede three-piece suit, with a watch chain and a hanky poking from his top pocket. Abble Graphics was in a small shop at the top of Cranborough village high street. They sold antique cameras, cine cameras and photo equipment, and they also processed photos, one of the few places that still did. There was a display case next to the door which showed examples of printed photos on mugs, T-shirts, calendars and cushions, but clearly this was an afterthought.

'Why is Maureen Cook an unpopular name?' asked Kate. A younger, muscular man in a tight black T-shirt came out from the back room with a large camera tripod. He looked to be in his thirties, had strong, dark features and his head was shaved. He saw Kate and Tristan and smiled.

'Afternoon, I'm Ben,' he said. He put down the tripod and leaned over the counter to shake hands with them both.

'Ben,' said Alfie, turning to him with a smile. 'This lady and young man are private detectives.'

'I don't know if I've ever met a private detective before, let alone two.'

'They're here to ask about Maureen Cook,' he said, enunciating the name. Ben raised an eyebrow.

'Let me guess. Someone hired a hitman to kill her, and you're having trouble narrowing down the list?' he said. Then he saw Kate and Tristan's serious faces. 'Oh. That was a joke. Is she okay?'

'As far as we know, she's gone off on a cruise. Would it be possible to talk to you somewhere more private?' asked Kate.

'Yes, do come through into the workshop,' said Alfie. They followed him into a wood-panelled room. A large dining table was next to a bookshelf, with a white tablecloth and a vase of freesias. Ben indicated a large sofa, and Kate and Tristan sat.

'Where is Maureen cruising this time?' asked Ben.

'The Caribbean,' said Kate. Alfie nodded and smiled.

'I wonder if they know Hurricane Maureen is about to hit them?' he said.

'This might sound odd, but can we ask you about the Cranborough Writers group?'

'I've tried to blank it from my mind,' said Alfie, sitting in an armchair beside the sofa. Ben perched on one of the arms.

'Me too,' said Ben.

'We understand you were members?'

'Yes, for the eighteen months it was in existence. We actually started it and planned to use the village hall for meetings. After a clash with the cub scouts who needed the hall, Maureen Cook stepped up and co-opted it in her living room,' said Alfie.

'We've been to her house. It seems like quite a nice place for a meeting,' said Kate, goading them a little. Ben pulled a face.

'Maureen can sniff out a group or society at fifty paces,' said Alfie. 'She's never interested in the subject matter. She just gets a kick out of being in charge. I'm sure if someone formed a Satan Worshipping society, Maureen would be there, offering herself up as the treasurer and planning the refreshments.'

'What other groups has she been involved with?' asked Tristan.

'She attempted a book club the year before, and then she fell out with the other members when they accused her of not reading the books,' said Ben. Alfie smiled at the memory.

'Maureen's problem is that she's both stupid and so sure of herself. They were quite a young group, and their first book was *Jordan: Pushed to the Limit*. Maureen hadn't read it, but tried to busk it and started talking about Christians fleeing persecution from the Islamic State, not knowing that the book was one of Katie Price's autobiographies.'

Kate couldn't help but smile.

'Back to the writing group. How many members did you have?' she asked.

'What kind of case are you working on, if you don't mind me asking?' said Ben.

'We'll get to that. I promise.'

'There were seven of us in the group. Me and Alfie, Maureen, Anna, another two local women called Helen and Doris, and a widower called Mick.'

'And how did it work? Did you all write stuff and read it out?' asked Tristan.

'Yes, we'd read what we'd written at home and then critique it positively,' said Alfie. 'Maureen liked to contribute poems of the cat sat on the mat variety. And schmaltzy, very melodramatic short stories.'

'In what way?' asked Tristan.

'Very often about a woman going on a cruise and falling in love with the ship's captain. Maureen loves her cruise ship holidays. I don't know if she's ever scored at sea in real life.'

'Why did the writing group fall apart?' asked Kate.

'The idea came up to publish a charity anthology. Ben and I thought we could raise more for charity if we printed a "real" book, not just some clip art crap on a photocopier.'

'Or "photostat copier", as Maureen likes to call it,' said Ben. 'She's very proud of her photocopier. A lot of people in the village used to go to her to get things photocopied, and she used to charge them, of course. Now we also offer photocopying with print processing.'

'Okay, so you guys offered to print the anthology?' said Kate.

'Yes, and a clash of opinion occurred, so we decided to vote on it,' said Alfie. 'Maureen loved to have a vote. She'd often call one if things weren't going her way. Anna, a woman who used to come to meetings, was often Maureen's deciding vote, but she wasn't there this particular week. Maureen lost the vote, and that led to the group splitting.'

'So. Maureen lost the vote, and the writing group collapsed. What happened next?' asked Tristan.

A look passed between Alfie and Ben.

'Maureen was furious with Anna for not turning up and helping her win the vote. And at the time, we thought she couldn't be bothered to turn up when in actual fact...' Ben hesitated.

'Anna was murdered in her own bed,' said Alfie. He shook his head. 'She lay there for almost two weeks. The second meeting she missed was where it all kicked off with the vote, so whilst we were bickering about who would print the anthology, poor Anna was lying dead. We only heard about it a week later when it was on the news.'

'What happened to the group?' asked Kate.

'Well. This goes to show what a nasty cow Maureen can be. We wanted to all come together and release the anthology for a charity for women. We chose a women's shelter because Anna was a victim of violence. But Maureen was still making problems and insisting that she print it.'

'How did you resolve it?' asked Tristan.

'A few months later was Anna's funeral, and we all attended. I say all – there was only us from the writers group and a few of her friends from work who showed up,' said Alfie.

'And it was at this point that Maureen completely changed her tune,' said Ben. 'She came to us and said that she had a story she wanted to include in the anthology. Inspiration had come to her during a cruise on the Danube, and she said that she was perfectly happy for us to include it in the anthology, as long as it was a "proper" book that could be sold in shops. And that became our anthology, *The Seven*.'

'And was it sold in shops?' asked Tristan.

'We published it back in spring 2008, which involved printing a load of books, and we managed to sell them to local independent bookshops... But it wasn't the success we'd hoped.'

'But the book is on Amazon as an ebook and paperback?' said Kate.

'A couple of years ago, it became easier to self-publish, and we uploaded the book. Have you read the stories?'

'Yes,' said Kate.

'Ben contributed the seventh story, about the man from space,' said Alfie. 'And mine was about the farmer whose land is falling into the sea.'

'Yes. And they were very good,' said Tristan.

'I agree,' said Kate, struggling to remember their stories

amongst the others she'd flicked through. 'So, about Maureen's story...'

Alfie sat back and looked at them.

'What does this have to do with the case you're investigating? Is it something to do with Anna's death?'

'Yes,' said Kate. 'So was Maureen's story different to the kind of stuff she usually contributed to the group?'

'Yes, we were all shocked when she produced this dark story about a woman who accidentally kills her baby and then buries the body in the woods.'

'Did you think she wrote it?' asked Tristan. The guys exchanged a glance.

'I don't want to belittle anyone's lived experience, as they say these days,' said Alfie, 'and even if this happened to Maureen, I doubt she has the writing chops to articulate it in the way she did. So no.'

'Did anyone confront Maureen about it?' asked Tristan.

'No. Everyone is quite scared of her,' said Ben. 'And it was a charity anthology.'

'Oh, come on!' said Alfie.

'Maureen intimidates people.'

'She might intimidate you, but not me. Always stand up to bullies. That's my motto.'

'If Maureen didn't write that story, then who do you think did?' asked Kate.

'I used to joke that Anna wrote it, and Maureen bumped her off to claim it as her own,' said Alfie. He caught the look that passed between Kate and Tristan, and added, nervously. 'But of course, I'm joking.'

47

Kate and Tristan were just getting into his car when her phone rang.

'It's Bernard Crenshaw,' said Kate. She put it on speakerphone.

'Hi, Kate. I'm sorry about the delay getting back to you,' he said.

'No problem,' said Kate. Tristan raised an eyebrow.

'Listen, I have to make this quick. My contact at Exeter police station came through. You can access the Anna Treadwell murder scene evidence. It's housed in our cold case storage, a building on the other side of Exeter. Can you be there at 3pm?'

Kate checked her watch. It was 2pm, and they were now feeling pretty ragged after a night of no sleep. She looked over to Tristan and he nodded. They had an hour, which wasn't a lot of time.

'Yes, we can be there,' she said.

'Good. If they offer you the opportunity to copy any data, I'd take a brand-new unboxed data drive or USB cable with you.'

Bernard gave her the address and contact details, and then Kate hung up the phone.

'Do you think he knows about the body we found?' said Tristan.

'Why would he? The police haven't found a link between Anna Treadwell and the body buried on Danvers Farm. If it's positively identified as Charlie, that could change things.'

'What did you think about the guys back there, what they said about Maureen?'

'I don't know. What we still need to solve is how Maureen came by, or wrote, the short story that told us where to dig,' said Kate. Tristan started the engine, and they set off for Exeter.

———

They arrived at the address on time. The Cold Case Evidence Unit was a plain-looking building on a back street. Kate and Tristan waited in the small reception for twenty minutes before a plain clothes police officer came to get them. The name on her ID was Detective Inspector Paula Simpson. She looked older than Kate and had a don't-mess-with-me demeanour. Kate and Tristan had to show their ID and sign several forms, and after being issued passes, Paula led them through a long corridor lined with offices.

It felt odd for Kate to be back inside a police building. There were all the familiar smells: coffee, floor polish and sweat, and she missed the hustle and bustle and the stress. As they passed a busy office and saw all of the officers working at their computers, she realised she missed the access to records she'd had as a police officer.

Kate pushed the thought away, and they followed the officer through a fire exit and into a concrete staircase which went down into the basement. They came up to a grille door at the end of another long corridor. Paula scanned an ID card, and they were buzzed through into a vast warehouse lined with shelves. There was a desk at the front where they had to show their ID again to a thin greying man in a police uniform and sign in. Paula didn't introduce them.

She took a folder from the man and opened it, running her finger down a list. She put it under her arm and picked up a large plastic tray, like the type you see in airport security.

'Right. If you can follow me.' They moved along the rows and rows of metal shelving, all filled with plastic evidence bags containing knives and other sharp objects. On another shelf they passed were scores of laptop computers and bundles of clothes, all wrapped in thick plastic. A blown glass paperweight caked in dry blood caught Tristan's attention as he passed, and he looked back at Kate with wide eyes.

Paula reached a row of shelving at the end. She checked the serial numbers on the side of three bags and loaded them into the plastic tray.

They followed her to a large metal table at the back of the store room and she placed the tray down.

'Gloves are here,' she said, pointing to a box. 'Wear them when handling evidence. You have thirty minutes.'

'Are you staying with us?' asked Tristan.

'I am,' she said. She stood back and folded her arms.

'Let's get on with it then,' said Kate. They pulled on a pair of gloves each and turned their attention to the contents of the tray. Inside were three thick plastic bags. One contained a bloodied claw hammer, and the bag was tagged with the date and location. Kate picked it up and saw some silvery fingerprint dust on the wooden handle of the hammer.

'Can you tell us if you managed to pull a fingerprint off this?' asked Kate, turning the hammer over in the bag.

Paula came over, peered at it, and then took the file out from under her arm.

'I can check the file,' she said. She went to a nearby computer on the wall. This was the HOLMES computer system, the UK police's central database, holding all criminal records and case files. There was something about the setup with the shelves and the computer for scanning barcodes which reminded Kate of those terminals where you can check the price of bananas per kilo.

Paula keyed in the number, waited a moment and then the case details appeared on the screen.

'Yes. Forensics was able to get a full thumbprint off that hammer handle. It's never been identified, though. Nothing is matching in the system for that print.'

'Thank you,' said Kate. She thought back to the crime scene photos showing the trail of blood spatter and bloodied footprints leading from Anna's body to the window and back out of her bedroom. And how the images where the sets of footprints had been marked up and numbered to show their route were marked as coming in and leaving.

She held the hammer and imagined how Anna's killer or killers had felt. They took the hammer with them but then dropped it in the garden for the police to find. And whoever did it didn't wear gloves. Why? Was it planned or a crime of passion?

The second bag Tristan picked up held the diary that Kate recognised from the crime scene photos from Anna's bedroom. It was thick with lots of additional paperwork stuffed inside and bound by a faded elastic band that bit into the edges of the black plastic cover. The year 2007 was embossed in gold on the front.

'Can we make copies on a photocopier?' asked Kate, looking over at Paula.

'Very funny.' She checked her watch. 'You should get moving. You've already used up five minutes,' she said.

Tristan's eyes were wide, and Kate could see he was starting to panic. There seemed to be so many papers stuffed inside the diary. Kate also saw a smaller plastic bag at the bottom of the tray, which contained a blue NOKIA mobile phone, one of the old ones with no internet or email access.

'Can we have a copy of the data from this phone?' Kate asked.

'Did you bring a USB key?' said Paula.

'Yes,' said Kate, indicating the new USB key they'd grabbed from a newsagent on their way. She'd kept it in the packaging as requested.

'If you give it to me, I can get the desk officer to copy the contents of the phone onto your USB,' she said. She pulled on latex gloves and took the bag with the phone and the USB key. She went to a phone on the wall and made a call.

'Come on, we don't have much time,' said Tristan. He took out his phone and opened the photo app. Kate's hands were shaking as she gently slid the diary out of the evidence bag.

Kate carefully removed the elastic band, trying to avoid ripping the pages. She moved the plastic tray to one side and put the diary on the metal surface. There were faded spots of blood on the pages at the side and one on the cover.

Checking the time and seeing they now had eighteen minutes, Kate opened the diary to the first page. Written in a sloping hand, in blue ink was:

If found, please return this diary to Anna Treadwell, 4 Kirby Cane Walk, Taunton, TN1 3ER. It was odd to see her neat mundane writing, and a splash of blood was on the edge of the page. Kate imagined her sitting down at a table and writing this out. Did she ever imagine it would be spattered with her blood?

Tristan took a photo of the first page, and Kate flipped it over. The first week of January was blank, apart from a couple of scribbled times "Manager's Meeting 10.30am" on January 4th and "Caseload Meeting 3.45pm" on January 6th. Tristan flipped his camera around and took a landscape shot of the double page. Kate carried on flipping the pages. It was disappointing stuff, endless times of meetings.

Kate stopped pausing to look at the pages and started to flip them so Tristan could take the photos. There was nothing of interest as they moved through February, March and April. In May, there were some details about the writing group meeting at Maureen's house. Maureen's address was written down, but the pages until Anna was killed were empty. Two weeks before her death, there was a note about a security company coming to install the alarms and lights at her house.

Kate checked her watch and saw that they had seven minutes left. The rest of the papers in the diary were work print-outs about fire safety and a charity fun run.

Then Kate saw the man from the front desk hurrying down the shelving aisle, holding up a clear plastic bag.

'Paula, there's one more from that case file.' He handed her the bag. She came over with a slim package containing a blue school exercise book. The little lined window on the front was blank with no writing.

'Can we get extra time?' asked Kate as she took the plastic bag.

''Fraid not,' said Paula. 'You have five minutes left.'

'Quick, open it, and I'll take as many pictures as possible,' said Tristan.

Kate got it out of the bag and opened the first page. She saw with a leap of her heart that this was a personal diary, written in a neat hand in black ink. There wasn't time to read the contents, and they whipped through with Tristan taking landscape photos of the double pages. It was a sixty-page lined notebook, and they just ran out of time as Tristan took the last image.

48

The weather had turned, and a storm was brewing on the horizon as Tristan drove them back to the office.

'How are you feeling?' she asked.

'Need coffee,' he said with a smile. Kate had Tristan's phone, and she was zooming in and out of the photos he'd taken of the diary pages, trying to read them, but the writing was small and neat.

'The diary seems to jump around over a few months,' said Kate reading snippets. 'We need to print these out because my eyes can't cope with the zooming and the tiny screen.'

'Is there anything in there about the writing group or Maureen Cook?' asked Tristan.

'No.'

When they were parking outside the office, the wind roared through the trees and blew sand off the dunes into their faces. There were only a few people left on the beach who were hurriedly packing up to leave.

Just as they got inside the office, the heavens opened, and it began pouring rain. It rattled on the roof as they set to work;

Kate printed off the images Tristan had taken using his phone, and Tristan set to work downloading the data from Anna's phone from the USB key.

The first set of images came from the diary, and the other sheets of paper stuffed inside.

'How are you getting on with the NOKIA data?' she asked.

'Each text message chain is saved as a different file, and there are a few low-resolution pictures,' said Tristan, moving his finger lightning fast over the laptop trackpad.

Kate took the hot pages with the diary and the blue exercise book entries out of the printer tray and brought them to the desk. Tristan started to print the data from the NOKIA.

As Kate saw in the evidence store, Anna's diary pages mainly contained practical information about work meetings. There were also several work documents stuffed into the diary, which made up the bulk of the additional paperwork; printed guidelines of what to do during a social work visit. There were copies of a form to have a father of three boys referred to the mental health services, but the name was left off. This was the only piece of paper related to Anna's social work.

'I suppose she would have written official reports and kept a lot of stuff on her computer files at work and email,' said Kate.

Tristan had joined her and taken half of the printed paper, and he started to go through everything with her.

Then Kate found a sheet of paper with a poster image about a charity fun run organised by Exeter Council. It had been due to be held on August 14th 2007. The following printout was the reverse side of the poster, which was scribbled over with hurriedly made notes. The bottom of the photocopied version had a black stain. The original had been soaked in blood, cutting off the bottom details about the fun run. Kate looked at the writing and froze. At the top was written:

DANVERS FARM, South Zeal.

Underneath was a bullet point list with writing in a scruffy hand.

- diagnosis of bipolar disorder

- Child always seemed happy/thriving. (Visited 14.6 as part of routine follow-up. No one was in and left a note asking to call me for routine follow-up, but no call was made to my phone, which caused concern).

- Visited again. 23.6 Rang the bell, no answer, then I saw mother through the side window of the house hiding. She reluctantly came to the door. I said I needed to see the mother and child for a follow-up appointment due to the husband's concerns on 1.6 about her. She let me in but wouldn't let me see the boy, who was poorly in bed and half asleep.

- Demanded to see him. The child's head was shaved. A drastic change in appearance. Weight loss?

- They are a strict Christian family, but behaviours have changed since the husband's alleged affair. Husband flagged concern about pagan influence.

Anna had underlined a lot of this in black, and the writing seemed more frantic as it moved down the page. And then, at the bottom of the paper was written:

Is father well? Spoke of diabetes due to poor diet

Is the mother's dia

Does David have p

The bloodstain bloomed on the edge of the paper, cutting off the rest of what she had written.

'What is that written at the bottom?' said Kate. It was now dingy in the office, the sky outside was black and rain was hammering against the windows. When she got up to turn on the light, she could barely see down to the sea, the beach was such a blur of grey. She held the piece of paper up to the light, to try and see what was written under the bloodstain, and then saw it was a photocopy.

'What is that? *Is the mother's diabetic?* That doesn't make sense. It's not, *does mother have diabetes*? And what's *Does David have p*? What can "p" mean?'

'Oh my God,' said Tristan, reading through the pages they'd photographed from the blue exercise book. 'Look.'

Kate could see, written in neat black ink, the text from Maureen's short story published in the anthology:

My little boy had been scared in the house. I knew it. His bed is in the back room, further from where we sleep than I would like, but the mould is so bad in the room next to ours. And in the summer months, the walls run with condensation and the moment I try and scrub the black mould away, it comes back. The spores lie in wait for when my back is turned and bloom through the plaster and wallpaper.
So I put him in the other room to save his little lungs.

'We need to be absolutely sure,' said Kate. She went to her bag and found her Kindle. She pulled up the short story and put the two side by side.

The text in the short story was the same word for word to that which was written in the blue exercise book.

'Look. The handwriting in the blue exercise book is different from the handwriting in Anna's work diary,' said Tristan.

Kate looked back at the piece of paper from Anna's work diary, where the blood stain had covered some of the writing. The handwriting was slightly different.

She looked at the second line of Anna's handwriting:

Is father well? Spoke of diabetes due to poor diet

Is the mother's dia

Does David have p

'Let's leave the blue exercise book to one side for a moment. What if the first line and the second line of this aren't related?' said Kate. 'And if Anna's not writing about the mother's "diabetes", what if the rest of that word is "diary"? *"Is the mother's diary".*

'Is the mother's diary... Is the mother's diary what?' asked Tristan.

Kate looked back at it all.

'What if Anna read what was written in the blue exercise book, which is like a personal diary, and she saw the part about the woman burying the child. Anna could have been writing on the paper, "Is the mother's diary real? Meaning, is what she wrote in the blue exercise book real?"' said Kate.

'But who is the mother? The woman who used to live at Danvers Farm?' said Tristan. Kate stared at him.

'Libby Hartley, she was the previous tenant of Danvers Farm. She has a son called David with her husband, Steve. So that third line of writing, "Does David have p", that could be referencing Libby's son, David.'

'What could 'p' mean?' asked Tristan. Kate looked at it for a moment longer and she felt a shiver go down her spine.

'I don't know. We need to share this information with the police,' she said.

49

Maureen Cook had spent the night in her favourite bed and breakfast and then a pleasant day shopping for clothes in an elegant boutique for ladies of a certain age. She'd found a stylish blue pleated skirt to wear with her white jacket with the blue piping and an anchor embroidered on the lapels. It was the *perfect* outfit for boarding the ship. Nautical and very nice.

At five o'clock that evening, the passengers were due to board the *Duchess of the Ocean* at Southampton. Maureen arrived in a taxi with plenty of time to spare. The ship seemed enormous, and as she climbed out of the car, she stood on the dock and took it all in. The tourists lining up to enter the departures terminal, a flock of seagulls cawed loudly above the shouts of men unloading trucks. A horn blasted, shaking the ground underfoot, and Maureen could smell the sea mixed in with the diesel fumes, and it always smelt like freedom.

She turned to look at the large blue sign high up on the wall behind her, where white letters read:

WELCOME TO THE
PORT OF SOUTHAMPTON
GATEWAY TO THE WORLD

'Can you close the door!' shouted a voice behind her. She turned and saw the taxi driver scowling at her. He could not dent her happy mood today, and she thanked him, shut the passenger door and walked towards the terminal. Maureen liked to step onto the ship unencumbered with luggage. Her suitcases had been sent ahead a few hours before, so she could walk the executive gangplank carrying her new white tote handbag with an anchor monogram that almost matched the ones on her jacket lapels.

Maureen took out her ticket and passport, smiled at the young woman welcoming the stream of passengers, and stepped in line behind an older couple. The terminal wasn't too congested, and she was proud and pleased to avoid the riff-raff and take the priority lane for exclusive Diamond Club members, emerging back into the open quayside in just a few minutes.

Maureen stopped for a moment to look up at the enormous curved bow of the cruise ship where DUCHESS OF THE OCEAN was written in elegant script. Two vast ropes strained as they kept the boat tethered to the colossal jetty. Using her ticket and passport to shield her eyes against the bright sunshine, Maureen tried to find the window of her executive en suite portside cabin with a small balcony. She always liked to imagine that she was following in the footsteps of many intrepid travellers when she boarded. This time around, she'd sent an email to the cruise company to ask if the *Duchess of the Ocean* would be docking in the same place as the *Titanic* had for her maiden voyage, but she hadn't heard anything back from them.

Maureen joined the line of passengers on the wide executive gangplank, which had a red velvet carpet trimmed with gold braiding. The crowds slowed, and Maureen noticed they were rechecking people's passports and tickets. She saw two handsome stewards flanked by a man and a woman in uniform, watching the people boarding.

Maureen reached the entrance to the boat and handed her passport to the smoulderingly handsome sailor. She could see inside the welcome area where the other passengers were enjoying complimentary glass flutes of Asti Spumante from silver trays.

She looked back at the sailor and saw he was still checking her passport.

'Is there a problem?' she asked. 'I have been a Diamond Club member for many years.' He handed her passport and ticket to the portly man. Maureen thought he was dressed rather scruffily for greeting passengers on such a prestigious vessel.

'Mrs Maureen Cook?' he said, looking up from her passport under craggy hooded eyes. She noticed his shirt wasn't correctly tucked in at the back and was bunched above his belt.

'Yes?'

'I need you to come with me,' he said, indicating a roped-off area next to the gangplank. The stern woman with him wore a plain black trouser suit, and she unclipped a section of the rope.

'May I ask why? I've already been through security and the metal detectors,' said Maureen.

He indicated the roped-off area. The passengers boarding behind her were backing up on the executive gangplank. The stewards with the silver trays of complimentary drinks were so tantalisingly close. Maureen glanced behind her. Everyone seemed to be watching. She turned back to the man.

ROBERT BRYNDZA

'Do you work for Empress Cruises?' she asked, irritated that he was ruining her *Titanic* moment. 'I am a Diamond Club member.'

The man rummaged in the back pocket of his trousers and pulled out an ID card.

'I'm Detective Chief Inspector Gareth Morrison. I'd like to talk to you in relation to a murder enquiry.'

His voice suddenly seemed very loud on the crowded gangplank. Maureen moved closer to him.

'*Please,* keep your voice down.'

'This concerns a body found at Danvers Farm in South Zeal. We believe you might have information that could help with our enquiries,' he said.

'A body? What could I possibly know about that?'

'We'd like you to come in voluntarily to talk to us.'

'This is ridiculous!' said Maureen, raising her voice. 'I'll say again that I am a Diamond Club member, and I don't expect to be ambushed on the executive gangplank when the ship is about to sail!'

'I'm afraid you won't be leaving tonight,' said the man.

'Step aside,' said Maureen, enraged at the embarrassment this man was causing her. The woman standing beside him came close and put her hand on Maureen's arm.

'Don't you dare touch me!' shouted Maureen, pulling her arm away. The woman held on, and what happened next was fast and horrifying. Maureen found herself lying flat on the executive gangplank with her hands cuffed behind her back.

The crowds were now moving and being welcomed onto the ship. All faces were turned towards her, watching with curiosity and disdain as Maureen was pulled up and marched back down the executive gangplank towards a waiting police car.

As DCI Morrison put his hand on top of her head and loaded her into the car's back seat, Maureen saw that the lights had been activated, and they were flashing bright blue across the hull of the *Duchess of the Ocean*.

50

Kate and Tristan had reported what they found in the cold case evidence store, and they had sent Detective Chief Inspector Harris the scans they'd taken of Anna Treadwell's 2007 work diary, and the written pages from the blue exercise book. Kate didn't expect to hear back from the police so quickly. Early the next morning, after finally getting a good night's sleep, she received a message from Harris, asking her and Tristan to come to Exeter police station.

When they arrived they were signed in at the front desk, and Harris took them to the Custody Suite. Kate could see that Tristan was nervous and she felt the same, worried that they were in some kind of trouble. However, Harris quickly explained that he'd asked them to attend as observers.

'I wanted you to come in and be part of this process, in light of the discoveries you've made,' he said. Kate thought how weary he looked. 'Late yesterday afternoon we arrested Maureen Cook.'

'Arrested her?' repeated Kate.

'For what? For stealing a short story? Or should I say, handwritten personal diary entries?' said Tristan. Harris now had the blue exercise book from the evidence store in his hand. He explained what had happened at Southampton.

'She elbowed a police officer in the face, so they arrested her for assault. She's been in a cell here overnight. I wanted you both to observe the interview,' he said.

'In the interview room?' asked Tristan. Harris smiled.

'No. Via the video suite, it's just here,' he said. He led Kate and Tristan into a long room with video screens on the wall and a row of chairs. Three police officers were working at keyboards on the bench in front of the screens. The first two screens had views of the interview room where a somewhat dishevelled Maureen Cook was sitting at a table wearing a grubby white jacket. The screen next to it showed the opposite view of the room where a smart woman in her fifties with ash-blonde hair had just entered carrying a briefcase.

'You are my solicitor?' they heard Maureen say through a speaker broadcasting the sound feed from the room.

'Yes, I'm Beatrice Weaver. I've been assigned as your legal representative,' said the woman.

'Can they hear us?' Tristan whispered.

'No. You can both sit down here,' said a police officer. The door closed behind them. He indicated a couple of chairs, and they sat. On the screen a moment later, Harris entered the room with another police officer and sat opposite Maureen and Beatrice.

'Good morning,' said Harris.

'Is it? I just spent a night in a police cell! It's outrageous!' Maureen said, leaning forward and jabbing her finger on the desk. 'I didn't get a wink of sleep. I was forced to lie on a disgusting plastic mattress, with all kinds of crude graffiti scrawled on the wall above. I didn't have a blanket or a pillow, and there was no...' At this point she lowered her voice. 'There was no lavatory paper.' Harris ignored her, looked up at the camera, and said his name. The police officer with him gave her name as Detective Hailey Cusworth.

'The time is 9.30am on the 28th of June 2018. Present with us is Beatrice Weaver,' said Harris. Maureen watched as they took out their folders and pens.

'Are you lot listening to me? I was arrested whilst boarding a luxury cruise. I'm a Diamond Club member. I paid a great deal of money for my ticket, and the cruise departed without me. And all I did was refuse to answer a series of ridiculous questions. The last time I checked, that wasn't illegal,' said Maureen.

'You were arrested for assaulting a police officer,' said Harris, taking the lid off his pen and looking at her.

'I resisted your officer, who placed her hands on me. That is not assault. I note that I haven't been charged. What are you going to charge me with?' she said. Kate thought how unbalanced she looked with her red hair on end and her fake tan.

'You've been cautioned. And what happens next depends on how you answer my questions here and now,' said Harris. He opened a folder in front of him, took out a print copy of *The Seven* anthology, and opened it to the first pages. He placed it in front of Maureen.

'Is this your short story?' he asked.

'What?'

'Is this, your short story?' he said, speaking slowly.

'Should I answer that, solicitor lady?' said Maureen.

'Is your short story published in this anthology?' asked Beatrice.

'Yes, it is,' said Maureen, folding her arms and sitting back in her chair. 'Yes, it is,' she repeated childishly, looking up at the cameras.

'And what inspired you to write this?' asked Harris. Maureen laughed.

'This is a question that all writers get asked: where do you get your ideas from? The origins of ideas are difficult to quantify.'

'So, you are a writer? We were under the impression that you didn't have that much talent in the writing department,' said Harris.

'And *who* told you that?' she replied, grandly, her nostrils flaring. Harris watched her for a moment. He leant forward.

'This is my problem, Maureen.'

'I prefer Mrs Cook.'

Harris nodded.

'This is my problem, Mrs Cook. I have an unsolved murder. The body of a young boy was discovered buried in a shallow grave at Danvers Farm in South Zeal. The two private detectives who found the young boy were led to the exact spot where the body was buried, from this short story you wrote.'

A little of the colour drained from Maureen's orange face. She looked between Harris, Hailey and her solicitor.

'How? That's a story. Fiction,' she said.

'Is it?'

Harris took out the handwritten pages from the blue exercise book, containing the text from the printed short story, and placed them in front of Maureen.

'What's this?' she said, peering at it.

'These pages are from a blue exercise book which was found at the Anna Treadwell murder scene, in her bedroom,' said Harris. 'You can see the short story in *The Seven* anthology is identical.'

'This is what you want to talk to me about?' she said, sitting back, her voice subdued.

'Very much so. We would have been happy for you to talk to us informally, but you made quite a scene at Southampton Harbour.'

'I did not assault your officer—'

Harris put his hand up.

'Mrs Cook. This is very simple, either you start telling us what's happening here, or I will charge you with assaulting a police officer and obstructing a murder investigation. If you decide not to talk, I'll make sure that you are denied bail, and you will miss your cruise, and quite possibly Christmas, too, judging how long your case will take to trial. Now. That doesn't have to happen if you just tell us about this short story.'

Maureen took a deep breath and wiped a tear from her eye with a shaking hand.

'What does this short story have to do with the murder of a small boy?' she said.

'I need to ask you first if you took the contents from this blue exercise book, and passed them off as your own short story?'

Maureen was silent for a long beat.

'Speaking broadly and hypothetically,' she said, eyeing one of the cameras, 'is plagiarism illegal in the United Kingdom?'

There was a pause.

'Ooh, now that's a good question,' said the police officer sitting next to Kate in the viewing room.

'Is it illegal?' asked Tristan. Kate looked back to the screen.

'Plagiarism is illegal only if it infringes the copyright or some other law,' said Kate, and as they watched the screen, Harris repeated the same words, adding, 'Even infringement may be lawful if it amounts to fair use or fair dealing.'

Maureen nodded.

'And can I just add that UK law provides little certainty on the subject of "fairness",' said Beatrice.

There was another long silence. Maureen looked between the three of them sitting opposite her. Harris sighed and opened another folder. He took out a photo and held it up to the camera.

'This is a mortuary photo of the victim found at Danvers Farm, yesterday.' He slid it across the table to Maureen. She closed her eyes against it.

'Did you bury this body?' Harris added.

Maureen's eyes opened with a look of alarm.

'What? No! Of course not.'

'Then can you explain your involvement in this this short story that details the place he was buried?'

'Please, take the photo away,' said Maureen. Harris moved it, and she opened her eyes.

'Are you telling me that this *story* is real?'

'We don't believe this is Anna Treadwell's writing,' said Harris, indicating the blue exercise book.

'Then whose is it?' Maureen looked genuinely shocked and horrified. 'I never imagined that the woodland in the story was a real place... Anna Treadwell was part of my writers group, and one day she arrived late. We had the meeting, and then afterwards, everyone left. I was tidying up before bed when I found her bag behind the chair she'd been sitting in. It was a sort of satchel. It wasn't her handbag, it was another bag she carried, and it had paperwork inside. Files about children whose parents were bad. And then there was this blue exercise book.'

'What did you do with the bag?' asked Harris.

'I photocopied the contents. All of it.'

'Why?'

Maureen shrugged, now tearful.

'I don't know. I had a phone call from Anna later that night. She asked if she'd left her bag, and I said yes, she had. It was very late, and she asked if she could pick it up first thing in the morning. So, I copied it all. And then the next day she came to collect it.'

'What did you do with the photocopies?' asked Harris.

'Nothing at first. I just kept it all and read it. It was quite eye-opening stuff, some of it. The poor children who were in bad homes. And what Anna was doing to try and get them out and into foster care.'

'Can you remember any of the children's or parent's names?' asked Harris.

'Offhand, no. But I remember the exercise book. And the short story. I was captivated by the writing. But... I thought it was Anna's work for our creative writing class!' Maureen put her hand to her mouth at the realisation. 'She'd never shared anything much with us before. Nothing about her private life. That was the last time I saw her. She missed the next meeting. And then she was found dead.'

Maureen's eyes were wide.

'The anthology came about quite a while after Anna had died. There wasn't a funeral for several months because they couldn't release her body. Her neighbour told us she was a real loner, with no family, no real friends, so I stepped up and helped organise the flowers and the order of service. Time passed, and then a few group members wanted to produce an anthology and give the proceeds to a women's shelter.'

'And what did you do next?' asked Harris. Maureen shifted uncomfortably in her chair.

'I, er... I submitted the extract from Anna's creative writing, or what I thought was her creative writing, as a short story.'

'Why?'

Maureen bit her lip and lowered her head, concentrating on the table.

'I overheard some of the other members talking about how I

didn't have any talent in the writing area.' She looked up. 'I thought that I'd show them. It was Anna's work, and she was gone. I never really stole it. I photocopied the contents and I gave her back the original the next day... I didn't mean to hurt anyone.' There was another long silence. Maureen leant forward and picked up the blue exercise book which was inside a large plastic evidence bag.

'Poor Anna. What happened to her? Do you know who killed her?'

'No, we don't,' said Harris.

'If Anna didn't write this, then who did?'

'We believe it was written by Libby Hartley, who was the tenant of Danvers Farm at the time.'

Maureen seemed to put this all together and she closed her eyes.

'Dear god,' she said, quietly.

51

Detective Chief Inspector Harris came out of the interview suite and met with Kate and Tristan in the corridor.

'What's going to happen to Maureen?' asked Tristan.

Harris shook his head and rubbed his eyes.

'We need a statement from her, and I think she'll be cautioned. I don't think she knew about the true origin of the short story.'

'We saw the shock on her face when you told her who you think wrote those entries in the blue exercise book.'

'What's happening with Libby and Steve Hartley?' asked Kate, feeling the tension from the interview with Maureen.

'A couple of hours ago I sent a police officer to talk to them – they now have a farm in Shropshire on the Welsh borders.'

'Yes. We know. The farm has a page on Facebook, their son David is now a teenager, and they also have a daughter called Daisy. It all looks very idyllic,' said Kate.

'Idyllic or not, I need to talk to them,' said Harris. A young man in a blue suit came running down the corridor.

'Guv, I've got a PC Collins on the line from Shropshire

Constabulary. They turned up at Hill Brook Farm, which is where Steve and Libby Hartley live with their kids. There was only a neighbour there, and he says that the family just decided to go on holiday.'

'But it's still school term time. Shit,' he said. He hurried off down the corridor.

'Come on,' said Kate to Tristan, and they followed them into an office. A busy incident room had already been set up with photos of Danvers Farm and the crime scene on the wall. Harris was standing at a desk by a bank of photocopiers, talking heatedly into the phone.

'Does this neighbour know what time they left?' he said. The other officers in the room were watching along with Kate and Tristan. 'Does the neighbour know which airport they're leaving from?' Harris listened and then mouthed *fuck*. 'Okay. And the two kids are definitely with them? David and Daisy. Okay. Thanks.'

Harris went over to a giant map of the UK pinned up in the corner of the incident room.

'The neighbour says Steve and Libby Hartley left very early this morning and they've taken the kids with them. They're headed for Spain, but the neighbour doesn't know which airport.'

'They'll have either gone to Birmingham or Bristol airport,' said Kate, looking at the map.

'Agreed,' said Harris. 'My money is on Birmingham if they plan to leave the country. There are more international flights. Put out an alert to the Civil Aviation Authority. Hop to it, everyone.'

Terminal 2 at Birmingham Airport was packed with people and felt sweaty. Ten-year-old Daisy Hartley came out of the busy toilets wiping her wet hands on the back of her denim shorts. She scanned the bustling departure lounge, looking for her brother, David. All of the seats in the departure lounge were taken, and she saw him crouched on the ground in a corner playing on his phone. She sighed and walked over to him.

'Mum and Dad told you to wait for me outside the loos,' she said. David looked up at her from under his baseball cap. The thick fuzz on his face had grown darker in the past few weeks. He rolled his eyes.

'Dais You can't wait outside the toilets. It's a communal entrance crowded with people,' he said. He scowled and turned his attention back to his phone. David had recently turned thirteen, and his birthday present had been a mobile phone. Daisy was three years younger, and she'd been told she'd also have to wait until she was thirteen before she got her own. She crossed her arms and looked around. Every seat and piece of floor space around the walls and windows looking out on the runway were taken. There was nowhere to sit, and their parents were acting weird.

Well, her mum Libby always had a capacity for weirdness which was kept in check by the pills she took, but now her dad, Steve, who was usually the grounded one, was also acting odd. They'd suddenly decided that they were going to go on holiday to Spain. Like, literally overnight. She was supposed to be in school, and tonight she'd arranged to go to the cinema with her friends. Dad told them they'd decided to go at the last minute because that's where the best deals could be had... But he was usually very excited when he landed a bargain. Instead, their parents were acting shifty and scared. Like they were running from something.

Daisy felt she was in the way, and the departures hall was getting busier.

'David. Can you shift up so I can sit down?' she asked. He sighed and scooted along a little, leaving a small space for her and she squeezed in between his shoulder and the wall. The floor felt cool. 'Do you know where we're going?'

'What?' asked David. He was in the middle of a computer game on his phone, which involved driving through a ghetto in a Cadillac.

'Do you know where we're going in Spain?'

'Malaga,' he said, pointing up at the departures board without looking away from his phone screen.

'Are we staying in a hotel or a B&B?' He shrugged.

'Mum and Dad are being weird, aren't they?' she added, scanning the shops to see where they were. She saw their dad was at a bureau de change stand, handing over a thick stack of notes, and the woman behind the perspex glass put it into a counting machine.

'Weird as opposed to who? The Addams Family?' said David with a grin. 'Libby told me she wanted to buy us hats.'

David had started calling their parents by their first names, which drove them crazy. Daisy wasn't sure how she felt about it. Sometimes it was funny, but she laughed, mainly because she wanted David to be nice to her, and it helped to laugh at his jokes. Daisy saw her mum come walking across the departure hall. She was wearing a green New Yorker baseball cap pulled down on her head and carrying an oversized plain white plastic bag. David looked up from his game and followed her gaze.

'Jesus Christ, what does Libby look like? I thought that wicker sombrero she had last year was bad enough,' he said.

Their mum, Libby, was a bit of a hippy when it came to what she wore. The green baseball cap looked odd with her tie-dye A-line skirt and the oversized baggy cardigan. She'd also tucked all her long greying hair underneath it, making the cap bulge and her head look swollen.

'There you both are,' said Libby as she reached them. She glanced up at the departure board. 'We're boarding in fifteen minutes. I got you these hats to wear against the sunshine. It's going to be hot there.' She rummaged in the plastic bag and handed Daisy a pink New Yorker hat. 'Go on, put it on.'

Daisy looked at the hat and then slipped it on her head. She caught sight of herself in the reflection of a stainless steel payphone above where they sat. The front of the cap was such a rigid dome, and it was too big for her head.

'There we are. That's good, Daisy. And it's got a nice peak to protect you from the sun,' said Libby, adjusting the brim. 'David, can you stop fiddling online?'

'Just two more minutes,' he said, concentrating on the screen.

'No. Get. Off. Your. Phone,' she hissed. David looked up at her.

'Libby. What's your problem? We've got fifteen minutes. You suddenly want me to try on a baseball hat just when we're going to get on the plane?'

Libby bit her lip, took a black baseball cap from the bag, and jammed it on his head. She then took another blue one out.

David kept calm, which Daisy knew would make their mother even madder. He took the cap off his head.

'Libby. We're gonna look like a bunch of dorks all wearing the same branded hats. Is that one for Steve?' he said, indicating the blue one. Their father came walking over to them, zipping up the backpack on one shoulder. He looked very pale and was sweating. Daisy had heard someone throwing up in the toilet early that morning, and she wondered if he'd eaten something bad.

'All right, love,' he said to Daisy, putting his hand on her shoulder.

'I got you this hat, Steve,' said Libby. He took it and slipped it on. He furtively looked around at the departures lounge and then at the electronic board.

'Oh, that's us. The gate is open. Gate fourteen,' he said.

'We should wait until the last minute to board the plane,' said Libby. Daisy looked at David again. He had the cap on his head but swivelled around backwards, and he was looking up at their parents with his arms folded.

'If we're waiting until the last minute, have I got time to buy a burger?' he said.

'No,' said Libby.

'Burger King is just over there,' he said, getting up and indicating the fast food place fifty feet away. 'I'm starving, and we're not going to get lunch for ages. It's a three-hour flight.'

Daisy watched as her mother's eyes darted around, scanning the other travellers suspiciously. She wondered if she'd stopped taking her pills. This had happened a couple of times before, when she just stopped and decided she could do without them. It had been particularly bad two Christmases ago.

'Go on, go and get a burger,' said Steve. 'Daisy, are you hungry?'

'Yeah,' she said. She wasn't. But she wanted to be with David. She felt safer with him, even if he was mean to her sometimes.

'OK, but listen. You've got five minutes,' said their mother, her eyes wild. '*Five*. And come right back here. We are *not* going to miss this flight!'

'Okay, Libs,' said David sotto voce.

'And stop calling me that!' shouted their mother.

'It's your name, Libby.'

'David. Give it a rest. Just go,' said their father. He looked so pained and grey that David didn't protest further.

'Come on, Dais,' said David.

'Have you got money?' asked their father. David took out his faded *Star Wars* wallet and held it up.

'I'm loaded from the strawberry picking I've been doing.' He moved off across the concourse, and Daisy followed.

'She's fucking crazy. Bat-shit crazy,' said David when they were out of earshot. He took the cap off when they got to the screens above the Burger King counter.

'Do you think she's stopped taking her medicine?' said Daisy, voicing what she was scared of out loud. David put his arm around her shoulders.

'No. I think she's just been logging into lastminute.com like a hyperactive chipmunk, she found a cheap deal, and got all wound up about going away on holiday. And you know the old Libster doesn't cope with things being last-minute. She needs time to plan...'

Daisy looked up at him. She knew he was lying, but she appreciated the effort he was making to help her feel better. He smiled. 'Now, what do you want? I'll treat you to a kids' meal.'

'With nuggets?'

'One portion of saturated fat with golden nuggets coming up for the lady,' said David. He went to the counter and ordered. Daisy saw an older girl with long blonde hair and skinny jeans admiring her brother, and she felt a warm feeling of being with him, of him looking after and protecting her.

In the end, they had to run for the gate as soon as they had their food. Their parents suddenly changed their minds and wanted to get on the plane, so Daisy had to leave the fries uneaten and nuggets in the meal box whilst they ran for it.

Libby got very annoyed with all the people standing on the moving walkway, saying in a loud voice that it was reserved for people who wanted to walk faster, and they made it to the gate as people were boarding.

They had just joined the end of the line of people waiting to have their boarding passes scanned when a young policewoman with a kind face approached her and David.

Daisy instinctively looked to her parents standing in front of them in the queue, but she saw two big burly police officers had approached them from the other side.

'Are you Steven Hartley?' asked one of them. He noticed their dad holding his passport in his hand, and reached over to take it.

'And are you, Libby, Elizabeth Hartley?' asked the second burly police officer. Daisy saw their mother instinctively move her hand away, where she had her passport and the passports belonging to Daisy and David. He grabbed them.

Both their parents were silent and pale, and it was the weirdest thing. They suddenly seemed limp and compliant as the police officers checked through their passports, like the game was up. That was the best way Daisy could describe it. And that moment would always stick in her mind.

The female police officer with the kind face took David and Daisy's passports from her colleague and checked them.

'So, you are Daisy Elizabeth Hartley? And you are David Hartley?' she said, checking their passport photos.

'Yes,' said Daisy.

'What's going on?' asked David, watching as their parents were taken out of the line and to one side whilst the police officers talked to them in low voices.

'Everything is going to be fine,' said the woman. 'My name is Tupele. I'm a police officer,' she said, taking out an ID card and showing it to them. 'And I just want you to know you and your sister have done nothing wrong—'

Suddenly, a scream erupted from their mother, and Daisy watched in horror as Libby made a run for it, hitching up her long tie-dye skirt and attempting to escape back down towards the departure hall. It all seemed to happen in slow motion as another couple of police officers appeared ahead and tackled Libby to the ground, as David, Daisy and her dad looked on.

52

'They've picked up Libby and Steve Hartley with the two children at Birmingham Airport,' said Detective Chief Inspector Harris, coming off the phone in the incident room. He checked his watch. 'They've just set off.'

'It takes about three hours from Birmingham to Exeter when the roads are clear,' said Kate.

'And they'll be blue lighting them all the way,' said Harris. Kate looked around at the incident room with the resources, the manpower, and the ability to get things done. Was she hankering after being a police officer again? She looked to Tristan, who was sitting on an empty desk. Harris went off to speak to his colleague.

'What should we do? I feel like we're intruding,' said Tristan in a low voice. Kate had the same feeling. They had been invited to observe the interview with Maureen Cook, but what now? They were only still there because Harris was too busy to ask them to leave.

He came over to them with his mobile phone.

'You know Alan Hexham, the forensic pathologist?' he asked.

'Yes, he was a guest lecturer for me, back when I was a criminology professor at Ashdean University,' said Kate. Harris raised an eyebrow. This seemed to impress him even more.

'I was Kate's research assistant,' said Tristan.

'Alan has just got back to me with the results of the post-mortem he's done on the body we found at Danvers Farm. I'd appreciate your thoughts, if you'd like to attend with me,' he said.

Kate and Tristan arrived at Exeter morgue with Harris just before eleven. Kate could see that Tristan was pleased to be visiting mid-morning. All of their other visits to Alan's morgue had been after breakfast – and Tristan had never been able to keep his food down.

They signed in at the small office and were shown into the examining room. Jemma, one of Alan Hexham's assistants, was cleaning one of the stainless-steel mortuary tables. She took her work seriously. On the last few visits, she had always been upbeat. This morning her eyes looked swollen and red.

'Morning,' said Jemma. Kate could see she had been crying, and she turned her face away when she saw them all enter. She was newly qualified, a few years older than Tristan, and a tall and well-built young woman – strength was essential in a mortician – and she had rapidly risen through the ranks to become Alan's right hand.

'We're here about the, er... the young boy's body found on Danvers Farm,' said Harris. Kate noted how difficult it was to say it, and she could only count on one hand the times she'd attended a post-mortem for a child.

'Alan's in his office, at the back,' she said to Harris, her voice cracking with emotion. They moved past a long line of refrigerator doors to Alan's tiny office at the end. The door was ajar, and he was sitting at his desk, surrounded by piles of paperwork and studying a file under the light of an angle-poise lamp. He was a massive bear of a man with a kind face and long greying hair tied back in a ponytail.

'Ah. Ken, hello,' he said to Harris, taking off his glasses. He got up and registered surprise at seeing Kate and Tristan with him. Harris explained their presence.

'It was you who found the boy?' said Alan. Kate was surprised and pleased that information hadn't yet hit the news.

'We've been working on a case, trying to find a missing boy,' said Kate. 'Charlie Julings. He vanished ten years ago—'

'Devil's Way. Yes. I've just been reviewing the police files... The police believed that he fell into the gorge and drowned. I can also see that the family petitioned the court for a death certificate in absentia,' said Alan. He hesitated and seemed to contemplate that. He slid his glasses up on the top of his head and peered closer as he flicked through the file. His office was windowless, and the angle-poise lamp cast long shadows on the walls.

'We've been hired by the grandmother of Charlie. She was the one who petitioned the court and now regrets it.'

This hung in the air for a moment.

'Would you like to view the body?' said Alan. Harris looked between Kate and Tristan, took a deep breath and nodded. Alan led the way out of his office.

Kate hadn't been to the Exeter morgue for eighteen months, and the mortuary looked the same. The room had a high ceiling and floor-to-ceiling white tiles contrasted with the row of six stainless steel benches. Since her last visit, a sizeable electrified flycatcher had been installed on the wall above a row of stainless-steel fridges, and its glow reflected over the tiles and steel, giving them a purple hue.

Jemma was waiting for them, next to a tiny shape under a sheet. She gently lifted it back, and Kate was shocked to see the little boy's body lying on an adult-sized mortuary table. As they drew closer, he looked smaller than when they'd seen him pulled out of the hole. The body had been washed. He was so pale and looked like a strange gargoyle taken from the side of a church.

Tristan put his hand to his mouth, and even Harris blanched. There was something almost eerie about the way the little boy looked like he was resting, like those Victorian photos of dead children posed to look like they'd fallen asleep.

'How can this be a body that's been in the ground for eleven years?' asked Kate, shocked at the slow rate of decay.

'I know, I was doubtful about how long the body had been in the ground if Charlie Julings went missing eleven years ago. However, we did a lot of work looking at the blanket and the type of soil, and we've had forensic information back about the land where you found him. The soil has a very high peat content which stops the oxygen and bacteria from being able to grow and attack the flesh. There was also a layer of sphagnum moss all over the area surrounding the boulders. Water or dirt caught beneath sheets of this moss won't get a normal supply of oxygen from the atmosphere. Also, sphagnum soaks up calcium and magnesium, which makes the underlying soil and water mildly acidic. Add this to the peaty soil, and this little boy was slowly mummifying in the earth,' said Alan.

'So you think he could have been down there for eleven years?' asked Kate.

'With the delayed rate of decay, I can't pinpoint the exact time and date of death.'

'You can cover him up now, poor little thing,' said Harris. Jemma lifted the sheet and pulled it over the tiny body. Kate could tell the sight of him was affecting the police officer.

'We were able to conduct a post-mortem. There was no water in the lungs. And there was little evidence of trauma to the body apart from the right leg. The bone was broken. A clean break across the tibia. I'm unable to say how he died.'

Harris nodded.

'Have you been able to extract any DNA that we can use to check his ID against the family of Charlie Julings?' he asked.

'Yes. We were able to extract bone marrow and get a good clean DNA sample. It was sent to the lab late last night, and we should be able to get a result later today,' said Alan.

53

Libby and Steve Hartley were driven from Birmingham Airport in a police squad car.

Steve was silent as the motorway swam past them. Libby had been put in handcuffs, but after protesting as to why they were being arrested, the police allowed her to ride in the car without cuffs. There was still a steel cage around them in the back seat. The grille and perspex glass separated them from the two police officers in front, and they couldn't hear what they were saying.

'They're going to interview us separately,' said Steve, breaking the silence. 'What are you going to say?'

Libby turned to him. Her face had that haunted look, with a pale face and wide eyes like a cornered animal. He could see she was chewing the side of her cheek.

'Nothing. We're going to say nothing... And we're in a police car. We can't hear them, but they can probably hear us,' she said. Steve knew she was right. He had heard her talk like this before when her mental health had been at its worst. When she thought that there were listening devices in the walls, and that they were being monitored by the police.

Steve closed his eyes and tipped his head back. He thought he might be sick. He breathed in and out. It was horribly claustrophobic in the back of the police car and smelt of sweat and fear.

He jumped when he felt Libby's nails digging into his arm. He opened his eyes. Her face was inches from his.

'I mean it. Don't say anything. You have the right to remain silent,' she said.

'What if they—' he started to say. Libby put her fingers on his lips.

'They can't do anything if you don't say anything, if we don't say anything. Okay?'

The policewoman in the passenger seat turned around, and she knocked on the glass. Libby moved away from him and stared out of the window.

How much longer can we keep this up? thought Steve. He turned around and looked out through the grille covering the back window. The car with David and Daisy was still behind them. Steve was pleased to see that they were travelling in an unmarked car, and as far as he could tell, they didn't have wire mesh on the windows.

What must they think of us, of all this? thought Steve. *How will we ever come back from this?* He wished he could be with them and hoped they weren't scared.

When the two-car convoy with Libby, Steve, Daisy and David arrived at Exeter police station just over three hours later, the cars drove past the front of the building and around to the back entrance.

The police officer, Tupele and the driver left Daisy and

David's car and went to talk to a tall man with greying hair waiting at an open door in the loading bay. Daisy watched as two more police officers went to the squad car in front and opened the back door. Their parents were led away into the back entrance of the police station. Libby looked in control of her emotions, but as Daisy watched, her mother didn't look back at them in the car, and that scared Daisy. Why didn't she look? Does she know we're here? Didn't they tell her? Why?

Their father, in comparison, looked broken. The police officer took his arm and led him away. He did look back, and when he caught Daisy's eye, he tried to smile, but his face crumpled in tears. He turned away, and then they were both gone.

Daisy looked back at David. He was slumped in the seat and very quiet.

'What's happening to us?' asked Daisy. She tried the door handle and was surprised when the door opened. 'It isn't locked.'

'Why would it be locked?' said David. He wound down his window, and the breeze came in. Daisy looked down at the concrete in the yard, and she was suddenly scared of the outside world. She wanted to remain in the safe cocoon of this car. She closed the door and sat back with her hands pressed between her knees.

'What do you think they've done, David?' asked Daisy. She realised this was the first time either of them had asked this question out loud. Their mother was an unknown quantity. Daisy had heard her father say this when he was angry with Mum. Or when she was in the grip of one of her obsessions. 'David?' Daisy repeated.

He shook his head.

'I don't know. But I bet you, whatever it is, Mum's done it. I heard them talking about the news, last night,' he said.

'What was on the news?'

'I don't know. Mum was asking Dad, did you see it?' His forehead creased, and Daisy noted that he'd switched back to calling their mother 'mum'.

'What was on the news that could make her want to take us all to Spain? I thought she didn't want to have a holiday this year... I'm scared.'

David reached over and took his sister's hand.

'I'm scared too, but we've done nothing wrong,' he said. Daisy felt her stomach drop as Tupele came back to the car. She was smiling, and she had two Mars bars.

'Are you two okay?' she said brightly, looking in through the open window.

'Law enforcement bearing chocolate bars,' said David. Tupele opened the door.

'David and Daisy, do you want to come with me whilst you wait for your mum and dad?' she said. Her tone and her smile were slightly manic, as if she didn't want them to see what she was really thinking.

'How long are Mum and Dad going to be?' asked Daisy.

'It could be a little while. That's why we've got a nice cosy office for you to wait in, and it has a TV!'

Daisy felt her throat close up with fear as they left the car.

'I've always wanted to watch TV in a police station,' muttered David. The smiling policewoman either didn't hear him or pretended not to, and she led them into the station.

54

Kate and Tristan returned to Exeter police station that afternoon to watch the interviews with Libby Hartley and Steve Hartley from the video observation suite.

Libby was interviewed first. She refused a legal representative and sat at the table with her hands folded neatly on the surface. She was still wearing the pink New Yorker baseball cap she'd had at Birmingham Airport. Her long greying hair hung past her shoulders.

'Can you please take off your hat,' said Harris. He was sitting opposite her with Duncan, the other police officer who had been first to arrive at Danvers Farm.

'Why can't I wear a hat?' asked Libby. She spoke well, and Kate couldn't work out where she was from. Her accent was neutral.

'We need to see your face,' said Harris pointing up at the cameras on the wall. Libby followed his gaze, and her face came into view. Her eyes had dark circles underneath, and even on the video, Kate could see that the skin on her face was red and cracked.

'You can see my face here, no probs,' she said, tilting her head back down. She sat back and crossed her arms.

'Can you please take off your hat.'

'No.'

Harris leant across and gently removed it. Her hair underneath leapt up from the static and formed a halo around her head under the intense lights. She stared at him defiantly.

'Why were you leaving to go on holiday?' asked Harris.

'I needed some sun.'

'The neighbour we spoke to said you made the arrangements late last night, and it was very last minute. Why?'

'I told you. We needed some sun.'

Harris sat back, and there was a long pause.

'Can you confirm to us when you were the tenants of Danvers Farm in South Zeal?'

She sighed and pursed her lips.

'Exact dates I can't remember. I'd say, from Christmas 2004, until early July 2007.'

'Can you remember when in December 2004?'

'No. I can't. It was a couple of weeks before Christmas. We took on the farm deliberately at this point in the year. We could have the winter to get ourselves acclimatised,' she said.

'I do have the date you gave up the lease on the farm,' said Harris. He found a piece of paper from his folder and slid it in front of her. 'This is from the Crown Estate land registry. You gave four weeks' notice on the property on the thirtieth of June.'

'Yes.'

'Why did you choose to give up your tenancy on the farm so close to the harvest?'

Libby shrugged.

'You left the country on June 25th 2007, but you didn't return to the property to serve out your lease. Why?'

'It was a difficult time,' she said.

'Were you aware that a young boy's body was buried in the woods on the farmland?'

'What? Of course not,' she said. Kate was watching her face and Libby kept her eyes on the table.

'Are you aware that three-year-old Charlie Julings vanished close to your farm on the night of the 21st of June? That's a week before you decided to leave and give up the lease on your farmland. And you left the country on June 25th. Four days after Charlie Julings went missing.'

'If I remember correctly, the police did come to the farm and talk to us. They checked the outbuildings in case, on the off-chance we'd stashed a little boy there. Which of course we hadn't. I didn't know about the boy you found buried...'

'You didn't see it on the news?'

She sat back and took a deep breath.

'Can I ask you a question?' she said.

'Of course,' said Harris.

'Do you have forensic evidence showing *when* that boy's body was buried?'

Duncan glanced across at Harris.

'I'm not at liberty to give that information,' said Harris.

'Because we left Danvers Farm eleven years ago, and another family has been living there. Why aren't you interviewing the current tenants in a fucking police interview room with cameras?' she shouted. She slammed her hand down on the table.

'You need to calm down.'

'No. You need to release me because you have nothing! I've done nothing!'

Harris kept calm and watched her impassively.

'Libby. This could have been a routine talk with a local police officer in your home, but you gave up that right when you decided to do a midnight flit and try to leave the country.'

'Midnight flit!' she spat. 'We left in the morning.'

'And again, one of my police officers tried to talk to you at the airport.'

'Liar! They tried to take my passport. I was detained.'

'Only after you attempted to run away. You seem like an intelligent woman, but your bizarre behaviour indicates guilt.'

'And you seem like a cunt,' said Libby. There was a nasty silence. Libby slammed her hand down on the table, making Duncan jump, and then she started crying. Uninhibited tears with snot and drool. 'Don't you know I have a diagnosis for bipolar disorder? I have a disability, and this is how you treat me! We left Danvers Farm because my husband was fucking a local girl! Do you hear me? That place, our home, the farm, was tainted by his betrayal! Is that not enough of a reason for you, for me to want to leave?'

Harris pulled a tissue from a box in the middle of the table and handed it to her. He indicated to Duncan that they should leave the room.

'I'm pausing this interview at 2.45pm,' he said. They watched him leave the room.

A moment later, he entered the observation suite.

'I'm not happy to continue this interview without her having a solicitor present,' he said. 'I think we need to take five minutes.'

Kate and Tristan followed him out of the video observation suite and into the corridor, where he went to a vending machine.

'Where are David and Daisy?' asked Tristan.

'Watching TV in one of our meeting rooms. We're trying to work out the best thing to do. We don't know if we have enough to charge Libby and Steve at this stage, but it's looking that way. We've set a deadline of 4pm to call social services and have them take the children into short-term care,' said Harris. He fed a few coins into the coffee machine. A plastic cup dropped down, and began to fill with steaming coffee. Harris took the cup, and then Kate got herself one. Tristan fed in some money and pressed the code for a can of Coke. It dropped into the machine below with a clunk. Harris blew on his coffee and took a sip.

'What gets me is that we can't prove when the body of that young boy was put in the ground,' he said.

'What about the diary? The diary could belong to Libby,' asked Kate.

'How do we prove in court that the diary belongs to her?' Harris replied. Kate nodded.

'Yes, the blue exercise book was found at the murder scene of a completely unrelated crime to Charlie's disappearance,' said Kate. 'And Anna Treadwell was attending a creative writing class. You would first need to prove that the blue exercise book is not Anna's, even though it was found in her house, and then you'd have to prove that it belonged to Libby Hartley. And in the meantime, Maureen Cook somehow got hold of the "short story" in the blue exercise book, and published it in her own name.'

Harris sighed and rubbed his face.

'Jesus, what a mess…' A uniformed police officer appeared in the corridor. She looked concerned. 'Ah, Tupele. This is Kate Marshall and Tristan Harper. They found the body out at Danvers Farm. This is Detective Inspector Tupele Grant.'

Tupele smiled, said hello, and then turned her attention back to Harris.

'Boss, we've just had the DNA come back from the boy's body. We ran it against the DNA swabs provided by Jean Julings and Joel Mansfield. It doesn't match her maternal DNA profile or Joel's paternal DNA. The body of the boy we found at Danvers Farm isn't Charlie Julings.'

55

'Who's going to tell Jean?' asked Tristan, his face pale with shock. 'I really thought it was Charlie.'

They were still standing in the corridor by the vending machines, and Kate felt just as much in shock as Tristan.

Kate looked down at the cup of coffee in her hand. The cup had been wet when she'd taken it out of the machine, and she'd wrapped an old petrol station napkin around it that she'd found in her pocket. She peeled it off the plastic cup and was about to drop it into the bin when she saw how the dark liquid had stained the petrol station name and logo at the bottom, obscuring the print.

'Hang on, that could be—' she said, thinking.

'Could be what?' asked Tristan.

'Can you stay here and watch the interviews with Steve, and Libby if they talk to her again? I need to ask if I can access the police evidence store we visited the other day. I need to see the crime scene stuff from Anna Treadwell's bedroom. Take a look at it again.'

Libby lay on the hard plastic bed in the prison cell in the bowels of Exeter police station. The room was strangely calming to her. Just a low bench, a stainless steel toilet bowl and scrubbed walls. Walls scrubbed clean of graffiti, but not quite. There were the faint ghosts of scratch marks and foul language. She didn't have to pretend to be sane in this room. Often when she went to the supermarket or a restaurant or drove somewhere in her car, she could feel eyes on her, watching her behaviour.

In this cell, she could just be.

The police didn't have anything. They couldn't. Libby got up and went to the hatch on the door. There was a small hole, and she could just see a circle of the dank concrete hall outside, lit with orange light.

'Steve. Steve, are you there?' she said. After a long pause, she heard his voice.

'Yes?'

It sounded faint and weak.

'Did they talk to you yet?'

'No.'

'They have nothing. Say nothing—' Libby heard footsteps in the corridor outside, and she took a step back as the bolt was shot back on her cell. A petite older lady with a severe black fringe stood in the doorway with the custody sergeant.

'Hello, Mrs Hartley. I have been appointed as your solicitor. May I come in?'

'I don't need a solicitor,' said Libby.

'I'm afraid it's been insisted on. You are strongly urged to seek legal counsel. With your history of mental health, you are in a precarious position. I have been assigned to you, but you can, of course, choose someone else.'

'They have nothing on me.'

'That might be so.' The solicitor looked around at the custody sergeant. 'May I come in for a moment, Mrs Hartley?' Libby nodded, and she came inside the cell. The custody sergeant closed the door and shot the bolts home. She perched on the bench.

'What's your name?' asked Libby.

'Donna Webber,' she said, handing Libby her card.

'Where are my children?'

'They are here in the station, in the canteen, for now. That's why I urge you to retain legal representation. With your history of mental health issues and the police investigation... If the children are taken into care later today, which looks like it may happen, it would just be for a short period,' she added, holding up her hand to stop Libby from protesting. 'You don't need or want the authorities to request a mental health assessment before they return custody to you. Once the children enter the system, social services would look to extend the emergency custody agreement if you give them cause.'

Libby stared at her.

'So even though I'm innocent, I could lose my children?' she said. The thought was too awful for words. Libby took a step back and felt the chalky wall against her back.

'I must stress that this probably won't happen,' said Donna. 'I'm going to be with you for the duration of any future interviews. And, of course, your husband is also their primary carer.'

There were more footsteps in the corridor, and Libby heard voices outside.

'Who is that?' said Libby.

'I don't know. I know your husband has retained his own legal counsel on the recommendation of the police. For the same reasons I've outlined,' said Donna. Libby noted that she sat bolt upright in a finishing school pose with her ankles crossed.

'Can they charge me? Can they keep me here?' asked Libby.

'They can keep you here for twenty-four hours before they have to charge you. They can extend that to thirty-six hours if they suspect you of a serious crime. But with the short time I've had with your file, I can't see that they have strong enough evidence to do so. However, either way, I don't think they have enough evidence to keep your husband, and if you are willing to be more cooperative with the police in the interview room, I can ask that they release Steve, so he can find accommodation for him and the children tonight.'

Libby felt a flood of relief when she heard this.

'Okay. Yes. I can do that,' said Libby. The thought of losing custody of the children was something she had never comprehended. It was never on her radar. Donna picked up her briefcase from the floor.

'Oh. There is one other thing. As you know, the police in the custody suite took a DNA swab when you were arrested. They also took a DNA swab from your husband. The police are asking for consent from you or Steve to take a DNA swab from David and Daisy, is it?'

'Why do they need to do that?'

'They say that they need to search your house, and they need to eliminate DNA,' said Donna.

'No,' said Libby, starting to panic. The sheer terror she felt was overwhelming. 'Absolutely not.'

Donna smiled condescendingly.

'Mrs Hartley. This isn't a DNA swab concerning a crime. This is perfectly normal. They are both under eighteen, so they do need your consent. The DNA sample will only be kept for twenty-eight days to rule them out of any investigation. It's just like a cotton bud, and they swipe it on the inside of their cheek. Painless and over in a flash.'

'No!'

Donna frowned.

'Mrs Hartley. On what grounds?'

'Because my children have nothing to do with all of this. Nothing! Why do they have to be dragged into it, and have these invasive procedures? No, that's it. Get out of my cell. Get out!'

Donna picked up her briefcase.

'Mrs Hartley, this is not helping you—'

'Get out!'

Donna went to the door and knocked.

'Please reconsider this. It will help your case in the long term.'

The door opened, and Donna stepped out. The bolts echoed as they shot home.

Libby stood in silence for a minute, feeling the blood pounding in her head.

'Libby,' said Steve's disembodied voice echoing down the corridor. 'I'm sorry... I gave them consent to do the DNA swabs on the kids. This has to end.'

Libby felt the floor drop underneath her, and she had only just reached the stainless- steel toilet bowl before she threw up.

56

Four hours later, Kate and Tristan were in the waiting area at Exeter police station. Kate's heart was beating so loudly that she was sure the people outside on the street could hear. Tristan glanced across at her and then back at the door.

A moment later, Jean came into the station with Joel. They both looked as scared as Kate felt as she greeted them.

'Hello, Kate. Hello, Tristan, love,' said Jean. She was pale, but she looked more robust and healthy than a few weeks ago, and she now only had a wooden walking stick to support her. Joel was wide-eyed and tapping his foot nervously.

'I didn't know you would both be here,' said Joel. 'I thought the police wanted to talk to us?'

'I told you they'd be here,' said Jean.

'You need to sign in, and then we're going to the detective chief inspector's office,' said Kate.

'Can you just tell me, please?' said Jean, taking Kate's hand and closing her eyes at the pain of it all.

'No, we can't do this standing in the reception area,' said

Kate. Once Jean and Joel had signed in and were given passes, Harris met them at the entrance into the station.

'You're a policeman?' asked Jean, looking him up and down and hesitating before she took his hand to shake it.

'Yes, I'm Detective Chief Inspector Ken Harris. I will be there in the room, but considering you hired Kate and Tristan to investigate Charlie's disappearance, I'll take a back seat whilst they tell you what is happening Please come through.'

Kate saw Jean glance back at Joel as they walked down the corridor and then came to a large airy office. There were two sofas and a couple of chairs.

'Please sit down. Do you want tea or coffee?' asked Harris.

'No, just please, tell us. Tell us what you know. I haven't been able to sleep,' said Jean. She eased herself onto the sofa. Joel sat beside her. He was now white as a sheet. Tristan and Kate sat opposite, and Harris was the last to sit down after closing the door.

Tristan looked at Kate, and she nodded.

'Okay, as you know, you asked us to investigate—'

'Just answer yes or no, is the body of that little boy Charlie?' said Jean putting up her hand.

'No. The body of the young boy we found on Danvers Farm is not Charlie,' said Kate. 'The body we found is of David Hartley.'

There was a long silence.

'David Hartley?' asked Joel, sitting forward on his chair. 'But I thought the police arrested Libby and Steve Hartley with their children David and Daisy?'

'They did. But that not the full story,' said Kate. She took a deep breath. 'A few hours ago, the police took DNA samples from David Hartley and Daisy Hartley. Their samples were run against the samples that you and Joel gave us—'

'No, no, no, you don't. Don't you dare!' said Jean, cutting her off and putting a hand to her trembling lip. Kate nodded.

'David Hartley, who is now thirteen, is not actually David Hartley. His DNA matches you, Jean and you, Joel. And we are certain that David is actually Charlie.'

There was another long silence. Jean just stared at them, and Joel looked between them.

'Hang on,' he said. 'What the hell... Are you saying that Charlie isn't dead?' asked Joel.

'That's correct. The boy that Libby and Steve have been bringing up for the past eleven years as their son David, is actually Charlie.'

'No! Are you sure?' said Joel. Jean's mouth was wide open.

'We have DNA samples from you both, and the boy we thought was David Hartley, his DNA matches with your maternal DNA, Jean, and your paternal DNA, Joel,' said Kate. 'Joel. Did you and Becky have any other children?'

'No! Of course not.'

'Did Becky have any other children?'

'No,' said Jean quietly.

'Then that boy, David Hartley, is Charlie,' said Kate.

Jean went very pale and then got up, leaning on her stick.

'Where is he? Can I see him? He's alive. Charlie is alive?'

Joel stood up with her.

'Please, Jean, Joel, can you sit down,' said Kate. 'There are things we need to explain.'

'But I can see him? He's here?' repeated Jean.

'Yes.'

'Oh my God.' Turning to Joel, she leant into him, and began to sob. He put his arm around her shoulders.

'How did you find all this out?' asked Joel, his voice choking.

'It was Kate and Tristan's investigations,' said Harris. He

indicated that Jean and Joel should sit back down, and then went and sat back down at his desk.

'It all came down to the evidence taken from the Anna Treadwell crime scene,' said Kate. 'Anna had been concerned about the now-deceased David Hartley's welfare. On one of her social worker visits, she found a diary written in a blue exercise book by Libby Hartley, and she read it and took it. The nature of the entries must have been disturbing but confusing. We also found a scribbled note in Anna's official work diary...' Kate reached out, and Harris handed her the original piece of paper from the evidence store, which was wrapped in thin plastic.

'This is a poster for a fun run,' she said, holding up the bloodstained poster. 'It was found in Anna's work diary. You can see where Anna has written some hasty notes on the reverse, but some of them were obscured by her blood. This was found blood-spattered at the crime scene.'

Kate read from the paper: '"diagnosis of bipolar disorder". Anna wrote notes about her visits to Danvers Farm when she saw Libby. We know that Libby Hartley has a diagnosis of bipolar disorder. Anna, then writes, "child always seemed happy/thriving". This is her writing about David, the original David Hartley. "Visited the fourteenth of June as part of a routine follow-up. No one was in and I left a note asking to call me." Lower down Anna writes, "visited again on twenty-third of June. Rang the bell, no answer, then I saw mother, that's Libby, through the side window of the house, hiding. She reluctantly came to the door. I said I needed to see them for a follow-up appointment. She let me in but wouldn't let me see the boy, who she said was poorly in bed and half asleep. I demanded to see him. The child's head had been shaved. A drastic change in appearance. Weight loss, question mark."'

Kate looked up at them.

'Jesus,' said Joel. 'She visited on the 23rd of June. That was a couple of days after Charlie went missing.' Kate nodded.

'Yes. Anna also wrote more at the bottom of the page, but you can see here where it was obscured by blood-splatter from the crime scene.'

Kate held up the frantic black writing with the bloom of blood obscuring it.

Is father well? Spoke of diabetes due to poor diet

Is the mother's dia

Does David have p

'The first time me and Tristan saw this evidence, we took photos of it and then printed it off at home. I didn't realise that the text obscured by the blood spatter might be recoverable on this original copy. Detective Chief Inspector Harris's forensics team was able to highlight the ink underneath the bloodstain using a luminol lamp, and this was what they found.'

Harris took a sheet of paper off his desk. He handed it to Kate. The luminol lamp had highlighted the rest of the writing under the ink in white.

'You can see the missing text highlighted here,' said Kate.

Is father well? Spoke of diabetes due to poor diet

Is the mother's diary genuine? She talks of burying a child, but is this her mania/bipolar?

Does David have passport? If the child has a passport, then easy to pass off one baby as another

'Jesus,' said Joel, taking the paper and looking at the ink. 'Why didn't anyone make the connection to Anna Treadwell? And why didn't Anna flag her concerns earlier?'

'The connection was made by chance, with the short story,' said Tristan. 'And Anna must have had to get things in place with her office in social services before going back to Danvers Farm with the police. Her suspicions had to be checked out. But before she could do that, she was murdered.'

It hung in the air.

'When was she murdered? Didn't anyone suspect anything?' asked Jean.

'We believe Anna was murdered in the early hours of the 25th of June,' said Harris. 'But her body lay undiscovered for two weeks until the 8th of July, when her neighbour found her body. And then it didn't make the news until a few days after that.'

'In the meantime, Libby and Steve Hartley left the country later on 25th June, and went to Spain for three weeks,' said Kate. 'They had a passport for the now deceased David Hartley, which they used for Charlie. You can see where Anna had written in her notes obscured by blood, "Does David have passport? If the child has a passport, then easy to pass off one baby as another."'

'My nephew recently had to have a passport done for my sister and brother-in-law's holiday,' said Tristan. 'It's laughable that you must have a passport picture of a baby. They all look the same and change constantly.'

'Jesus,' said Joel. 'So, they left the country with Charlie as David and... then what?'

'They came back three weeks later and went to live on a new farm in Shropshire where they brought Charlie up as David,' said Kate. 'And then they had a daughter, Daisy.'

Jean was staring into space; she looked dazed.

'But what about us? *We're* Charlie's family. Have you asked David if he remembers us? What if you're wrong?'

Kate put her hand on Jean's arm.

'No, we haven't. And this might sound harsh, but what do you remember from when you were three?'

Jean opened and closed her mouth again.

'Charlie was my little boy. How can he just not remember?' she asked.

'There's one thing I don't understand,' said Joel. 'If Libby Hartley abducted Charlie the night he went missing, how did she get him?'

'Yes, I saw this thing written on Anna's paper which was obscured,' said Kate. 'They are a non-religious family, but behaviours had changed since the father's alleged affair. "Husband flagged concern about pagan influence." During our investigations, we spent a lot of time at Devil's Way, working out a timeline of what might have happened to Charlie. We think that Charlie came out of the tent, got lost in the long grass outside and between the tree and Devil's Tor, and he walked along the river, crossed a small wooden footbridge towards something called the Pixie Tree, which is close by on the other side at the end of a small stream. It's a pagan site where people make offerings or ask for luck or forgiveness. We believe that Libby drove to the Pixie Tree that night. One of the police officers who visited Danvers Farm the next day said Libby and Steve's car was messed up and in a real state, covered in mud. Like it had been driven across the moors. We think that just as Libby arrived that night and went to the tree, Charlie came stumbling up to the pond, lost, and in her mental state and having just buried the body of David, she took him.'

They were silent in the room for a long time.

'But that's a guess, isn't it?' said Joel.

'No. David is Charlie. We know this now through DNA. There was only a short window where Charlie could have gone missing. The long grass disorientated him. There was a bridge over the river, which isn't there now. He got lost, crossed it, and by chance, fate, or bad luck, he arrived at the Pixie Tree just as Libby Hartley was there. She'd accidentally killed her child by rolling on him in bed. And she was mentally ill and in the grip of bipolar, which made her bury David. All of this is happening to her. She's losing her mind. And then she sees Charlie appear at the edge of the water, just as she wishes to bring David back or ask for forgiveness.'

Jean shook her head.

'What if you're wrong? Or the DNA test is wrong? I can't believe it, only for it to be snatched away when you realise it's a mistake.'

'We have a confession from Steve Hartley,' said Harris. 'He has confirmed that David Hartley is Charlie.'

'And he went along with this?' said Joel, showing a flash of anger for the first time.

'He states that he panicked,' said Harris.

'I panic plenty in my life. I don't abduct children,' said Jean.

'He didn't know that David had died, or that Libby had buried the body. He only found that she'd abducted Charlie when the police came knocking on the door at the farm the next day. He said he'd been out working. He was suddenly placed into this nightmare and he panicked and they decided to leave the country and take Charlie. He said he thought they would be questioned at the airport, but when Charlie was waved through on David's baby passport, he felt there was no going back,' said Harris.

'Well, he'd better not come anywhere near me or Jean,' said Joel.

'What about Libby?' asked Jean.

'She collapsed. She's being treated in the hospital.'

Jean opened her mouth to say something and then closed it again.

'And you think that Libby and Steve Hartley killed Anna Treadwell?' asked Joel.

'A thumbprint was recovered from the claw hammer used to kill Anna Treadwell. The thumbprint matches Libby Hartley's prints that we took earlier today,' said Harris. 'We still don't know if Libby acted alone.'

There was another long silence.

'What happens now? Can we see Charlie? I want to see him!' said Jean.

'We have an unprecedented situation,' said Harris. 'David and Daisy will have to be taken into custody by social services now that both of their parents are in prison. However, David, Charlie, is your child, and your grandchild. So, naturally, you should automatically have custody of him.'

'What about Daisy?' asked Joel.

'That's the other issue.'

'No! Charlie is coming with us. I'm not leaving here without him!' said Jean. 'And this little girl, we can't leave her.' She pushed on her walking stick and struggled to her feet. 'Where is he? I'd like to see my grandson.'

'Jean, please. We need to work out how best to do this,' said Kate.

'No!' cried Jean. 'No! He's ours! *Ours!*' She beat it out on her chest with her fist. 'I asked you both to find him, and bloody hell, you've found him! I'm not sitting here a moment longer, knowing we're in the same building as Charlie! Do you hear me?'

Joel got up and stood with Jean.

'Take us to see him,' he said. 'Now. Take me to see my son.'

It was an odd moment as Kate and Tristan watched the reunion between David, Jean and Joel through the safety glass of an office door. Jean looked at David, and they heard her say,

'Charlie. Is it really you?' She put out her hands and placed them on his arms, studying him. David stared at her as if she was mad and shook his head. Jean then turned to Joel with tears in her eyes. 'It's him, Joel. It's our Charlie.'

Jean grabbed Charlie in an embrace and he shrank back. Daisy stood to one side, bewildered. Joel towered over Jean and Charlie, and he stepped closer, put his arms around them both, and buried his face in Charlie's hair, sobbing.

'They're all so confused,' said Tristan. Kate watched as tears rolled down Jean's cheeks, and she pressed her face into Charlie's neck and pulled him close.

'My boy, my boy,' she was now saying. His arms hung at his sides as he was sandwiched between Jean and Joel, who were both sobbing. Charlie pulled himself free and stepped towards Daisy, who grabbed his hand.

'What do you think will happen now?' asked Tristan.

'They need work it out. They have to,' said Kate. 'Come on, let's leave them be.'

They moved away from the door, leaving Jean, Joel, and Charlie and Daisy on either side of the room in a strange, fearful standoff.

EPILOGUE

SIX WEEKS LATER
10th August 2018

It was a beautiful morning in late August, and Kate and Tristan were digesting the latest news about the Charlie Julings abduction case – as it was now known. They sat in front of Tristan's laptop and watched as Libby and Steve Hartley were led separately in handcuffs into Exeter Crown Court. The camera image then switched to a bank of journalists outside in front of a group of bystanders.

'This morning, Libby and Steven Hartley were brought to Exeter Crown Court and formally charged with the murder of social worker Anna Treadwell in June 2007,' said the news anchor. Anna's photo appeared on the screen, taken from her social services pass, and another picture of her overgrown house on the cul-de-sac. The news reporter went on, '—and the subsequent abduction of Charlie Julings, who went missing eleven years ago on June 21st 2007. A separate charge of manslaughter has been brought against Libby Hartley for the death of their biological son, David Hartley. Steven Hartley pleaded guilty in court to all counts. Libby Hartley has put in a plea for diminished responsibility due to an undiagnosed bipolar disorder at the time of the manslaughter, murder, and abduction.'

The camera angle then changed to Libby being led back out of court to a police van, half-covered by a blanket. She was flanked by two police officers, and she was being jeered and photographed by members of the public.

'Charlie Julings has spent the past eleven years believing that his natural parents were Libby and Steve Hartley, and that he was David Hartley. He has since been reunited with his biological family.'

The news report changed to the next story, and Kate and Tristan sat back in their chairs.

'Jesus, do you think they'll go down, Steve and Libby?' asked Tristan.

'I don't know. I can't imagine what it's been like for David and Daisy. I mean, Charlie and Daisy. They've lived happily and normally for many years as a family.'

Kate's phone beeped with a message, and she saw it was Jean saying they were down on the beach. It was the first time that Kate and Tristan would get to meet Charlie with Jean and Joel since they'd been reunited at Exeter police station six weeks ago.

Kate and Tristan left the office and walked down the sand dunes to the beach. It was busy with people swimming and sunbathing, but Jean, Joel and Charlie stood out from the crowd. They all stood awkwardly. Together, but apart. It had been Jean's idea to meet in public in case tempers became frayed and Charlie wanted to leave.

Jean was smoking a cigarette and leaning on her walking

stick. Joel was beside her, holding a thin sweater, and Charlie was a few feet away, kicking at the sand with the toe of his trainers. He wore shorts and a T-shirt and looked taller than he had two months ago.

'Hello, my loves,' said Jean, reaching up to hug them both. Joel came over and shook hands with them. Charlie sighed, nodded, and leaned forward to shake their hands.

'We just wanted to come and say hello, and see you both, didn't we, Joel?' said Jean, looking nervous.

'Yeah. It's been a lot to get used to having Charlie, sorry, David, back,' said Joel. He put out his hand and touched Charlie's shoulder. Charlie pressed his lips together and angled his shoulder away, nodding. He looked like he wanted to walk away, but he stopped himself.

'He wants us to call him David, don't you, love? But it's tough. It's really hard, Charlie,' said Jean. 'You're my little Charlie. Always will be.' She looked like she wanted to reach out and touch him on the shoulder like Joel did, but she stopped herself. She shook her head and took another drag on her cigarette.

'How are you, David?' asked Kate.

'I don't know,' he said. 'I don't like the name Charlie, though. It's a bit pikey.'

'Charlie! That's offensive,' said Jean. 'Don't talk like that, please,' she said softening her voice. There was an awkward silence.

'How is Daisy?' asked Kate.

'She's okay. She's gone out with a school friend today. Joel bought her a phone, so he's in her good books.'

Joel went to say something, but Jean cut him off.

'Daisy misses her old friends up in Shropshire – she's got the phone so she can keep in touch with them,' said Jean. 'Now they're both staying with us. She wants to go back to her old school in September. We're not sure what's going to happen. Anyway. Char– *David*, what do you have to say to Kate and Tristan?'

'Thank you for, er, unmasking my true identity...' he said, his voice heavy with sarcasm. Jean opened her mouth to scold him again, and stopped herself. Kate couldn't imagine how he felt.

'We're just glad you're okay,' said Kate.

'I'm like Harry Potter, the boy who lived,' said Charlie with a grin.

'You might have lived, but another young boy died,' said Joel, quietly. Charlie blushed and looked at sand, kicking at it with his feet.

'He didn't mean anything bad,' said Jean.

'I know he didn't,' said Joel. There was a tense silence.

'Nice trainers,' said Charlie, indicating Tristan's new blue Adidas.

'Thanks,' said Tristan, smiling.

'Can I be excused now? And go and skim stones?' asked Charlie.

'Okay. Yes. Don't go too far...' said Joel. His voice trailed off, and Charlie pushed his hands into his pockets and walked down the beach to the rock pools.

'Jesus Christ. I never thought it would be like this,' said Jean, taking out a tissue and pressing it to her face. Tears were rolling down her cheeks. 'It's like he hates me, us. We're calling him two names. Sometimes I don't even think it's him.'

Joel nodded. Kate felt at a loss as to what to say.

'He still thinks that Libby and Steve are his parents. And Daisy is his sister. And they have been, for most of his life,' said Joel. 'Although we're making sure they're still together as brother and sister. They're very close, that's why we want Daisy to stay with us, permanently,' he said. They watched Charlie at the edge of the water as he knelt down and picked up a stone, skimming it into the waves.

'He has no memory of when he was little,' said Jean, taking another drag on her cigarette. 'I've started bloody smoking again. We got them to do the DNA tests again, just in case. He's ours. It is Charlie,' she said insistently.

'We know,' said Kate.

'What's happening about custody? I read there were custody problems?' asked Tristan. Joel nodded.

'The courts have been useless. Libby and Steve Hartley tried to file an injunction through their lawyer, saying we don't have legal custody of Charlie! We both had to go to court and explain to them that Charlie was abducted, so, technically, we've always had custody,' he said.

'But we never had a passport for Charlie,' said Jean. 'He was only just three when he went missing, but he's got a passport in the name of David Hartley, medical records, and dental. And a passport is a passport. Definitive. So, it's caused all kinds of problems.'

'Where's Charlie living?' asked Kate.

'With us, of course. Well, with Joel, above the pub, which is nice. Daisy is there too, and she gets on well with Joel's girls. I'm staying with them too, for now... We're all there, trying to make a go of it. The Crown Estate will take back the farm where Charlie and Daisy spent the last eleven years. I'm scared he'll want to legally keep his name as David when he's old enough.' Jean became tearful. 'I just wish Becky...' Her voice trailed off. 'I just wish Becky was here. And then there's that poor little boy, the real David, who died. And that social worker, Anna.'

'You have to keep faith,' said Kate. Joel and Jean nodded, and they all looked over at Charlie. He'd taken off his shoes and he was now paddling in the sea.

'I still don't know how they got Charlie to be David,' said Tristan. 'He might have been small, but didn't he get upset that these strangers had suddenly taken him in and made him live with them? And call them Mum and Dad?'

'From what we've heard, they dosed him up on cough mixture for the first few weeks when they left the country with him,' said Joel. 'Once they were on holiday in Spain, they seemed to work on eradicating us from his memory. It didn't take long, with him being only three. Who remembers much from that time of their life?'

'He didn't start school until almost two years later, and by then...' Jean took another puff of her cigarette. 'It's still so hard to talk about. He'd forgotten about us, or at least, he'd accepted the new reality. We're all having counselling together. It's not going well.'

'It will, Jean,' said Joel, putting his arm around her. They were quiet for a moment, watching Charlie pull up the legs of his shorts and wade a bit deeper into the waves.

'Anyway. We just wanted to come and see you both and say thank you,' said Jean, taking hold of Kate's hand. 'I don't feel I'll ever be able to thank you enough. And just saying "thank you" never seems enough. Without you, we'd never know what happened, and we'd never have got him back.'

'Yes. Thank you,' said Joel. He had tears in his eyes now. Charlie was out of the water and picking his way through the sand back towards them, carrying his shoes. Jean and Joel hurriedly wiped their eyes. They were silent when Charlie reached them.

'Could I have an ice cream? Please?' he said, finally. 'I saw a place up there.'

'Course you can, love,' said Jean. 'And a flake.'

341

'And a flake, cool, that's almost worth getting abducted for!' said Charlie. He grinned at them all. 'That was a joke.'

Joel grinned, and Jean gave him a weak smile.

Kate and Tristan watched as Jean, Joel, and Charlie walked up the sandy cliffside to the ice cream shop.

'The boy who lived,' said Tristan with a laugh. 'He's certainly got an interesting sense of humour. Do you think they'll be okay?'

'I hope so,' said Kate. 'I hope so.'

A NOTE FROM ROBERT

I want to send an enormous thank-you to the most important people, my readers. When I started, it was the real readers who championed my books, which is still the same today. Thank you to all those who love books and work so hard as booksellers, librarians and book bloggers.

I always say that word-of-mouth is the most potent form of advertising. If you enjoyed this book, please tell the people in your life who love to read, or tell someone who has lost their reading mojo! The greatest compliment is hearing that one of my books has helped someone back into reading.

Thank you to my first reader, Ján Bryndza, and the rest of Team Bryndza/Raven Street Publishing; Maminko Vierka, Riky, and Lola. I love you all so much, and thank you for keeping me going with your love and support!

Thank you to the fantastically skilled translators from around the world who bring my work to life, and thank you to Henry Steadman for another beautiful cover. Thank you also to Jan Cramer, who brings this Kate Marshall audiobook edition so wonderfully to life.

I want to say a special thanks to my mum and dad, who took my sister and me on holiday every summer to Devon and Cornwall. At the time, I moaned that all my friends were off to Spain or Disneyland, but I've come to appreciate how much fun and freedom we had on those holidays surrounded by the beauty and mystery of Dartmoor.

The Devil's Way Tor, the river, the gorge, and the Devil's Way sinkhole are all fictitious. I've walked the length and breadth of Dartmoor and Exmoor in sunny and rainy weather. They are beautiful and often dark and mysterious places to be. I have used those memories and all the places I explored to inspire these fictional locations in *Devil's Way*.

And finally, as I always say, there are many more books to come, and I hope you stay with me for the ride. There will be more Kate Marshall and more Erika Foster, but next up is *Fear the Silence*. This is my first standalone psychological thriller, and I'm very excited for you all to read it!

If you want to be the first to know more sign up via the QR code below. This is my newsletter and the only place you can get details and updates for all my exciting new book releases! Your email will never be shared, and you can subscribe anytime.

Rob

ABOUT THE AUTHOR

Robert Bryndza is best known for his page-turning crime and thriller novels, which have sold over five million copies.

His crime debut, *The Girl in the Ice* was released in February 2016, introducing Detective Chief Inspector Erika Foster. Within five months it sold one million copies, reaching number one in the Amazon UK, USA and Australian charts. To date, *The Girl in the Ice* has sold over 1.5 million copies in the English language and has been sold into translation in 29 countries. It was nominated for the Goodreads Choice Award for Mystery & Thriller (2016), the Grand prix des lectrices de Elle in France (2018), and it won two reader voted awards, The Thrillzone Awards best debut thriller in The Netherlands (2018) and The Dead Good Papercut Award for best page turner at the Harrogate Crime Festival (2016).

Robert has released a further five novels in the Erika Foster series, *The Night Stalker, Dark Water, Last Breath, Cold Blood* and *Deadly Secrets*, all of which have been global bestsellers, and in 2017 *Last Breath* was a Goodreads Choice Award nominee for Mystery and Thriller.

Most recently, Robert created a new crime thriller series based around the central character Kate Marshall, a police officer turned private detective. The first book, *Nine Elms*, was an Amazon USA #1 bestseller and an Amazon UK top five bestseller, and the series has been sold into translation in 18 countries. The second and third books in the series are *Shadow*

Sands, and *Darkness Falls* and the fourth, which has just been published, is *Devil's Way*.

Robert was born in Lowestoft, on the east coast of England. He studied at Aberystwyth University, and the Guildford School of Acting, and was an actor for several years, but didn't find success until he took a play he'd written to the Edinburgh Festival. This led to the decision to change career and start writing. He self-published a bestselling series of romantic comedy novels, before switching to writing crime. Robert lives with his husband in Slovakia, and is lucky enough to write full-time. You can find out more about the author at www.robertbryndza.com.

facebook.com/bryndzarobert

instagram.com/robertbryndza

bookbub.com/authors/robert-bryndza

tiktok.com/@robertbryndza

CPSIA information can be obtained
at www.ICGtesting.com
Printed in the USA
BVHW040032091222
653825BV00003B/50